CONFLICT OF INTEREST

CONFLICT OF INTEREST

By

SCOTT PRATT

ISBN 13: 978-1-944083-13-7

This book, along with every book I've written and every book I'll write, is dedicated to my darling Kristy, to her unconquerable spirit and her inspirational courage. I loved her before I was born and I'll love her after I'm long gone.

PART I

CHAPTER ONE

I lifted my arms and allowed the guard to run his hands all over me. He was a young man, maybe twenty, just starting his career at the sheriff's department. They start all of the new deputies at the jail. It familiarizes them with the "local talent," so to speak, and teaches them how to deal with the same kind of incorrigible conduct they'll encounter later on patrol. I looked at the name stitched into his black pullover shirt as he finished frisking me. It was Freeman. I mused at the irony while he grunted something unintelligible and waved me through the metal detector.

I walked down the gunmetal gray halls and heard the shouts of inmates, the echoes of clanking iron doors, and the buzzing of electric locks. I'd been practicing criminal law in one form or another for almost twenty years, and the sounds I was hearing had become familiar. They were still disconcerting to a degree—I disliked everything about confinement and mistrusted almost everything about governmental authority—but over the years I'd come to accept them as a part of my life, much the way one who lives in a polluted city comes to accept the foul odor in the air.

My name is Joe Dillard, and I was at the Washington County Detention Center on a Sunday night at ten o'clock to see a man who, from what his family and a couple of his friends said on the phone, wanted to hire me. They said he would be willing to pay me a substantial amount of money to act as his defense lawyer in a criminal case. They said he was being railroaded.

I'd never met the man, but from what the people I spoke to during a flurry of telephone calls said, he was a hardworking businessman. An entrepreneur. A success story. He wasn't world-class rich, but he was far from poor. He could pay a good fee, they kept saying. He could pay a really good fee. One person suggested that he could afford as much as a hundred thousand dollars.

I didn't know whether I wanted to get involved, but the lure of a hundred grand elicited a promise from me that I would at least go down to the jail and talk to him. Before I did, however, I spoke to the police officer who was in charge of the investigation and to a couple witnesses. I didn't like what I heard.

His name was Howard French. He was forty. He had a wife and two teenage girls. He owned and operated a company he'd inherited from his father. The company manufactured cabinets and countertops and employed fifty people. I looked him over as he walked into the interview room in his bright orange jail jumpsuit. He was a shade under six feet tall and more than a little overweight. His hair was brown and cut like a banker's and his eyes were brown. He had lots of deep acne scars in his cheeks. He looked extremely uncomfortable in the handcuffs and shackles. You'd think most anyone would look uncomfortable in handcuffs and shackles, but it isn't so. I'd met guys that wore them like old socks.

Howard French had been charged with second-degree murder. He'd been in jail for less than twenty-four hours and would certainly make bond as soon as he was arraigned by a judge the following morning. He sat down stiffly in the steel chair as the guard walked out and closed the door.

"Thank you for coming, Mr. Dillard," he said. "Thank you for coming." He was nodding like a bobble-head. I reached out and shook his cuffed right hand.

"I'm sorry about what happened," I said.

He cocked his head to the left and said, "What do you mean?" Somehow I knew he'd say that.

"I'm sorry about the girls."

"Oh, me too. I can't tell you how sorry I am about those two young ladies. But I didn't have anything to do with it."

"You didn't?"

"No, I swear it. Not a thing."

I resisted the urge to get up and walk out the door. I'd been there for less than a minute, and he'd already lied to me.

"Why don't you give me your version of what happened, Mr. French?"

"Call me Howie," he said. "Everybody calls me Howie. Okay, well, I went to the Bay House to eat supper, you know? I finished eating and walked outside and there was all this commotion up at the top of the parking lot by the street. Tires squealing and a big crash and a fireball and all, so I ran up there to see what was going on. When I got to the street there was this car that was upside down on its roof. It was on fire and there was this police officer and a woman dragging someone away from the fire and then the police officer went back to the car but the fire was getting hotter and he couldn't get close to it."

"So you walked out of the restaurant just as it happened?"

"Yeah. Just as it happened."

"What time was it?"

"I'm not real sure. Around ten o'clock I guess."

"Doesn't the Bay House close at nine?"

"Maybe. I'm not sure."

"You were eating alone on a Saturday night? Where were your wife and kids?"

"They were busy. They went to a movie or something."

"Did you go anyplace else before you went to the restaurant?"

"I rode around some."

"You were driving your red Viper?"

He nodded his head enthusiastically.

"I love driving that car," he said. "It's a cool car, you know? Really fast. Five hundred horsepower. It'll fly."

His eyes lit up when he talked about the Viper, the fool. He was forty years old and running around town in a hopped-up muscle car like a kid half his age.

"Do you race it?" I said.

"No, no. I don't race it. I just drive it around."

"Do you ever race it on the street? You know what I mean. Pull up next to somebody at a red light and rev the engine, see if they want to go a few blocks?"

"Nah, I've had plenty of people try to get me to race, but I don't pay attention."

I sat back and folded my arms. I wasn't all that pleased about being there so late on a Sunday, and his nasal tone—plus the fact that he was lying through his teeth—was quickly getting on my nerves.

"How about we cut the crap, Mr. French?" I said. "I came down here because some members of your family and a couple of your friends called me and asked me to consider defending you. You've been charged with second-degree murder because the police and several witnesses say you were drag racing on a busy street when there was a lot of traffic around. A young girl was killed and another was burned so badly she'll never be the same. The one who was killed, do you even know her name?"

"Yeah, I know her name. Of course I know her name. It's been all over the news."

"What was it?"

"I think it was maybe Britney?"

"That's right. Britney James. And the girl who was with her in the passenger seat? The one who is in a coma right now? Do you know her name?"

"I think maybe it's Jane."

"Jane Clouse. Do you know what they were doing when David Burke slammed his Mustang into the back of their car?"

"People are saying they were maybe looking at some pictures."

"Right. Britney James had been crowned homecoming queen at her high school on Friday night, about twenty-four hours before this happened. Her best friend Jane Clouse had taken a bunch of pictures. They had them developed at Walgreen's. They'd just picked up the pictures and were sitting at a red light when the Mustang you were racing hit them going a hundred and thirty miles an hour."

"I wasn't racing—"

"Stop," I said, holding up my hand. "Just stop. The impact ruptured the gas tank in the little Honda Britney was driving. It also snapped the driveshaft in two, lifted the car off the ground, turned it over, and sent it more than two hundred feet down the street. Do you know that at least four different witnesses have told the police that you were sitting at a red light next to the Mustang revving your engine less than a half mile away a few seconds before the crash?"

"They saw me? They saw my face?"

"I don't think anyone saw your face, but they saw a red Viper."

"So?"

"Is this really the way you want to play it? Is your defense going to be that you weren't even on the road when the crash happened? That the red Viper everybody saw must have belonged to someone else and that you just happened to be dining a couple hundred feet from the wreck? I don't know this for a fact, but I'd be willing to bet that you're the only guy within a hundred-mile radius of Johnson City, Tennessee, who owns a red Dodge Viper."

His shoulders slumped and his chin dropped. He hesitated a few seconds before taking a deep breath.

"I can't go to jail," he said. "I might have been at the red light next to the Mustang. The Mustang might have been revving its engine. The guy who was driving it might have been trying to get me to race him. I might have started to race him, but I might have gotten scared and backed off before he ran into those girls. It wasn't my fault."

"Doesn't matter," I said. "That's like saying you and a buddy walked into a bank intending to rob it, but you got scared and left in the middle of the robbery. You'd still be held responsible under the criminal law for bank robbery. And if the buddy you went into the bank with killed someone during the robbery after you left? You'd be held responsible for the killing too. This is the same thing. That's why they charged you, and that's why you're going to wind up in jail. They won't be able to convict you of murder, but you'll get convicted of vehicular homicide for the girl who died and aggravated assault for the girl who was burned. If she dies, you'll get convicted of two counts of vehicular homicide. You're going to prison. You might as well get used to the idea and start planning for it."

"But I didn't hit them! He hit them!"

"He'll get convicted and go to prison too, if it makes you feel any better."

He leaned forward on his elbows and started looking at me with what I perceived as a conspiratorial gleam in his eyes.

"What kind of money are we talking here?" he said. "How much will it take for you to get serious about this? Everybody has been telling me to get old Joe Dillard. He's the baddest man around. He'll fight for you. He's not afraid of anything or anybody. He's a junkyard dog, that's what he is. He'll chew the state's witnesses up and spit them out all over the courtroom. That's what I need, Mr. Dillard. I need that junkyard dog. How much will it cost me?"

I stood and pushed the button on the wall to summon the guards. The words I'd spoken had absolutely no meaning to him.

"What are you doing?" he said.

"Leaving. I'm going home."

"What? Wait a minute! You'll take my case, won't you? I'll pay you two hundred thousand dollars, up front, cash on the barrel head."

There was a time in my life when two hundred thousand dollars would have enticed me to defend Jack the Ripper. But those days had passed. I'd made good money during my legal career, and I enjoyed the things money brought to me and to my family, but I was no longer interested in trading my conscience for a fat fee. I just wanted to be a good man, a good lawyer, a good husband and father. I wanted life to be simpler than it had been in the past.

This guy was guilty, and he'd already showed me he wasn't the least bit interested in the truth. He wanted to be free of responsibility for the death and pain he'd caused, and for two hundred thousand dollars, he would expect me to ensure both his freedom and his public absolution. And to be honest, for two hundred grand, I could have probably done it.

But I just didn't want to. The door buzzed and I pushed it open.

"So you're going to walk out on me?" he said. "Just like that? Didn't you kill five men not too long ago? Five men! Why aren't you in jail? What makes you any different from me?"

I stopped and turned to face him.

"I'm not any different from you, Mr. French," I said. "But I'm surprised nobody has ever taught you that life isn't fair sometimes. Good luck in prison."

CHAPTER TWO

The accusation Howard French hurled at me was true. It had been nearly a year since I'd ambushed and killed five men as they approached my home intending to kill me and every member of my family. I lay in wait for them, set traps for them, and I killed them exactly the way the United States Army had taught me to kill when I was still a teenager—efficiently and without passion.

The events that led up to that night were so perfectly arbitrary and chaotic that I'd often thought that perhaps something else was at play, something like fate or destiny, but I'd learned over the years that dwelling on the past was as useless as fretting over the future. In the aftermath of the "Gunfight at the OK Corral," as the media labeled it, I resigned my job as district attorney general and went back to private practice, albeit on a limited basis. My daughter had given birth to a baby boy back in May and had honored me by naming the child Joseph. My son was still pursuing his professional baseball career at the minor league level, and my wife's breast cancer was a painful, distant memory. I'd decided I wouldn't let what happened that night have any effect on me, and until French mentioned it at the jail, I hadn't thought about it in months. Once I walked out of his jail cell, I pushed it from my mind again.

Six days after my meeting with French, I learned of Lindsay Monroe's disappearance when I walked through the kitchen after mowing the lawn on a Saturday morning. My wife, Caroline, who had been sweeping the kitchen floor, was standing stone still, staring at a small television on the kitchen counter with a look of abject horror on her face. The weekend anchorman at the local CBS affiliate, a fresh-faced kid with a nasal voice and an accent that said, "Hi, I'm from nowhere," was doing his best to sound and look deadly serious. This is what he said:

"Police and a small group of volunteers are combing Tennessee's oldest town this morning in search of a six-year-old girl who was apparently taken from her bed last night. Lindsay Monroe of Jonesborough was reported missing shortly after 7:00 a.m. by her mother, Mary Monroe. Sources say Mrs. Monroe called 9-1-1 after going to Lindsay's room and finding the child's bed empty. Mrs. Monroe reportedly told the emergency dispatcher that a window in the second-floor bedroom was open and a screen had been removed. We go live now to News Twelve correspondent Nate Baldasano, who is outside the Monroe home."

"No," Caroline murmured. "Please, no."

The screen switched to a slim, mid-thirties, generic-looking man with black hair named Nate Baldasano. Baldasano had been a reporter for News Twelve for at least ten years. I'd been interviewed by him several times because I'd been involved in a lot of criminal cases both as a defense lawyer and later as a prosecutor. Ten years is a long time for a television reporter to stay in the Tri-Cities media market. It means one of two things: the reporter either lacks drive or lacks talent.

"There is a pall hanging over Jonesborough's National Historic District this morning," Baldasano said. "The police aren't releasing any information as of yet, but so far we know that a six-year-old first-grader, Lindsay Monroe, has gone missing. Her parents, Richard Monroe, a respected local businessman, and Mary Monroe are both inside the house at this time along with several police officers. Neighbors and friends of the Monroes have started a search of the immediate area."

The broadcast cut to a blonde woman. At the bottom of the screen was the caption, "Melissa Franklin, Neighbor."

"We're frantic," the woman said. "We've already printed hundreds of flyers and are going door-to-door passing them out and asking people to help us find Lindsay. Everyone around here knows her. She's such a sweet, lovely child."

A photo of the girl flashed onto the screen. I recognized her. She was dark-haired and blue-eyed, a beautiful little girl, grinning widely, missing a front tooth. The next shot was of the house. I recognized it too because it was smack in the middle of downtown Jonesborough, only a couple blocks from the old Washington County courthouse on Main Street. It was a large, two-story brick house that was built in the 1870s and was one of a dozen or so "historic homes" that the tourists liked to ogle from the sidewalk. I'd been inside it once, many years earlier, before the Monroes bought it. Caroline and I had been invited to a progressive dinner a week before Christmas—a dinner that starts with drinks at one home, then moves to another home for appetizers, then to another home for soup and salad, then to another home for the main course, that kind of thing—and the house where the Monroes now lived had been the last stop of the evening. At the time, it was owned by a retired liquor distributor named Lovelace. It had been updated and remodeled several times, and it was impressive. The interior reminded me of the Biltmore Estate in Asheville, North Carolina, all gleaming hardwood, expensive rugs, pristine antique furniture, and sparkling chandeliers.

"Sources tell me that an unknown perpetrator may have used a ladder to reach Lindsay's second-floor bedroom window," Baldasano said. "My information indicates that Lindsay was last seen around 10:00 p.m. last night when her mother put her to bed. One source, speaking on condition of anonymity, told me that a ransom note was left on Lindsay's pillow, although I have not been able to confirm that information."

The guy actually used the phrases "unknown perpetrator" and "my information indicates." He reported unconfirmed information about a ransom note. It was broadcast journalism at its finest. Caroline walked over to the television and turned it off.

"Let's go," she said.

"Where?"

"To Jonesborough. Lindsay is one of my girls. We're going to go help look for her."

Caroline had owned and operated a dance studio for more than twenty years. The relationships she formed with her students were deeper than those formed between most teachers and students. Typically, a teacher is involved with a student for a year, maybe two. Even high school coaches have kids for only a couple years before the athletes graduate and move on. But Caroline's girls, for the most part, came to her when they were three or four years old, and some of them stayed through their senior year in high school. Many of her students left dancing around the age of ten and moved on to things like cheerleading or gymnastics or volleyball or softball or swimming, but there were dozens of girls who had taken dance from Caroline for ten years or more. She watched them grow from babies to little girls to young girls to teenage girls to young women. She knew their families, their friends, their favorite colors, their birthdays, their favorite foods. She became an integral part of their lives.

I'm convinced that those young girls kept Caroline alive during the worst of her five-year battle with breast cancer. No matter how tired she was, no matter how sick she'd been, she always, always went to the studio to teach, and she would always come home rejuvenated. It was as if the enthusiasm and the optimism and the *life* in those young people transferred to her through some sort of spiritual osmosis and kept her going for one more day, one more week, one more month, one more year. It was a beautiful thing to behold.

Lindsay Monroe was a cute, feisty, spirited child, and had quickly become one of Caroline's favorites. Caroline often spoke of her when she returned home from the studio. She'd tell me stories about things Lindsay said or did. Caroline often affectionately described her as a "hot mess."

"They're already turning it into a circus," I said to Caroline. "Why don't we just let the police handle it? They're trained—"

"I'm going with you or without you," she said. She was standing at the door leading to the garage.

"At least let me change my shirt," I said. "I smell like a horse."

"Now," she said over her shoulder.

As I started after her, I felt a sinking sensation in my stomach. I'd defended one child murderer and prosecuted two others in my career. I'd been involved in dozens of other murder cases. I'd dealt with rape and robbery and violent assault, but I'd never, not once, had to endure a case that involved a young girl vanishing in the night. I had no idea what was going on, and I had no idea what would happen in the future, but the gnawing in my stomach told me that nothing good would come of this, nothing at all.

CHAPTER THREE

When Caroline and I arrived in Jonesborough around 10:30 a.m., we parked in the old courthouse lot and walked the three blocks to the Monroes'. There was a large group of people gathered on the sidewalk in front of the house and crime-scene tape had been stretched around the edge of the lot. Caroline ducked under the tape and started up the concrete sidewalk toward the front door. I went after her. We were met halfway up the walk by a young, uniformed Jonesborough policeman named Will Traynor. I knew Will from my time at the district attorney's office. He smiled, although it appeared to be a reluctant smile, as we approached.

"Mr. Dillard," he said as he reached out to shake my hand. "It's been awhile."

"Nice to see you, Will."

"I'd like to talk to Mary Monroe," Caroline said. "We're friends. Lindsay takes dance at my studio."

"I'm sorry, ma'am, but I can't let you go inside. It's a crime scene. I have strict orders not to let anyone past the tape."

"But I need to talk to her," Caroline said.

Traynor looked at me for help, and I took Caroline gently by the elbow.

"He's right," I said. "They'll skin him alive if he lets you in there."

"Sorry, Mr. Dillard," Traynor said.

"No need to apologize."

"Can you at least tell me if Lindsay is all right?" Caroline said. "Do you have any idea?"

Traynor looked around and lowered his eyes. "As far as I know, she's still missing," he said quietly. "We're doing everything we can."

"Thanks, Will," I said. "Good luck."

I turned Caroline around and we walked back under the yellow tape. Nate Baldasano immediately stuck a microphone in my face.

"What can you tell us, Mr. Dillard? Are you involved in this case?"

"No, I'm not involved and I can't tell you anything," I said. "Please get out of my way."

Caroline and I started walking back down the street in the direction of the courthouse, just to get away from the crowd.

"Is Lindsay the kind of kid that might wander off early in the morning?" I said.

"She's precocious and independent-minded, but I don't think she's reckless," Caroline said.

"Let's assume she wandered off, since we're here. Where would a little girl go?"

"She'd probably go into the backyard, but I'm sure they've searched it."

"But what could draw her away from the backyard? An animal, maybe? A stray dog or a cat?"

"Maybe. Kids like water. Maybe she came around front and went to play by the creek."

A small creek ran all the way through town about a half block from Main Street. It cut right through the Monroes' front yard.

"There are people all around the creek, Caroline. If she was there, somebody would have found her."

Not only were there people all around the creek, there were people everywhere. The news about Lindsay was out, and the street was quickly filling up. I could hear calls of "Lindsay!" "Lindsay Monroe!" coming from side streets and the alleys between the buildings, from the banks on either side of the creek, from the railroad tracks a block away. Several people had dogs on leashes, and almost everyone was carrying a cell phone.

"I don't think there's anything we can do here," I said.

She gave me that look of hers, the one where she sets her jaw and her eyes become lasers. It means, "Don't give me any trouble right now."

"What do you want to do?" I said.

"Look for her. Let's just look. Maybe we'll see something somebody missed."

We walked down Main Street to Fox and turned right toward the railroad tracks.

"Do you think there's really a ransom note?" Caroline said.

"I hope so," I said. "There's a lot better chance of catching him if he tries to pick up a ransom."

"Him? You're sure it's a him?"

"Women don't do ransom kidnappings. It's a man thing."

CHAPTER FOUR

Inside the house, suspicion and angst hung in the air like thick fog. Leon Bates, the sheriff of Washington County, had just walked into Lindsay Monroe's bedroom along with Special Agent Ross Dedrick of the Federal Bureau of Investigation, Special Agent Mike Norcross of the Tennessee Bureau of Investigation, and Jonesborough Chief of Police Mitchell Royston. Bates stepped carefully, as did the others. They scanned the room, hoping to spot something, anything, that might offer some insight into the disappearance of a six-year-old girl.

Bates glanced briefly at the other men. Norcross was a giant, six feet seven and rock hard. Dedrick was around the same height as Bates—six feet four—but while Bates was gangly, Dedrick was thick and powerful. Royston was short, maybe five eight. Throw in a guy about seven feet tall, Bates thought, and they'd have the perfect makeup of a basketball team.

The room was large; Bates guessed maybe sixteen by twenty feet. The floors were gleaming oak, the walls painted in soft pastels, the bed covered in a lacy, white canopy. A white ceiling fan spun slowly above a decorative light. The pink comforter on the bed was ruffled where the child had slept; a typewritten note lay on the pillow where her head had rested only hours earlier.

Two windows, each of them four feet wide by six feet high, looked out over the back patio and yard. Both were open, but the screen that covered the one to Bates's right had been cut near the edges of the window frame and was lying on the stone patio fifteen feet below.

"No blood," Bates said. "No sign of struggle. I reckon that's a good thing."

Bates walked over and peered down at the ransom note. He'd read it earlier. It demanded three million dollars in cash within seventy-two hours.

"We need to decide how you guys want to organize and delegate," Dedrick, the FBI agent, said. "We have statutory authority to investigate missing-children cases, but it's your jurisdiction and I don't want to step on any toes."

Bates didn't know Dedrick. He'd heard rumors about why Dedrick had been transferred to northeast Tennessee, but this was the first time the two of them had laid eyes on each other. Bates didn't really care why Dedrick had been transferred. He wasn't much for gossip, and he stayed too busy to worry about the inner workings of a federal agency he regarded as top-heavy, inefficient, and sometimes arrogant. But at the same time, he knew the FBI had resources and manpower at their disposal far beyond anything Bates could muster.

"I think we all recognize that I don't have the people to deal with a case like this," Chief Royston said. "I'll defer to Leon."

Bates removed his cowboy hat with his left hand and started scratching his head with his right. From all appearances, it was a kidnapping. A ransom kidnapping of a six-year-old girl.

"This is a nightmare," Bates said. "Have any of y'all ever worked a ransom kidnapping?"

The question was met with silence.

"But the FBI has people who specialize," Bates said. "Am I right?"

Dedrick nodded. "They're called CARD teams," he said. "Child Abduction Rapid Deployment. All I have to do is put in a request. They'll have a team here in a few hours. Profilers, tech people, field agents. We can also make use of the AMBER Alert system and get the word out to every law enforcement agency in the region, in the nation if necessary. It'll spread fast."

"Do it," Bates said. "What else?"

"The CARD team will set up a command post somewhere close by. They'll start searching databases for sex offenders who live in the area or who might have passed through the area last night or this morning. They'll set up a communication system to field leads from the public. They'll make use of your people and Mike's people and Mitch's people and my people and coordinate grid searches, conduct and catalog interviews, run down leads and suspects."

"We need a forensic team in here pronto," Bates said. "This scene looks pretty clean, but you never know. They might find something."

"I already made a call to Knoxville," Norcross said. "They'll be here within the hour."

"What do y'all think about the parents?" Bates said.

"They're suspects," Dedrick said. "They seem genuinely terrified, it looks like they reported it immediately, and they're both saying all the right things, but it's too early to make any kind of judgment. We need to separate them as soon as possible and interview them in depth. Who do you want to handle it?"

"You do it," Bates said, "but I want to be watching and listening."

"No problem."

"You up to handling the media?" Bates said to Royston.

Royston nodded his head, and Bates felt a twinge of sympathy for him. Mitch Royston oversaw a police force of fourteen men and women in a sleepy little tourist town that rarely experienced a serious crime. He'd been the chief in Jonesborough for several years, and Bates knew him to be a quiet, thoughtful man who disliked attention and avoided controversy.

"You sure, Mitch?" Bates said. "It'll be like fending off a pack of wolves."

"It's my town," Royston said, "my responsibility."

Bates took a deep breath and put his hat back on.

"All right, boys," he said. "A little girl is out there somewhere and nobody's happy about it. Let's get to it."

CHAPTER FIVE

Caroline and I wandered the streets for the next four hours beneath a darkening sky. It was late September and had been pleasant in the morning, but as the afternoon wore on, the temperature began to drop and the breeze picked up. We probably covered about ten miles in ever-widening squares. By midafternoon, the search had become a free-for-all. The streets downtown were lined with parked cars. All the city lots were full, the church parking lots were full, the lot behind the courthouse was full. People kept showing up, asking how they could help, what they could do. Around one o'clock, the police finally realized that it would be prudent to block off Main Street at both ends, but by that time, any hope of conducting a thorough search or inventory of every vehicle that was in the area when Lindsay was reported missing was gone. Around one thirty, people started saying the Jonesborough chief of police was going to hold a news conference on the courthouse steps at four. Newshounds were everywhere, lugging cameras and microphones and sound equipment, diligently interviewing anyone who would talk to them, taking notes on their little notepads. It was complete chaos.

Jonesborough is a small town of about six thousand in northeastern Tennessee. It's a quaint, quiet little town nestled in the hills between mountain ranges. It's on the National Register of Historic Places, which has brought a significant amount of government grant money to the town. That money has been used to preserve much of the original architecture, promote tourism, and to develop the downtown area, which is only about five blocks long, into an attractive place with cobblestone sidewalks and small, individually owned shops and restaurants. But none of that government grant money has been used to fund a police department, and on the day Lindsay was kidnapped, the Jonesborough Police Department employed fourteen police officers and only one—that's right, one—criminal investigator. The department was completely unprepared to handle a crime of such magnitude, let alone deal with the deluge of do-gooders and rubber-neckers and news vans and trucks and reporters.

The ministers and deacons of the Jonesborough Methodist and Presbyterian Churches, which were across the street from each other and just a few doors down from the Monroes', set up a couple large tents on the front lawn of the Presbyterian Church and were doing their best to lend some kind of organization to the search, but it was a futile effort. Hundreds of people were wandering aimlessly through town, up and down the side streets, along the creek and the railroad tracks. They covered the same ground over and over and over. I heard Lindsay's name called at least five thousand times.

Finally, around two thirty, I said, "Caroline, this is useless."

I could see she knew it was true. She seemed to deflate a little. Her shoulders slumped just a bit and her chin dropped.

"You're right," she said. She was looking at the ground.

"Let's just go home and wait, let the police handle it, and hope for the best. I'm sure there's an AMBER alert out by now, which means the TBI and the FBI will be involved. They'll have her picture on billboards and highway signs. Everybody in the country will be looking for her. Think positively. They'll find her soon."

A tear ran down her right cheek and I reached for her.

"She's out there somewhere, terrified and alone," Caroline said. "What if he's ... what if he's *doing* something to her?"

She let the question trail off, and I didn't answer. I knew that if Lindsay had been taken by a stranger, the chances of her being sexually abused were great, and the chances of her making it home were minimal. I took Caroline's hand in mine, and we walked slowly back to my truck as a cold drizzle started to fall and the light faded even more. We drove out of town in silence, each of us lost in our own thoughts, both of us hoping against hope that we would watch little Lindsay Monroe dance on a stage once more.

The press conference, which was televised live by all the local networks, was typical of those held by police early in an investigation. The Jonesborough chief of police, a middle-aged, red-haired, rather fierce-looking man named Mitchell Royston, spoke from the courthouse steps surrounded by a gang of reporters and hundreds of people. He made a brief statement that divulged virtually nothing outside the fact that Lindsay was missing. He asked people to please allow the police to do their jobs, to have confidence in them. He told the group of volunteers that a temporary command center would be set up within the hour on the grounds of Christopher Taylor Park to organize the ground search into grids. He expressed hope that Lindsay would be found before nightfall and assured everyone that if Lindsay had been kidnapped, the person or persons responsible would be brought to justice. He declined to answer questions and immediately left in an unmarked police car.

My heart went out to the Monroes. I couldn't help thinking about what it would be like to be in their situation. I had a daughter, Lilly. What if someone had taken her when she was only six years old? Someone who had broken into the house in the early morning when Caroline and I were both in a deep sleep? We were living in a tiny, two-bedroom apartment in Knoxville when Lilly was that age. I was in law school. Jack and Lilly shared a room, slept in the same bed. We didn't have a dog or a security system. There was a window in the kids' room that opened onto a common sidewalk in the complex. What if some pervert had noticed Lilly, whether she was at school or with me or with Caroline or whether the whole family was together at a mall or a gas station or a movie theater or fast-food drive-through or a bank? What if he'd fixated on her and stalked her? What if he'd taken his time, been discreet, and learned everything he needed to learn to be able to sneak in and grab her in the blackness of the early morning? What if Caroline, Jack, and I woke up one morning and Lilly was gone?

Gone.

I couldn't imagine how something like that would feel.

CHAPTER SIX

What follows is a partial, edited transcript of an interview with Mary Monroe that I obtained early in the discovery process. The interview was conducted at the FBI field office in Johnson City the day before I was hired.

Interviewer: Special Agent Ross Dedrick, Federal Bureau of Investigation
Interviewer: Special Agent Mike Norcross, Tennessee Bureau of Investigation
Interviewee: Mary Monroe
File No.: 13357

Dedrick: Special Agent Ross Dedrick (FBI)
Norcross: Special Agent Mike Norcross (TBI)
MM: Mary Monroe

Norcross: Mrs. Monroe, we appreciate you sitting down with us. I'd first like to talk about the days and weeks—even months—prior to Lindsay's disappearance. Has there been any time that you've felt uncomfortable about anything concerning Lindsay? And by that I mean have you noticed anything unusual?

MM: Are you talking about people taking an interest in her?

Norcross: I'm talking about anything, anything at all that would have caused you concern.

MM: No. I can't think of anything unusual.

Norcross: Have there been any problems in your life that might have been caused by or involved Lindsay?

MM: She's a child. There are little problems that come up when you're raising a child.

Norcross: What kind of problems? Give me an example.

MM: I don't know, little disciplinary problems, like her not wanting to go to bed when she's supposed to or talking back to me or Richard or being whiny. Medical problems like strep throat or the measles. There wasn't anything serious though. Just normal kid stuff.

Norcross: Would you describe Lindsay as a good girl?

MM: She's a wonderful little girl.

Norcross: No problems at school?

MM: None. Her teachers love her. She gets along with the other kids.

Dedrick: I have a couple quick questions.

Norcross: Go right ahead.

Dedrick: Have you ever had an affair, Mrs. Monroe?

MM: Of course not. Why would you even ask such a thing?

Dedrick: What about your husband? Have you ever caught him having an affair?

MM: This is ridiculous ... no. Richard has never had an affair.

Dedrick: Have you ever suspected him of having an affair?

MM: No.

Dedrick: Are you happy in your marriage?

MM: Yes, very happy. I still don't—

Dedrick: If you had it to do over again, would you marry Richard?

MM: Yes. I resent this. I want that on the record.

Dedrick: Is Richard a good father?

MM: The best.

Dedrick: Which one of you disciplines Lindsay?

MM: We both do.

Dedrick: Has Richard ever become angry with Lindsay?

MM: Not really, well, I suppose a couple times. What parent doesn't become angry with a child once in awhile?

Dedrick: So you've become angry with her?

MM: Again, what parent doesn't become angry with a child once in awhile?

Dedrick: Have you ever struck her?

MM: No. We don't strike children.

Dedrick: Not even a little pop now and then, just to straighten her out?

MM: We don't strike children.

Dedrick: What about Richard?

MM: Does the word "we" confuse you, Agent Dedrick?

Dedrick: But you're not with him and Lindsay all the time. Is it possible that Richard may have struck her at some time?

MM: No.

Dedrick: Did you kill your daughter, Mrs. Monroe?

MM: I most certainly did not.

Dedrick: Did you stage her kidnapping?

MM: No!

Dedrick: Did your husband kill your daughter?

MM: He did not.

Dedrick: Did he stage a kidnapping?

MM: Are you enjoying this?

Dedrick: Answer the question, ma'am.

MM: Neither of us staged Lindsay's kidnapping. Neither of us killed her.

Norcross: Let me jump back in for a minute or two. Let's go back to Friday, Mrs. Monroe. Walk me through your day.

MM: We've been over this a dozen times.

Norcross: I know, and I apologize. Please, one more time.

MM: I got up at six thirty, like usual. I got dressed and went to Lindsay's room. I woke her up and got her ready for school. We ate breakfast together, and I dropped her off at Ashton Academy around seven forty-five. From there, I went to the gym and worked out from eight until ten. I went back home, took a shower, washed my hair, put some makeup on, and went back out. I went to the grocery store, to the bank, and to Walmart. I went back home and dropped the groceries off, and at noon I went to lunch with my friend Ruth Killian. At one, I drove to the hospital and visited Richard's aunt for about twenty minutes. After I left there, I went to Lindsay's school and met with Melinda Hall. She's the music teacher. I have a background in music and theater, and I'm helping her plan a Christmas show this year. We talked until it was time for school to let out. I met Lindsay and drove her to her violin lesson. I waited in the lobby for forty-five minutes. From there, we went to the mall, and I bought Lindsay an orange outfit for the ballgame we were going to on Saturday. We left the mall and went home. I fixed supper while Lindsay played in her room upstairs. We ate supper and put the dishes in the dishwasher. After that, we met another friend of mine, Brandy Stokes, and her daughter, Alexis, at the elementary school playground. The girls played for about an hour while Brandy and I talked. We left just before dark and went straight home. I helped Lindsay change clothes and got her ready for bed. I tucked her in and turned on a movie for her. I went downstairs and poured myself a glass of wine. When I went back upstairs about twenty minutes later, Lindsay was asleep. I turned off the television and went back downstairs. That was it. That was the last time I saw her.

Norcross: Where was your husband?

MM: He worked late on Friday since we were going to be gone all day Saturday.

Norcross: Did you speak to him at all on Friday?

MM: Not until he got home.

Dedrick: What time was that?

MM: Around nine o'clock.

Dedrick: Is it unusual for you to go an entire day without speaking to Richard?

MM: No. He works, Agent Dedrick. He works hard. He owns the business, and he doesn't have time to babysit me during the day.

Norcross: Why was he so late?

MM: He said he had dinner with the president of some company he's thinking about doing business with. He does that kind of thing all the time. It wasn't unusual.

Norcross: Did he say where they ate?

MM: The Peerless, I believe.

Norcross: Had you seen Richard on Friday morning before he left for work?

MM: He kissed me goodbye.

Norcross: What time did he leave the house?

MM: He leaves around six every morning.

Norcross: And he got back home around nine?

MM: Yes.

Norcross: Long day. What did you and Richard do between nine and bedtime?

MM: We talked for a little while at the kitchen table, and then Richard went into his study and I watched television.

Norcross: Did either of you check on Lindsay during that time?

MM: I didn't. Richard probably went in and kissed her before he went to bed. That's always been his habit.

Norcross: Did you and Richard go to bed at the same time?

MM: No. I went up at eleven. Richard came some time later.

Norcross: Do you sleep in the same bed?

MM: Yes.

Norcross: Were you awake when he came in to bed?

MM: No.

Norcross: Did you see Richard after he went into his study?

MM: I went to the door and told him I was going to bed.

Norcross: What was he doing?

MM: Playing a video game. Richard is a hopeless gamer.

Norcross: Did you go right to sleep?

MM: I brushed my teeth, washed my face, put on my pajamas, said a prayer, and read a couple chapters of a biography on Bob Fosse. Then I went to sleep.

Norcross: Who is Bob Fosse?

MM: He was a famous dancer and choreographer. He's dead.

Norcross: Did you get up at all during the night?

MM: No. I woke up at six thirty the next morning, just like I always do. Richard had left at six, just like he always does. He was going to check on a couple things at the office, and then he was going to come back home and pick Lindsay and me up at eight so we could drive to Knoxville and go to the ballgame. It was being televised so it started at noon.

Norcross: What time did you discover Lindsay was gone?

MM: Around seven, I guess. I went to her room to wake her up and she wasn't in bed. I called her name but she didn't answer, so I went into her bathroom and she wasn't there. When I walked back into her room, I noticed the note on the pillow.

Norcross: Did you touch it?

MM: Of course I touched it. I picked it up and read it and then I think maybe I screamed. I dropped it back on the pillow and that's when I noticed the window screen was missing. I walked over and looked out and saw the screen lying on the patio. I ran downstairs and went outside. I looked at the screen and up at the window and I just ... I don't know. I lost my composure. I'm not really clear on what happened after that. I think I ran around the house outside looking for Lindsay, and then I ran back inside and looked all over the inside of the house. At some point I picked up my cell phone and called Richard. He told me to call the police, so I did.

Dedrick: Did you and your husband argue about anything Friday night?

MM: No.

Dedrick: Have you had any problems lately? Financial problems? Sexual problems?

MM: We're rich, Agent Dedrick. We don't have financial problems. And our sex life is absolutely none of your business.

Dedrick: Would you voluntarily surrender your cell phone so we could examine it?

MM: You know something? I think maybe I should talk to a lawyer.

Dedrick: Why would you need a lawyer?

MM: Because I feel like I'm being accused of something I didn't do.

MM: You should have already eliminated me as a suspect. And Richard too. You're wasting your time talking to me like this. Lindsay's out there somewhere, and you're sitting here talking to me. I love that child with all my heart. I adore her. I would never do anything to harm her and I can't believe you think I would.

Dedrick: Have you ever heard of Susan Smith? Andrea Yates? Jeff MacDonald? It happens, Mrs. Monroe. We have to be thorough. Let me ask you this. How would you feel about taking a polygraph examination?

MM: I'd feel as though I was being accused of something.

Dedrick: If you pass, it would go a long way toward taking you off our list completely.

MM: And who would give me this polygraph? An FBI agent?

Dedrick: We have the best polygraph examiners in the world.

MM: I don't think I want to take a polygraph.

Dedrick: Why? Are you hiding something?

MM: That's it. I'm done. I'm going to talk to a lawyer.

CHAPTER SEVEN

And this is a partial, edited transcript of an interview with Richard Monroe that I also obtained early in discovery. The interview was also conducted at the FBI field office in Johnson City the day before I was hired.

Interviewer: Special Agent Albert Gideon, Federal Bureau of Investigation
Interviewee: Richard Monroe
File No.: 13357

Gideon: Special Agent Albert Gideon (FBI)
RM: Richard Monroe

Gideon: First off, I want you to know we're here to help you, Mr. Monroe. Do you believe that?
RM: I'm not so sure. Am I a suspect?
Gideon: I'll be honest with you. From everything I've seen, this appears to be a ransom kidnapping committed by a stranger. But we have to do our jobs. You were in the house when she was taken. We have to eliminate you as a suspect, and that's what we intend to do by conducting this interview.

RM: Fine. Let's just get it over with so you can get back to doing what you need to be doing.

Gideon: I'm primarily interested right now in where you were between six and nine o'clock on Friday night.

RM: I took a colleague out to eat.

Gideon: Who was your colleague?

RM: He's the president of a software company that we might do business with.

Gideon: His name?

RM: I don't want to drag him into this. It was a business dinner, Agent Gideon. We were talking about business.

Gideon: I believe you told us earlier that you ate at the Peerless, is that correct?

RM: Yes.

Gideon: That's in Johnson City?

RM: Yes.

Gideon: You said you left work at six, got to the restaurant around six thirty, and stayed for two hours?

RM: Yes.

Gideon: Did you pay for the meal or did your associate pay?

RM: I paid.

Gideon: Did you use a credit card?

RM: I believe I paid in cash.

Gideon: That surprises me a little, Mr. Monroe, because I would think you'd write something like that off as a business expense and you would use a credit card so you'd have a record of the transaction for your accountant.

RM: Have you ever heard of a receipt?

Gideon: Oh, so you have a receipt?

RM: I'm sure I do.

Gideon: Do you have it with you? In your wallet maybe?

RM: I probably put it in a folder in my office at home.

Gideon: Do you mind if I send one of my guys over to your house to get the folder? I'd really like to take a look at that receipt.

RM: Why are you so interested in the meal I ate on Friday night? What could that possibly have to do with finding Lindsay?

Gideon: I'm interested because I don't think you were at the Peerless on Friday night between six thirty and eight thirty.

RM: I don't care what you think. I was there.

Gideon: We try to be extremely thorough, Mr. Monroe. When you told us you ate at the Peerless, we sent people there to verify it. Nobody there remembers you coming in, so we gave you the benefit of the doubt, and we checked their security tapes just to see if maybe they were so busy they didn't notice you. They have cameras all over the place, mostly to ensure their employees aren't stealing from them. But they also have cameras in the parking lot and at the front door. Do you see where I'm going with this? You're not on any of the tapes.

RM: I was there.

Gideon: I'm having trouble understanding why you would be untruthful about something that seems so insignificant.

RM: I'm not being untruthful. I was there, at the Peerless. I ate a T-bone steak.

Gideon: Because if you would be untruthful about something that seems so insignificant, then I have to believe you would be untruthful about other things. Do you see where I'm coming from?

RM: I don't know what to tell you. I was there. I ate a meal. I left and went home. End of story.

Gideon: Okay. Maybe we missed you somehow on the tapes. I'll go back and look at them again myself. In the meantime, it would help move things along a great deal if you'd let us go to your house and pick up that folder so I can take a look at the receipt.

RM: I'm not positive I put it in the folder. I mean, I don't have a—what is it you guys call it?—a specific recollection of putting it in the folder. It might not be there.

Gideon: Why don't we just take a look then?

RM: I don't want you or any of your guys wandering around my house.

Gideon: I promise we won't wander around. Just tell us exactly where the folder is and we'll go in and get it.

RM: I'll look for it when I get home. If it's there, I'll call you.

Gideon: I'd really like you to take a polygraph, Mr. Monroe. Mr. Monroe? What are you doing? Are you leaving? Hold up, there. Wait! (Pause.) The subject has terminated the interview.

CHAPTER EIGHT

O ver the next two days, Lindsay Monroe became a
national story. Her face was on television screens, computers, cell phones, and billboards across the country.
Chief Royston's daily press conferences, which were now
being held in the upstairs courtroom at the old courthouse
to accommodate the ever-increasing number of reporters
who had traveled to Jonesborough, became adversarial.
Royston stubbornly refused to divulge any information
beyond what everyone already knew, and the reporters pep-
pered him with questions that were obviously intended to
bait him into popping off and telling them something new.

On Tuesday morning, someone leaked a copy of a
ransom note to a tabloid reporter, who immediately put
it up on a website. It said:

> WE HAVE YOUR DAUGHTER.
> RANSOM IS THREE MILLION IN
> CASH IN SEVENTY-TWO HOURS.
> HUNDRED DOLLAR BILLS. NO
> SEQUENCE. FAILURE TO RAISE
> AND DELIVER RANSOM WILL
> RESULT IN HER DEATH. YOU

WILL ONLY GET ONE CHANCE.
IF WE ARE UNABLE TO COLLECT
RANSOM FOR ANY REASON—
INCLUDING INTERFERENCE FROM
POLICE—SHE WILL BE KILLED. IF
ANY OF OUR PEOPLE ARE CAUGHT
BY POLICE, SHE WILL BE KILLED.

The tabloid had gotten a hold of Chief Royston and asked him whether the note was really from the crime scene. He refused to confirm, but he wouldn't deny it either, which told me the note was real.

I was sitting at my computer in the small office I'd rented near the new courthouse in Jonesborough when I read the note. I'd gone back to practicing criminal defense law and had been cherry-picking cases, taking only the ones I wanted, and I worked alone. I didn't even have a secretary. I had a grand total of three cases pending. One was a second-degree murder in Carter County that I thought was justifiable homicide and was scheduled for trial the following February, one was an aggravated robbery that involved a client who I thought had been mistakenly identified, and the third was a misdemeanor assault that involved a sixty-five-year-old high school teacher who had punched a student in the face and knocked him out. The kid who got punched in the face had pulled a girl's panties down in the lunchroom. I thought the kid deserved what he got, so I took the case.

My cell phone rang a little after nine that morning, just after I read the online ransom note. It was Caroline. She sounded excited.

"I just talked to Mary Monroe," she said.

"You're kidding. How is she?"

"Desperate, confused, angry, frustrated. About what you'd expect from a mother whose child is missing and who is being accused of having something to do with it."

"The police think she took her own child?"

"They're accusing both of them. They want to come and talk to you."

"When?"

"Now. They should be there any minute."

It took them a half hour. I watched them pull into a parking space out front. Richard was driving a red, CL600 Mercedes-Benz, a car that costs more than most people's homes. I opened the door for them when they approached.

Mary Monroe was, by any standard, a beautiful woman. Her hair was the color of polished ebony and fell in gentle waves around high cheekbones and a smooth, angular face. Her eyes were sky blue, her nose small and perfect. She was tall and slim and carried herself elegantly. She was wearing a beige jacket over a pale yellow, button-up blouse and a knee-length skirt that matched the jacket. The shoes looked expensive although I wasn't any kind of expert in women's footwear.

Richard was a boy-next-door type. He was the same height as his wife—a little under six feet tall—with wavy, sandy brown hair and dark eyes, an average build, and deep dimples in his cheeks. His smile was what drew my attention first, easy and attractive, the kind of smile that puts people at ease. He was wearing black jeans and casual shoes and a navy blue pullover shirt with a cardigan sweater tied around his neck.

"Sorry it took us so long," Richard said as he walked through the door. "I had to lose a convoy of reporters."

"They followed you?"

"They're disgusting," Mary said. "I've never seen anything like it."

I looked out over the parking lot of the quaint little complex that housed my office, one that included a hair salon, a used-book store, a real estate office, an insurance office, and just around the corner, a diner that my sister had opened in January. It was less than a mile from the Monroes' house. I didn't see any cars pulling in behind the Monroes, but I locked the door anyway and led Richard and Mary through the small reception area back to my office. I smiled and shook their hands.

"Joe Dillard," I said. "I'm pleased to meet you, but I wish it were under different circumstances."

They both looked exhausted. I noticed that Mary had taken the time to put on makeup, but the whites of her eyes were tinted pink and she looked pale and drawn.

"Please, sit down," I said.

They sat in the two chairs in front of my desk. I wanted to sit next to them and express sympathy, to reassure them, but I resisted the impulse. They obviously needed legal advice, and legal advice is best served dispassionately.

I walked around my desk and sat across from them, not really sure how to start the conversation. I sat there awkwardly for a few seconds before I finally said, "I can't imagine what you're going through. Caroline loves Lindsay. I've seen her dance at the recitals, and I've seen her at the studio a couple times, but I've never talked to her. She's a beautiful child."

"Thank you," Mary said. She opened the small purse she was carrying and took out some tissue that had been folded into a square. She held it up for a second and said, "Just in case. I told myself I wouldn't cry. I've cried so much over the past few days that I don't know how I could have any tears left in me."

"How can I help you?"

She looked down and shook her head slowly.

"It's all so ... so *surreal*."

"Caroline said the police might be accusing you of something."

Her head came up quickly and anger flashed in her eyes.

"They're insinuating that we either killed Lindsay or had something to do with her kidnapping. It's the most ludicrous thing I've ever heard."

"Have they interrogated you?" I asked. "By that I mean have they taken you to the police station and talked to you separately?"

"Yesterday," Richard said. "At the FBI office in Johnson City. They split us up and took turns badgering us. One of them, Special Agent Dedrick, the one who seems to be in charge, is the most aggressive."

"The news said Sheriff Bates is in charge," I said.

"In name only," Mary said. "The FBI is running the investigation."

"Dedrick?" I said. "Never heard of him. What's his first name?"

"Ross," Mary said. "Ross Dedrick. I can't stand him. He's smug and rude and thinks he knows everything. We've given him fingerprints, hair samples, and blood samples. They've searched the house, the cars, our beach house in Charleston, our chalet in Vail. We let them take our computers so their geeks can analyze them. When they started making accusations and asked us to take polygraphs, we knew it was time to hire an attorney."

"What do you think makes him suspicious of you?"

"I'm sure they're getting a lot of outside pressure," Richard said. "Pressure from the media, pressure from superiors, that kind of thing. They don't seem to have any viable suspects so they think we must have had something to do with it."

"I read the so-called ransom note on the Internet a little while ago," I said. "Is it legitimate?"

Both of them nodded and Mary's eyes became wet.

"I found it on her pillow when I went into her room Saturday morning," Mary said. "At first I didn't understand .... I didn't know what to think. But then I noticed the window. The screen was cut."

"Was the window locked the night before?"

She shook her head and bit her lip. "I've always liked fresh air. I open the windows sometimes. I never thought about someone climbing up there. It's at least fifteen feet up a brick wall ...." Her shoulders heaved involuntarily and she burst into tears. She cried for maybe a minute— it seemed like an hour— and then, with obvious effort, composed herself.

"I went over to the window and looked out and saw the screen lying on the patio," she said. "I started running around the house looking for Lindsay. I was so upset I don't remember everything clearly. I just remember feeling sick and terrified. I went outside and looked all around the house. I kept calling her name and calling her name, but she didn't answer, and then I went back in and got my cell phone and I called Richard and then I called 9-1-1. A uniformed policeman came first, and then another, and then a supervisor. The house filled with police officers—TBI agents, FBI agents, Jonesborough police, the sheriff. Everything just seemed to spin out of control."

"So you weren't there, Richard?"

"I left for the office at six," Richard said. "I usually go in and kiss Lindsay, but Mary was going to get her up at seven, and I was going to pick them up at eight so I didn't want to disturb her. We were going to drive to a friend's house who lives near the Holston Hills Country Club outside Knoxville. He has a boat and a girl Lindsay's age, and we were going to meet a group of people there and ride to Neyland Stadium on the river and go to the Tennessee game."

"What kind of business are you in?"

"I own a company that develops apps for cell phones. We're going through a little rough spot right now, but overall it's been good."

"Good enough to pay three million in ransom money?"

Richard and Mary exchanged glances and Richard took a deep breath.

"Six months ago it would have been no problem," he said, "but I'm involved in some litigation right now that has everything tied up. One of my former friends, a college roommate, sued me. He thinks he's entitled to half my company. He isn't, but his lawyers filed for a temporary injunction that's making it tough for me to even do business right now, let alone come up with a huge amount of cash. We already have the ransom money though. Mary's father put it together. He and some of his employees are staying at the Carnegie Hotel in Johnson City. He has the money with him."

"Do the police know about the money?"

"That's another reason we came today," Richard said. "The ransom note says no police. You and I both know what the police will do if the kidnapper contacts us. They'll make all the decisions. They'll be more interested in catching the guy than in getting Lindsay back safely. We don't think we want them involved."

I thought the assessment was a bit harsh, but it had at least a smattering of truth to it. The law enforcement officers who were involved would care very much about getting Lindsay back safely, but Richard was right. They would also care very much about catching the kidnapper.

"What exactly do you want me to do for you?" I said.

"Three things," Richard said. "We need you to protect us from the police, protect us from the media, and help us get our daughter back."

I sat back and folded my arms across my chest. I was an experienced trial attorney and had done a fair amount of investigative work, but I had never been involved in a search for a missing child. I thought about the cases of girls like Jaycee Lee Dugard and Elizabeth Smart and JonBenet Ramsey and asked myself whether I wanted to put myself through the gut-wrenching emotions that I knew would go along with representing the parents of a missing six-year-old girl. The case could go on for years.

Then there was the inherent conflict of interest involved in representing two people suspected of committing a crime. I almost decided to pass, to diplomatically explain that I just didn't want to subject myself to this particular brand of turmoil, but then I thought about Caroline and what she said when we were about to leave Jonesborough the day Lindsay was taken: *She's out there somewhere, terrified and alone.* I thought about my daughter, Lilly, and knew that I would have done anything to get her back if someone had taken her.

Mary must have sensed my reluctance, because she stood suddenly and put the tissue back into her purse.

"We had nothing to do with Lindsay's disappearance, Mr. Dillard," she said. "We came to you because of your reputation and because we think so highly of your wife. If you're not interested, perhaps you could recommend someone."

I swallowed hard and made my decision.

"Please, Mrs. Monroe, sit back down," I said. "Are you familiar with the term concurrent conflict of interest?"

She sat back down slowly, shaking her head.

"It basically means that if the police suspect either or both of you of being involved in Lindsay's kidnapping, then there is a possibility that at some point you might be put in the position of having to testify against each other. Or the district attorney might offer one of you a deal to testify against the other. As a lawyer, my loyalty has to be to my client, and in a situation like I've just described, it could become impossible for me to be loyal to both of you."

Richard held up his hand.

"You can stop right there," he said. "I understand what you're saying, but in order for that to happen, one of us would have to be guilty of something. We're not."

"But you could be charged even if you're not guilty," I said. "It happens."

"We'll cross that bridge when we come to it, *if* we come to it," Richard said.

"If either or both of you are charged, I'll have to withdraw or one of you will have to hire another lawyer."

"Agreed," Richard said.

"I'll need you to sign a form that acknowledges that I've explained the potential conflict to you and that you consent to me representing both of you."

"Fine," Richard said. "Mary?"

"That's fine," she said.

"Okay," I said. "Something tells me this isn't a good idea, but if both of you understand the potential conflict and you sign a consent form, then I guess I'm in. You've just hired yourself a lawyer."

PART II

CHAPTER NINE

As I sat there looking at and listening to Richard and Mary Monroe, I wished—for the millionth time in my career—that I could tell whether the people sitting in front of me were telling the truth. I used to think I was good at detecting deception, but the simple fact is that it's almost impossible. There have been many studies done on whether one person can tell if another is being untruthful by looking for physical signs like blinking or looking away or looking up and to the left or looking up and to the right or looking down or waving the hands or crossing the arms or fidgeting, and the scientific consensus is that nearly all those things are as unreliable as the person telling the lie. Human beings have been lying since they learned to talk and they're excellent at it, especially when the truth becomes a danger to their well-being or freedom. Even the results of polygraphs are open to interpretation and notoriously arbitrary, which is why they're inadmissible in court. I'd been deceived many, many times in my career, and as a result, I'd learned to make strategic and tactical legal decisions based solely on admissible evidence. But the most difficult time for a lawyer is early in a case when all he has to go on is what the client is saying. If the client is lying, and the lawyer accepts the lie as truth, the lawyer unwittingly becomes an advocate for deception.

We talked for the next two hours, primarily about Richard and Mary's backgrounds and, of course, about Lindsay. Mary was by far the more emotional of the two when Lindsay was mentioned. She cried repeatedly, and I could almost see her weakening with each passing moment. Richard was more stoic, even brooding at times, especially when Lindsay became the main topic of the conversation. I could only imagine the anger and frustration that must have been churning deep within him, knowing that his only daughter had been stolen from under his nose and there didn't seem to be a thing he could do about it.

I learned that Mary was thirty-two, had been born Mary Catherine Russell and raised in Brentwood, Tennessee. She was the valedictorian of her senior class at Brentwood Academy. Her father, who she said she worshipped, was a former Marine aviator and was now the CEO and majority owner of a highly successful risk-management company based in Nashville. He'd been in town since the evening after Lindsay disappeared. She said her mother was a former beauty queen who became an alcoholic and committed suicide when Mary was sixteen. When she was ten, she said, her parents took in a child named Earl Botts who had become like a brother to her. Botts now worked for her father and was also in town, staying at the Carnegie Hotel.

Mary graduated with a degree in psychology from the University of the South in Sewanee, Tennessee. From there, she'd gone to Europe for a year to travel, then to New York where she lived in Manhattan and tried her hand at musical theater for two years with no success. She came back to Tennessee when she was twenty-five and was visiting a friend in Johnson City when she met Richard at a pig roast. Richard was five years her senior. They fell in love and were married in Hawaii in what she called a storybook wedding a year later. Mary became pregnant with Lindsay six months after that. A complication during delivery had left her unable to have more children, so Lindsay was the focus of her life.

Richard's parents were both high school teachers. His father taught math and his mother taught physics. He described himself as geeky and awkward as a child, a skinny, clumsy lover of video games and fantasy novels. He was a computer science major at East Tennessee State University in Johnson City and had started the company he named Pegasus at the age of nineteen. He and his roommate had programmed a cell phone application that read bar codes for a class project during his junior year. His roommate's main contribution to the project, Richard said, had been to bring beer to the study sessions. Richard thought the app was good enough to sell, and by the time he was halfway through his senior year, he'd sold it to a software-development company for two million dollars. After that, he said, confidence was no longer an issue. He took what he'd learned developing the first app and started on another, and then another, and another. He talked fondly of meeting and marrying Mary and described Lindsay's birth as a "profound experience."

"Tell me about your enemies," I said to Richard.

He frowned and shook his head slightly.

"I don't have any," he said. "At least not in the sense of someone who would take my child for ransom. I have competitors and I have the roommate who sued me—his name is Preston Sparks, by the way—and I'm sure I have some employees who might not be as happy as they'd like to be, but I can't think of a single person who would do something so extreme."

"I know this is a difficult question," I said, "and I'm sure the police have already asked you, but what do you think about who took her? Any ideas?"

"Someone sick and evil," Mary blurted. "I don't think he really wants money. I think he wanted Lindsay and now he has her, and I don't think he has any intention of giving her back."

"Do the police have any theories that don't involve the two of you?"

"If they do, they aren't sharing them with us," Richard said.

"Tell me more about Lindsay."

Through sporadic tears, Mary told me that Lindsay was bright to the point of precociousness, vivacious, and mischievous. She was in the first grade at a private school called Ashton Academy in Johnson City and had already tested in the top percentile in the nation in math and reading among her age group. She took violin lessons, voice lessons and dance lessons, and loved stories about princesses. Mary said that Lindsay idolized my wife and put on mini dance recitals in the living room of their home a couple times a month. She loved to dress up in frilly gowns and wear a tiara, and she had a special affinity for strawberry ice cream and a dwarf hamster she called Belle.

As she was describing her child, I heard the unmistakable chirp of a cell phone.

"Excuse me," Richard said, "I'd better look."

He reached into his pocket and pulled out a phone.

"The number's blocked," he said.

Richard pushed a key and peered at the screen. His eyes widened, and I saw his hands begin to tremble.

"What is it?" I said.

With both hands, he laid the phone on my desk and slid it across to me. I looked at the screen. It was a text message that said, "If you want her back, it's time to pay."

CHAPTER TEN

What should we do? Think!

I'd never been in a situation even remotely similar. Just a few minutes earlier, I'd agreed to become the Monroes' lawyer, to take on their case, to provide counsel. And now, suddenly, an anonymous kidnapper who had already made a three-million-dollar ransom demand was trying to collect. I stared at the text message, wondering, first of all, how the kidnapper got Richard Monroe's cell phone number. I decided to deal with that issue later.

"We have to make some decisions," I said. "What have the police told you to do if the kidnapper contacts you?"

"Call them immediately," Richard said.

"Is that what you want to do?"

Mary shook her head.

"The ransom note said no police," she said. "I'm afraid he'll kill her if we notify them."

"They have experience with this kind of thing," I said. "Especially the FBI. Besides, this could be dangerous. Think about it. We don't know what he has in mind as far as delivering the money. We could wind up delivering ransom money to a psychopath in the middle of nowhere without any kind of protection."

"I'd deliver it to the devil at the gates of hell if it meant getting my daughter back," Richard said.

"Whoever sent the text will know you're close to your phone hoping to hear from him," I said. "You need to answer the text."

I slid the phone back across my desk.

"What should I say?"

"Just say, 'We're ready. We have the money.'"

Richard typed the message and sent it.

He stared at the phone in his hand as the tension in the room built with each passing second. I breathed deeply, trying to calm myself. I had to do this right. A little girl's life hung in the balance. The phone beeped a few seconds later.

"Delivery in one hour," Richard said. "Instructions in thirty minutes."

"Tell him to prove Lindsay is alive."

Richard typed the message, and the phone pinged in his hand thirty seconds later.

"It's a photo," Richard said. He looked at the phone for a few seconds and cursed. Mary leaned toward him and looked down at the screen. She shrieked as Richard stood and handed the phone to me. The photo was of Lindsay. She was gagged with what looked like a bandana and was lying curled into a fetal position in a wooden box. Attached to the photo was another text: "Pay or she dies."

"We have to call the police," I said.

"We came to you for help," Richard said. "Help us. We won't risk Lindsay's life by involving them."

"I don't have any experience dealing with kidnappers and ransom money. I'd feel better if we had someone involved who knows what they're doing."

"Do you think the police know what they're doing?" Richard said. The words were clipped and there was intensity in his voice. "Do they *really* know what they're doing? How many times have you heard of the police getting involved in a ransom situation and everything turning out fine?"

I thought for a minute. I couldn't think of a single instance that involved police, kidnappers, ransom money, and a happy ending.

"Call Mary's father," I said. "Tell him to have the money ready when we get there. Let's go."

CHAPTER ELEVEN

Charles Russell, Mary Monroe's father, opened the door to a large suite and Mary made a quick introduction. He was lean and hard-looking like an old soldier, probably early sixties, his receding gray hair shaved to within a quarter inch of his scalp, his eyes the same sky blue as Mary's. He was dressed semi-formally in a navy blue jacket and starched white shirt, no tie, slacks that matched the jacket, and black shoes with a mirror shine. I noticed that Richard walked past him without looking at him or saying a word.

I was in the middle of describing what had happened at my office when Richard's phone rang. The number was blocked, but this time it wasn't a text message. The kidnapper was calling.

"Put it on speaker," I said, and Richard answered the phone.

"Have you followed my instructions?" The voice sounded like Darth Vader. It was obviously being run through some kind of alteration device.

"Yes," Richard said.

"Are you ready to make delivery?"

"I want to speak to my daughter! Right now!"

"Your daughter is unharmed."

"Let me talk to her! Put her on the phone!"

"Shut your mouth and listen. If you don't do exactly as I say, I'll cut her head off and leave it in your mailbox."

Mary was standing next to her father. The color suddenly went out of her face, her eyelids fluttered, her eyes rolled back, and she dropped straight to the floor. Richard and Charles Russell went to her immediately and Richard tossed the phone to me.

"This is Joe Dillard," I said. "If you want the money, you'll have to deal with me."

There was silence for about ten seconds before he said, "So you're the bag man. Perfect job for a scumbag lawyer."

How did he know I was a lawyer? I looked over at Mary. Her eyes were open, and Richard was whispering in her ear.

"Just tell me what you want me to do and let's get this finished," I said. "All we want is Lindsay back safely."

"Take the money, take the phone, get in your vehicle and start driving north on the interstate. Alone. If anyone follows, I'll know."

The line went dead just as a man walked through the door carrying a large, black suitcase. He was dressed almost identically to Russell—the only difference was that his suit was charcoal gray.

"This is Earl Botts," Charles Russell said.

Mary had told me earlier that Botts was the same age as she. He had light blond hair, almost white, and his eyes were an unusual color, something like dark gold. He had a long, sharp nose and a sharper chin. The combination of the eyes and the nose gave him the look of an eagle or a hawk.

"What's going on?" Botts said.

"The kidnapper just called," Russell said. "Mr. Dillard is going to take the money and deliver it."

"This is unacceptable," Botts said. He seemed as frustrated and angry as everyone else in the room. He carried the suitcase, which was obviously heavy, to where Mary was still lying on the floor and set it down. He stared at me like I was the enemy.

"I'm open to suggestions," I said.

"I need some idea of where you're going so we can ... never mind. Give me the phone."

He reached out his hand, and I looked at Richard and Charles Russell. Richard nodded, and I handed the phone to Botts. He disappeared into what I assumed was a bedroom for a couple minutes. When he returned, he gave Mary's phone back to me and nodded toward the suitcase.

"I installed a transmitter on the phone so we can monitor the calls and the texts," Botts said. "The money's in the case."

"Are you going to follow me?"

"The less you know the better."

"And if he sees you? If he knows you're following me, he'll kill her."

"Let me worry about that."

"Go," Charles Russell said to me. "Take the suitcase and go. Bring my granddaughter back."

I exchanged phone numbers with Charles, walked out of the room to the parking lot, and got into my truck.

SCOTT PRATT

I pulled onto Interstate 26 and headed north. A wave of anxiety came over me as I realized just how bizarre a turn the day had taken. Just a few hours earlier, I'd been an interested but uninvolved bystander in the Lindsay Monroe case, and now I was driving down the road with a suitcase filled with three million dollars in ransom money that I was delivering to a ruthless kidnapper who obviously knew what he was doing. The thought crossed my mind again that we should have involved the police. If anything went wrong and if the police found out about it, I knew there would be hell to pay.

I forced myself to calm down. *Just do what the man says. That's all. Just do what he says.* I looked in the rearview mirror. The traffic behind me was thick. There was no way to tell whether anyone was following me.

For the next forty minutes, I received periodic text messages telling me which exit to take, which road to take, which direction to turn. I didn't know the destination until I pulled into the parking lot at Steele Creek Park in Bristol. There wasn't a single vehicle in the lot besides mine. A text message told me to get out and walk to the Lakeside Trail. I grabbed the heavy suitcase—it had to weigh close to seventy-five pounds—and got out.

It was one o'clock in the afternoon. The temperature was mid-fifties or so and falling. It was windy and a dark bank of thunderheads was rolling in from the northeast. The park was deserted. I walked along a trail that wound through thick woods beside a lake for about twenty minutes when Richard's phone, which I was carrying in my left hand, rang.

"Dillard."

"There is a trash can fifty yards ahead on your right," the altered, alien-sounding voice said. "Remove the lid, empty the money from the case into the can, and take the case with you. Walk—don't run—back to your vehicle and drive away. Don't do anything to call attention to yourself. If I see your vehicle again after you leave the park or if I see anything even remotely suspicious, I'll kill her."

I looked around at the tree-covered hills. He was watching me, and he was close. I could feel his eyes on me. I wondered about Botts and what he was doing, whether he had followed me, whether he had other people with him, or whether Richard and Mary had had a change of heart and had perhaps gotten in touch with the FBI. I wondered whether there might be a rifle pointed at my head and whether I'd see my family again. I cursed myself for allowing things to spin out of control so quickly, for allowing myself to become so vulnerable. I wondered whether I'd suddenly hear the roar of helicopters as an FBI SWAT team descended on the park.

"Where is Lindsay?" I said into the phone. "When do I get her?"

"After," the voice said. The phone clicked in my ear, and he was gone.

The trash can was sitting on a concrete pad next to a bench. It was made of galvanized steel. I removed the lid. The can was empty. It looked new and there was no trash bag or liner. I poured the bundles of cash into it—three hundred bundles of one-hundred-dollar bills, ten thousand dollars in each bundle. I'd never seen that much money. The wind was beginning to howl, the storm quickly approaching.

I put the lid back on the trash can and walked back to my truck. The storm unleashed its fury just as I shut the door. I called Charles Russell as soon as I pulled out of the parking lot.

"Any word from Botts?" I said. "What's going on?"

"He's waiting for him to pick up the money. As soon as he does, Earl will take him down."

"Botts is here? At the park?"

"He's where he needs to be. Did you see anything?"

"Nothing. But the kidnapper was watching me. He knew exactly where I was."

Botts must have been out there too. Somewhere. What was he, some kind of spook? I thought about turning around and going back. There was a high-stakes cat-and-mouse game going on at the park, and a part of me wanted to be in the middle of it.

"Isn't there anything I can do?" I said.

"Nothing."

"Did you call the FBI?"

"Earl and his people are on it. He's a professional."

Earl and his people? Charles Russell hadn't said anything about what Botts did, but if Charles had more confidence in Botts than he had in the FBI, Botts had to be a formidable man.

"How's Mary?"

"Not well."

"So there's nothing I can do?"

"All we can do right now is wait," Russell said. "Wait and pray."

CHAPTER TWELVE

I dropped Richard's phone off at the Carnegie Hotel a little after 1:00 p.m. and talked to Charles Russell for just a few minutes. He said he'd called Mary's doctor and obtained a mild sedative for her and that she was lying down. He was abrupt and irritable, so I left and drove back to my office in Jonesborough. On the way, I called Caroline and asked her to meet me at my sister's diner. I'd been up since 5:00 a.m. and hadn't eaten anything the entire day.

I loved my sister, Sarah, but she'd been a pain in everybody's butt for most of her life. She'd taken a traumatic childhood event—extremely traumatic, she'd been raped by our uncle when she was nine—and turned it into an anvil she'd been dragging around for almost forty years. She'd been a copious consumer of drugs and alcohol, and she'd stolen from people, including me, when things were at their worst. She'd also done more than one stretch in the county jail, but she seemed to have finally put it behind her. She'd opened a cafeteria-style diner in Jonesborough just a few doors down from my office that she called "Granny's" and was doing quite well clogging the arteries of the locals with fried chicken, roast beef, pork chops, ham, and gravy. She served vegetables, but the cauliflower was covered in cheese sauce, the green beans were cooked in bacon fat, and the mashed potatoes were stuffed with butter. Her food was a heart attack on a plate, but people loved it.

It was close to two o'clock when Caroline showed up, and the diner was winding down for the day. I always enjoyed going in there. The food was good, the atmosphere pleasant, and because Sarah and many of the courthouse employees were insufferable gossips, it was a great place to gather information. Sarah was in the kitchen when we went through the line and didn't see us come in. We sat down at a table in the corner.

"So?" Caroline said. She looked at me with those liquid, brown eyes that could soften my heart in an instant. At forty-five, even after everything she'd been through with the cancer treatments, even after bearing two children and putting up with me for twenty-five years, she was still the most beautiful thing I'd ever seen. Her wavy, auburn hair still shined, her skin was soft and clear, and her figure hadn't changed since high school.

"It's as bad as it could be," I said quietly as I stirred mashed potatoes and peas together on the plate. "I just dropped three million dollars in ransom money off at a park in Bristol."

She stared at me for a minute, silent.

"Say that again," she said.

I leaned forward and kept my voice down. "I met Mary and Richard at the office. We talked for a while and I agreed to represent them. Then Richard got a text message from the kidnapper. Everything happened so fast I'm having trouble believing it myself. But I wound up in the middle of it, and I just dropped three million dollars in ransom money off at a park in Bristol. We're waiting now to see if he picks up the money and releases Lindsay."

"But why you? Why didn't the police send one of their own to drop the money off?"

"Because we didn't call the police and tell them it was happening. The kidnapper kept saying if the police were involved he'd kill Lindsay. I just kind of stumbled into the whole thing. Bad timing."

"Where did you leave the money?"

"In a trash can by the lake at Steele Creek Park."

"So that's it? You just took the money and left it and you're trusting this person to give Lindsay back without notifying the police?"

"It wasn't my call. Mary's father is involved. He put up the ransom money. I'm not sure what he does, but he had this other guy at the hotel with him, a young guy named Botts that Charles apparently took in and raised, who acted like he knew what he was doing. I think Botts and maybe some other people are in the woods waiting for the kidnapper to show up and pick up the money. When he comes, they'll probably grab him."

"And then what?"

"I don't know. I honestly don't know, but I got the feeling that this Botts guy is—or was—some kind of spook. Maybe former FBI or CIA or special forces or something like that. You should see the guy. He looks like a blond-headed raptor."

"What happens if they don't catch him? Or what if he spots them and doesn't pick up the money?"

"I'm trying to stay positive right now. If the kidnapper just wants money, maybe he'll be smart enough to get his hands on it and he'll give her back."

"Is that what you think will happen?"

"That's what I *hope* will happen, but I did a little research after Lindsay went missing. If she was taken by a stranger—and it looks pretty certain that she was—the odds of her still being alive aren't good."

"She isn't dead, Joe."

"And you're basing that assertion on?"

"Intuition, whatever you want to call it. I can feel it."

"Great. Can you feel exactly where she is so I can go and pick her up and put an end to this mess?"

"Don't make fun of me. She's still alive."

I saw Sarah walk out of the kitchen carrying a cup of coffee. She made her way over to our table, greeting the few remaining customers and smiling. Sarah the hostess. Sarah the glad-hander. It was such a different life than the one she'd lived for so long.

"Don't you have work to do?" I said as she set her coffee down on the table.

"You ever heard of employees? They can handle it for a few minutes. I've been here since four thirty this morning and haven't had a break."

Sarah hugged Caroline's neck, gave me the finger, and sat down. She was dark-haired and green-eyed, her skin still remarkably unblemished, especially considering all the abuse she'd doled out to herself over the years. She was forty-six and looked like she was in her early thirties. She was wearing black jeans and a purple T-shirt that said, "Don't Bother, I'm Not Drunk" across the front.

"How's Grace?" I asked. Sarah's daughter was three years old.

"Cute as a button, mean as a snake."

"She comes by the second part honestly."

"Did anyone ever tell you you're a jerk?"

"Not since the last time I talked to you."

Caroline blurted, "Joe's representing Richard and Mary Monroe."

I gave Caroline a look that said I didn't want to talk about what had happened in front of Sarah while Sarah looked at me with raised eyebrows and took a sip of her coffee.

"Really? The parents of a kidnap victim? Why would they need a lawyer?"

"You ever heard of John and Patsy Ramsey?" I said. "You know how cops can be. They just want me to run some interference until things calm down."

"He's going to help them find her," Caroline said. She's a pathetic liar, but Sarah acted like she didn't notice.

"Do you have any idea what you're doing?" Sarah said. "I mean, how do you go about finding a child that was in her bed one second and gone the next? Do you have any experience with this type of thing?"

"None whatsoever," I said as I chewed a piece of baked chicken. "And the answer to your first question is also no. I have no idea what I'm doing."

Sarah turned and looked over her shoulder.

"He's here again," she said.

"Who?"

"This guy. Don't look over there. He's sitting in the corner by himself. This is the third day he's been here. He gets his food and goes to the corner and he sits there for an hour. He stares at me."

"You want me to talk to him? Ask him if there's a problem? Or are you just being paranoid?"

"Don't bother him," she said. "He hasn't caused any trouble. It's just kind of creepy. I swear I know him from somewhere, but I can't place him."

"I think I'll go wash my hands," I said.

I stood up and walked to the restroom, which was only about ten feet from where the man was sitting. He looked down when I caught his eye, but I had the same feeling Sarah had described, a vague notion of recognition. He looked to be in his mid-sixties with short, salt-and-pepper hair and a prominent chin, wearing a button-down, light blue shirt. His skin was pale and his cheeks hollow. Even though he looked away quickly, I saw his eyes, turquoise and intense. I went into the bathroom, washed my hands, and when I came back out, he was gone.

"Looks familiar to me too," I said when I sat back down at the table.

"What'd you say to him? You ran him off," Sarah said. "As soon as the bathroom door closed, he made a beeline for the door."

"Didn't say anything. I swear I know that guy from somewhere."

"See what I mean?" Sarah said. "It's eerie."

The call from Charles Russell came at one in the morning. I was shooting pool alone in the game room in the basement. Caroline had already hit the sack.

"Botts waited until midnight," Russell said. "They kept the area under constant surveillance and hadn't seen anything all day. He finally sent one of his men to look in the can where you left the money."

His words were clipped, his tone angry.

"Whoever did this is a professional," he said. "The can was sitting directly above a drainage culvert that's buried two feet underground. Someone had tunneled up from the pipe, through the concrete. There was a false bottom in the trash can."

"So the money is gone?"

"The money is gone."

"Any word from him?"

"Nothing. He took my granddaughter, and now he's taken my money. I swear on my mother's grave I'm going to find him and kill him."

CHAPTER THIRTEEN

I went to bed with a hollow feeling in the pit of my stomach and woke up feeling the same way. We'd failed. We had a chance to get Lindsay back and we blew it. I couldn't shake the feeling that there must have been something I could have done, that there was something I should have noticed that would have made a difference while I was delivering the money.

I went into the office the next morning, but I couldn't concentrate on anything. I surfed the Internet for news about Lindsay Monroe and immediately found something disturbing. The same Internet tabloid site that had put up a copy of the ransom note carried a story that said the police suspected both Richard and Mary Monroe of being involved in Lindsay's abduction. The story, written by a woman named Blaire Reed, quoted anonymous sources and was long on speculation and short on specifics. It was blatant sensationalism, but at least there wasn't anything about the ransom delivery. Botts and his people may have failed at getting Lindsay back, but they apparently knew how to keep their mouths shut.

As soon as I finished reading the story, I picked up the phone and called Richard Monroe. I talked to him for a little while about how the kidnapper might have obtained his cell phone number and asked him to e-mail me a list of the contacts from his cell phone and his relationship with each person.

After I hung up, I turned my attention to a stack of business cards Mary Monroe had left at my office the previous day. She'd picked them up in various places around her house—in the mailbox, on the porches, a few had even been slid under the front and back doors, all of them from reporters. She'd also showed me another two or three dozen messages reporters had sent to her on Facebook. Invariably, they all wanted to tell "Richard and Mary's side of the story." None of them had yet managed to get a hold of Richard or Mary's personal e-mail or cell numbers, but I didn't think it would be long. One of the cards was from Blaire Reed, the reporter who worked for *The World* and who had written both the story about the ransom note and the story that speculated that the Monroes were behind their daughter's kidnapping. I did some quick research on Blaire Reed. She'd done a lot of crime stories, most of them sensational, some of them utterly ridiculous. *The World* was one of the big national tabloids that are sold in grocery stores. I'd seen it hundreds of times and had never touched one. I dialed her number.

"I have a proposition for you," I said after I told her who I was.

"How much do you want?" she said.

"Beg your pardon?"

"You're a lawyer about to offer me a story. How much will it cost?"

"I don't want money and I'm not offering you a story. How about a face-to-face? Tonight, nine o'clock, a little bar on Oakland Avenue in Johnson City called Pappy's."

"I'll be there."

I hung up and checked my e-mail. Richard Monroe had already sent me the list of contacts from his cell phone. It was a long list that included friends, employees, business associates, doctors, lawyers, accountants, a dentist, two insurance agents, two hair stylists, a masseuse, three realtors, three luxury car salesmen, two florists, two lawn services, three landscape designers, two personal trainers, three catering services, four contractors, two liquor stores, two painters, two mechanics, and a tree-trimming service, plus all the people who were involved in his life because of Lindsay, people like Caroline and the voice teacher and the violin teacher and people from Ashton Academy.

As I was poring over it, my phone rang. It was Sarah.

"Where are you?" She sounded upset.

"In my office. Why?"

"He's back. The man who's been coming in here for lunch. He's standing right here in front of me. He wants to talk to both of us."

"I'll be right there."

"He says he wants to talk privately. Can we come over there?"

"Sure."

"Be there in a minute."

I met them at the door. He was about six three, the same height as me, wearing the same clothes he had on the day before. He nodded at me as he walked past.

"Who are you?" I said gruffly. "What do you want?"

"I'm not here to do anyone any harm," he said. His tone and demeanor were calm. I looked him up and down, trying to figure out why he seemed so familiar. "Can we sit down and talk like reasonable people?"

I glanced at Sarah. She shrugged her shoulders as if to say, "Why not?" They sat in the same chairs Richard and Mary Monroe had occupied twenty-four hours earlier.

"I'm here about your father," he said.

"You knew him?" Sarah asked.

My father had been dead for forty-five years. He was drafted into the U.S. Army and sent to Vietnam. He was there for six months, then went on a ten-day leave to Hawaii where he vacationed with my mother and his infant daughter, Sarah. I was conceived during that week. A month later, he was killed in action. I never laid eyes on him.

"I want to tell you a story about a young man, only nineteen when he was sent to the jungle. Your father was a LRRP. Do you know what that means?"

LRRPs, pronounced "lurps," stood for "long range reconnaissance patrol." The LRRP soldiers worked in small teams early in the Vietnam War. They were inserted behind enemy lines and tasked with intelligence gathering, clearing landing zones, kidnapping, and ambush.

"I was a Ranger," I said. "I know what a LRRP is."

"I wasn't aware that you served," he said. "Did you see combat?"

I nodded. "I was one of the first out the door when we jumped onto the airfield at Point Saline in Grenada."

"Then you know what kind of training your father went through, and you understand the terror of combat. In August of 1966, his company was operating out of a base not far from a place called Tuy Hoa. His team was inserted by helicopter near what was reported to be a large Viet Cong force that was planning to attack an air base nearby—"

"You were there?" Sarah interrupted. "You were with him?"

"I was there. Six of us rappelled from a helicopter into the jungle at midnight. We hid until daybreak and then started moving along a trail. We'd only been walking for about a half hour when we were ambushed. Our point man was killed immediately, shot in the head, and our radio operator went down a few seconds later. We returned fire, but before we knew it we were flanked. A rocket blew my best friend to pieces. He and I were running for better cover and all of a sudden he just seemed to explode. The blast knocked me unconscious for a short amount of time—I don't know exactly how long it was—but when I woke up, I realized I was the only one left alive. The Viet Cong had stopped firing, but I could hear them calling to each other. They were close, and right then, at that moment, I made a decision that changed my life. I started crawling away on my belly. I crawled until I couldn't hear them and then I started running and I didn't stop until my legs gave out. I was alone in the jungle with no radio, no way to contact anyone. I had some food and water, a weapon, and a rough idea of where I was, but I'd already decided I wasn't going back. I couldn't. I'd seen a dozen of my team members die and twice that many wounded, and for the life of me, I couldn't understand why. So I headed west. I made my way into Laos and eventually all the way to Malaysia. I settled in Kuala Lumpur and have lived there ever since. I married and raised two daughters. My wife is gone now, and my daughters are both married and raising their own children. I had a good life there, but I needed to come back."

"So you deserted," I said.

He nodded and frowned. "Yes, I deserted, and the longer I stayed gone, the more ashamed I became of what I'd done."

"But you shouldn't have been ashamed," Sarah said. "You couldn't have saved anyone. You said they were already dead when you woke up from the explosion that killed your friend. Was it our father? Was he your friend?"

"Before I started crawling," he said, "I saw his dog tags, covered in blood, lying on the ground next to me. I picked them up, and I took mine off and laid them there."

It took me a few seconds to understand the ramifications of what he'd just said.

"That means that you were reported as killed in action when you were still alive, and the man you switched tags with was reported as missing in action," I said. "What is your name? Your real name?"

"You have a son named Jack," he said. "You named him after your father."

"That's right."

"You named him after me."

CHAPTER FOURTEEN

My breath was taken away momentarily. I was so stunned I couldn't talk, couldn't hear, couldn't think. It was like an epiphany, a sudden understanding that causes a person to have to reorder everything he's ever believed or thought he knew. I looked across the table at Sarah, who was in a similar stupor. She was staring at me but I don't think she could see me. My surprise quickly turned to denial.

"You're lying," I said. "I don't know who you are or what you're trying to pull, but you're obviously mentally ill."

"Look at him." Sarah's voice was just above a whisper. "He looks just like you. That's why he was so familiar."

"No, he doesn't."

Anger, my lifelong nemesis, was quickly building inside me. My stomach was beginning to knot, and my vision was beginning to narrow. I could feel my thighs and hands trembling slightly.

"He doesn't look anything like me," I said. "He looks like a sick old man who's trying to get his jollies by playing some kind of psychotic joke on us. What is it? Did I represent some scumbag relative of yours? Some murderer who got convicted and you're trying to get back at me?" I stood and pointed at the door. "Get the hell out of here and don't come back. Old man or not, if I ever see you again, I'll break every bone in your body."

He took an envelope from his back pocket and started pulling out photographs and documents and setting them on my desk.

"I'm sorry," he said. "I know how difficult this must be for both of you. These two are pictures of your mother when she was a senior in high school. This one is of me and you, Sarah, when you were two months old, right before I left for boot camp. This is my driver's license that was issued in 1965, this is my Social Security card, and this is my military I.D. card."

The face in the photo of him and Sarah convinced me. I had an old photo of my father sitting on a shelf in my den. It was taken in Vietnam before he was killed, or at least supposedly killed. The person in that photo was the same person that was peering out at me from the photo on the table, holding a baby and smiling. I looked at the old man, back at the photo, and over at Sarah, once again speechless.

"I've been ashamed every day of my life since then," he said. "Too ashamed to come back here. Too ashamed to admit what I did."

Sarah stood up and walked toward the bathroom. I heard her sniffle as she pushed the door open, and I knew she was going in there to cry, which was something she did very, very rarely. I looked back at the man sitting across from me. His face reflected a profound sadness, but I felt no empathy. I can't adequately describe what I was feeling at that moment. My emotions were so polarized, so utterly conflicting, that I found myself nearly paralyzed.

I finally managed to say, "Who is lying in the grave at the V.A. that has your name on it? Whose family is probably still hoping that their son is alive somewhere? That he'll miraculously show up one day. That he was brainwashed in some Vietnamese prison camp and doesn't even know who he is anymore."

He reached back into the envelope and laid a beaded chain with a dog tag attached on the table. "His name was Lucas Venable. We went through boot camp and Ranger school together. He was the best friend I ever had."

"Have you bothered to contact his family? To tell them he's dead? That he's lying in a grave marked with someone else's name?"

His eyes watered and his lower lip quivered. "I've thought about writing to them a million times," he said. "But they deserve more than that. His parents are still alive. They're in a little town in Wisconsin called Fairfield."

"How do you know?"

"The same way I found out about you. I didn't even know I had a son until the Internet came along. Your mother hadn't told me she was pregnant. She may not have even known until after ... until after—"

"Until after you stole your best friend's dog tags, deserted your unit and the Army, and abandoned your family? Is that what you were about to say?"

"I don't expect you to forgive me," he said. "That isn't why I came here."

"Why *did* you come here? Why bother? Why couldn't you have just left it alone and let us go on believing you died in combat? That you were a hero instead of a coward and a deserter?"

He folded his hands on the table in front of him. They were large like mine, the fingers long and thick. Unlike mine, they were covered in liver spots.

"I just thought you should know the truth before I die."

I shook my head, incredulous now.

"You came here to die?"

"I was born here. I want to die here. I'd like to be buried next to your mother. I loved her dearly."

"Stop! Just stop right there." I held up my hands. "You need to leave. Right now."

He reached into the envelope one last time and retrieved a folded piece of paper.

"This is where I'm staying. Room number and phone number."

He laid the paper down among the other things, stood, and shuffled to the door. I watched him. He stopped and turned back to face me.

"I'm sorry, Joseph," he said. "I'm truly sorry."

And then he was gone. I turned and headed for the bathroom to retrieve Sarah and try to offer her some comfort, or to let her comfort me.

CHAPTER FIFTEEN

You can't miss what you've never had. I kept repeating those words to myself. You can't miss what you've never had.

Sarah had actually taken the encounter with the man who called himself Jack Dillard better than I thought she would, at least on the surface. At one point she smiled and looked at me with wet, gleaming eyes and said, "Who'd a thunk it?" But that was Sarah's way. Her primary psychological defense mechanisms were sarcasm and dark humor, usually ladled out with a thick dollop of profanity on top. I loved her deeply, though, and was concerned that the shock of what she'd learned that morning would send her back into the abyss of drug and alcohol abuse. She assured me it wouldn't, and when she left, she said she was going to work the rest of the day and then head straight to the babysitter's to pick up Grace.

I sat behind my desk for a while, thinking about what had just happened. I wanted to call Caroline—she was my best friend and my counselor—but before I did, I wanted to try to think it through on my own. Growing up without a father was something I'd never really allowed myself to dwell upon, at least not consciously. There'd been pangs of envy and regret when I was young, when I'd seen other boys with their fathers or heard other boys talk about their fathers, but I didn't wallow in self-pity. I stayed busy, I worked hard, and I avoided self-examination. My mother, on the other hand, was embittered by the Vietnam War and spent her life thinking that politicians, generals, and defense contractors—the military-industrial complex that Dwight Eisenhower had spoken of when he left office—had robbed her of her husband. She rarely mentioned my father, and when she did, it was invariably followed by an acid-laced diatribe against the government. I wondered how she would have felt if she'd known he'd abandoned her, that he'd abandoned all of us and was living in Malaysia with another family.

I like to think I derived one important benefit from growing up without a father though. I became an attentive and loving father to my own children. I had no regrets about the way Caroline and I had gone about raising them. We'd made some mistakes, certainly, but as the old saying goes, children don't come with instructions. I could look back on the two decades-plus that Jack and Lilly had been alive, and I knew that I'd done everything I could to help them become independent, to help them find their own way in the world, and to let them know that I loved and supported them. Jack had been gone for five years attending college and playing baseball, and I missed him terribly, but whenever I thought of him, I felt a sense of pride and satisfaction. It was the same with Lilly, who was now married, raising her own son, and working while her husband attended medical school. I wondered whether I might have taken fatherhood for granted somehow if mine had been around when I was young. There was no way of knowing.

You can't miss what you never had. You can't miss what you never had. The words kept running through my mind like a mantra.

The beep of my cell phone brought me out of the trance. It was a text from Richard Monroe. It said simply, "What now?"

I got up, went into the restroom, splashed some cold water on my face, and looked in the mirror.

"Deal with the old man later," I said out loud. "You have a child to find."

I texted Richard back and asked him to lose the reporters again and come to the office. He showed up in twenty minutes and said he and Mary hadn't gone back home. They'd gone to a close friend's house instead. Mary was resting, still under the influence of sedatives her doctor had prescribed. It was certainly understandable. Her father's money was now gone along with her daughter, and the situation seemed hopeless. I told Richard I thought it would be best to inform the police about the money being taken, and he reluctantly agreed. He asked me to handle it, which meant I would soon be having an unpleasant exchange with either Leon Bates or the FBI.

We spent the next couple hours organizing the list Richard had e-mailed me into columns of friends, professionals, business contacts, and a column I labeled "miscellaneous." We talked about each one briefly, and the more we talked, the more I realized what a daunting task it would be for me to effectively cover the list.

Even if I could, there was no way of knowing whether the person who had kidnapped Lindsay was on the list. Still, there were several people that interested me, and I wanted to talk to all of them. My biggest concern was time. How much longer would Lindsay be alive, if she was still alive?

"I don't care all that much for Charles or Earl, but they're supposed to be very good at what they do," Richard said when we took a break from the list. "And if they are, then who—or what— are we up against? I feel like the kidnapper is toying with us, but at the same time, because he's toying with us, I feel like Lindsay is still alive."

I nodded my head and must have smiled unconsciously.

"What?" Richard said. "Did I say something funny?"

"No, no. I was just thinking about something my wife said yesterday. She feels the same way you do about Lindsay being alive, and judging from experience, I tend to take her intuition pretty seriously. So what does Charles's company do? Mary said something about risk management. Is he in the insurance business?"

"Security," Richard said. "Mostly human security, as in protecting business executives and diplomats in foreign countries. They do a lot of high-risk work in dangerous places. One thing I've heard Charles talk about is ransom kidnappings in South America and Mexico. That's one of the reasons I was okay with leaving the police out of it. Charles used to talk about his business when Mary and I were first married. He doesn't say much anymore though."

"Did something happen between you?"

"Not really. Mary let a few things slip about him, things about how he treated her mother. I asked him about it a couple years ago when we were all on vacation in Belize and Charles and I were both half in the bag. It didn't go well. We haven't talked much since."

"But Mary said she worships him. That's the word she used—*worship*."

"I know, and she does, at least to an extent. He's a decorated Marine aviator and a multi-millionaire, a self-made man's man. In a lot of ways, he's a daughter's dream. It's a complicated relationship, but that isn't so unusual, is it? A lot of fathers and daughters have complicated relationships. We've never really gotten into it that deeply. Mary and I have been happy, and I didn't see the point in pushing it. She seemed to be doing just fine—*we* seemed to be doing just fine—until this happened."

"Do you want me to share information with your father-in-law and Botts? Do you want me to keep working with them to try to find Lindsay after what happened yesterday? I guess it would make sense since they have experience with ransom kidnappings and know how to track people, but there are going to be problems with the police from now on. As soon as they find out what happened, they're going to start yelling and screaming and threatening to arrest people for obstruction of justice and interference with an investigation."

As if on cue, I heard the buzzer that told me someone was walking through the front door. I got up and walked to the small foyer and was confronted by three men wearing ill-fitting suits and ugly shoes. Only cops wore suits and shoes like that, and because the suits were decent quality and none of them were fat, I knew they were FBI agents.

The one leading the way was Slavic-looking—sandy-blond hair cut like a politician's, icy, green eyes, pinkish complexion, and an equine face. He was a couple inches taller than me, thick-chested, broad-shouldered, and strong-necked. I stopped a few feet from him, and we locked eyes the way a couple bulls would lock horns.

"What can I do for you gentlemen?" I said.

"I understand you delivered three million dollars in ransom money yesterday," the Aryan said. "Three million dollars that wound up being stolen by a man who had already kidnapped a child."

"You must be Special Agent Dedrick," I said.

"I'm your worst nightmare right now, lawyer."

"I'm terrified. Do you mind if I ask how you obtained this scurrilous information?"

"From the kidnapper, pretty boy. I had a little trouble understanding him, though, because he couldn't stop laughing."

Richard Monroe stepped out of my office and into the foyer. Dedrick eyed him suspiciously for a couple seconds before turning his attention back to me.

"Do you think you can just waltz in and take over a kidnapping investigation?" Dedrick said. "Because if you do, you're—"

"Mr. and Mrs. Monroe have hired me to represent them," I said. "If you have anything more to say to them, you'll have to go through me."

"I want their cell phones," Dedrick snapped.

"Then get a warrant."

"I'll have it in a couple hours."

"Really? And your probable cause will be what? You have no idea who the kidnapper is so the parents must have something to do with it?"

"My probable cause will be that they obstructed justice and interfered with a federal investigation."

I turned and smiled at Richard. "See? What'd I tell you?"

"You find this amusing, do you?" Dedrick said.

"No, I find it tragic," I said, "but I've been around this block as many times as you have, and I know when a cop is blowing smoke. The Monroes have no legal obligation to cooperate with you in any way, especially since you've openly accused them of being involved in their daughter's kidnapping. You've made them suspects, and that gives them rights. One of those rights is to tell you to go piss up a rope, and right now, that's what they're inclined to do. So I'm going to ask you politely—one time—to please get out of my office. Mr. Monroe and I are busy."

The muscles in Dedrick's jaw started twitching, and a vein popped out in the middle of his forehead. I noticed his left hand as it closed into a fist. It was good to know that his buttons were so easily pushed. He was angry and off-balance, so I decided to give him another nudge.

"Go find Lindsay Monroe," I said. "Go do your job."

He took a step toward me, and for a second, I thought he was going to take a swing at me.

"I'll find her," he hissed. "I'll find her, I'll find the kidnapper, and I'll find the money. And while I'm at it,

I'm going to find a way to have you disbarred and thrown in jail where you belong."

"Sometimes I think being disbarred wouldn't be such a bad thing," I said. "At least I wouldn't have to deal with badge-toting muscle heads who think they know the law and get off on making empty threats."

He glared at me while his buddies shifted uneasily behind him. After several seconds, he turned abruptly and walked out the door with his little entourage in tow. I turned and looked at Richard, whose face had taken on the color of bleached bone.

"That went well," I said. "Don't you think?"

CHAPTER SIXTEEN

Later that afternoon, I drove to the East Tennessee State University campus to an appointment I hadn't told Richard or Mary about. Tom Short, a forensic psychiatrist whom I'd worked with many times in the past, was waiting for me in his office. Tom was a short, wiry academic with a neatly clipped gray beard and a pipe that he used like a pacifier. He never lit the thing, but it was almost always in his mouth. He was sitting at his desk staring at a computer screen flanked by two shaded lamps. He turned his head when I walked in and peered at me over his reading glasses.

"You remind me of a Timex watch," he said.

"Beg your pardon?"

"Takes a lickin' and keeps on tickin'? Remember that old saw? Nobody even wears watches these days. Cell phones have made them obsolete."

I smiled and reached for his hand as he stood.

"It's good to see you again, Tom."

"And you as well. You really don't look much worse for the wear. I expected you would have aged more after ... after ...."

"The gunfight at the OK Corral?"

"I never really got the details, just what I read in the paper."

"You don't want to know."

"But you're okay about it? Nightmares? Anxiety attacks? Depression? Anything like that?"

"Nightmares for a while, but not anymore."

That wasn't entirely true. I still had nightmares once in awhile, but they were neither as frequent nor as intense as they'd been in the immediate aftermath. Tom looked at me with what I perceived as a touch of skepticism for a few seconds, but then he motioned to the chair in front of his desk.

"Take a seat, Joe. After we talked on the phone, I decided to do some research to refresh my memory. I haven't worked on a kidnapping case in years, and then it was just as a consultant, but since you said you think this might be the work of a pedophile, I thought I'd brush up on a few things. I've worked with plenty of pedophiles, and I'm current on the professional literature. But let's just sit back and take a look at this analytically, shall we?"

Looking at things analytically was what Tom did best. As an attorney, I tried to do the same, but over the years I'd come to realize that emotion sometimes clouded my judgment. Tom didn't have that problem. Outside the office, he was fun, especially when he had a couple drinks in him. Caroline and I had been out with Tom and his wife, Jennifer, several times. He was an attentive and loving husband and father, and he was passionate about politics and bluegrass music. Inside the office, however, Tom's demeanor reflected his training as an academic and a scientist. There was no room for emotion.

"Just to be sure I didn't miss anything, we have a six-year-old girl who was taken after someone cut the screen covering a second-floor window and then presumably climbed into her room. Was there any sign of struggle in the room?"

"Not that I know of. Just the note on the bed from what the parents tell me."

"So, unless the kidnapper is a neighbor, he had to get a vehicle fairly close to the house, remove a ladder, carry it to the back of the house, set the ladder up, climb it, and cut the screen. He knew which room the girl slept in, obviously, so he'd done some pretty extensive reconnaissance. How far is the window from the ground?"

"About fifteen feet."

"So it was an extension ladder unless he's a ninja or Spider-Man. Once inside the room, he immobilized the child, probably either by drugging her or binding her. He then had to climb out the window and back down the ladder while carrying her. He had to break the ladder down and then carry her and the ladder back to the vehicle. I assume you looked around outside too?"

"I'm familiar with the neighborhood, but I drove around it a couple times before I came here and took a closer look."

"Is this plausible? Is it plausible that someone could have done all of these things without being seen?"

"The house sits on a corner in the middle of downtown Jonesborough," I said. "There's an old county extension-agent office half a block to the east that has a small parking lot in the back that's accessed by a narrow street. He could have parked there. The lot is only about two hundred feet from the window, and it sits on the edge of a little grove of trees. If he backed a van up to the trees and walked toward the house, he would have been in the trees for about sixty, seventy feet. After that, he would have crossed two neighbors' backyards—about a hundred feet. Both yards have a few trees in them where he could have hidden. There are a couple street lamps at the corner in front of the Monroes' house, but they're those old-fashioned lamps that are only about ten feet off the ground and are designed for ambiance more than security. You know how Jonesborough is, it's small and quiet, very little if any traffic that time of night. So yeah, if he went in anywhere from midnight until five in the morning, he could have gotten in and out pretty easily without being seen."

"All right, assuming it happened the way we're discussing, we can be fairly certain about several things. The kidnapper is male. He's young. He's agile. He's strong. He's driving either a pickup truck or a van. He's intelligent, he's patient, and he's organized. He's either a local or has been working in the area for a fairly significant amount of time. Since he has your client's cell phone number, the chances are good that he's either a friend, he's worked for the Monroes directly, or he works for someone—or *has* worked for someone—who works for them. A logical hypothesis would be that he's in the construction business or the home maintenance business, a carpenter or a plumber or a painter or a roofer or something like that."

"Richard gave me a list of his cell phone contacts," I said. "I already divided it into groups. There are some people like that on the list."

"I'd start with them," Tom said. "The other thing we need to consider right now is the kind of person you're dealing with. Criminal profiling 101 tells us that you're dealing with a Caucasian male, early to late twenties, who lives alone. He was most likely physically, mentally, and/or sexually abused as a child. He's a social misfit. His sexual urges and fantasies have grown so powerful that he can no longer contain them within himself; he's acting them out now. His first step was picking out a child, second step was surveillance, third step preparation, fourth step execution of the kidnapping, and now he's actively engaging his fantasies through sexual acts."

I muttered a curse word and shook my head.

"Are you all right?" Tom asked.

"It's just so ... so disgusting," I said. "It makes me want to find him and rip his head off, along with a few other body parts."

Tom stuck his pipe between his teeth and sat back.

"You'll have a much better chance of finding him if you can control that kind of anger," he said. "You're going to have to approach this systematically, the same way the police would if they were thinking along the same lines as you are. It becomes a process of eliminating suspects until you're left with only one."

"There's something I didn't tell you over the phone," I said. "He took the money yesterday."

Tom removed his pipe from between his lips and raised his eyebrows while I gave him a quick explanation of what happened. When I was finished, I said, "He's going to kill her, isn't he?"

He nodded slowly. "Yes, I suspect he is."

"When?"

"If he thinks he's about to be caught, he'll kill her immediately. Otherwise, he'll wait until he's exhausted his fantasies."

"And how long will that take?"

"Maybe a week. Maybe a month."

"It's already been three and a half days, which doesn't leave much time for a systematic approach. What are the chances that he's one of those people who wants to keep her and raise her as his own?"

"I'd say zero. The ransom note, the texts, taking the money, all of those things are taunts. Have you ever heard the term 'malignant narcissist'?"

"Is that some sort of sociopath on steroids?"

"Worse. A psychopath on steroids," Tom said. "Clinical symptoms are typical of narcissists: an extremely inflated sense of self-importance, grandiosity, lack of empathy, that kind of thing, but with one very important and very disturbing difference. Malignant narcissists are also sadistic. This man is obviously taking pleasure in the parents' pain. He's probably inflicting pain on the child as well."

"I'm starting to wish I hadn't called you," I said.

"The fact that he may be a malignant narcissist could be a good thing, at least in one way. If you're able to identify any suspects from the list your client gave you based on the other criteria we've talked about, I can almost guarantee you a clincher."

He paused for dramatic effect, as had always been his habit when he was about to offer a revealing insight. The pipe went back into his mouth.

"Malignant narcissists have a great deal of trouble controlling their impulses from an early age," Tom said. "He'll have a criminal record dating back to his teens, and it will be violent."

CHAPTER SEVENTEEN

Blaire Reed looked better in person than she did in the photographs I'd seen. Her long, wavy hair was the color of a maraschino cherry, her eyes aquamarine. Her face was angular Irish, her skin creamy. Her teeth were perfect and ivory white beneath a set of collagen-filled lips and her body was one that said, "Touch me if you dare." She oozed sexuality the way a maple tree oozes sap.

We'd just sat down in a booth at Pappy's, a dingy, cigarette smoke-filled honky-tonk in Johnson City that claimed to be the oldest bar in town. It had a reputation as a redneck paradise, a place frequented by blue-collar construction laborers, assembly-line workers from a nearby water heater factory, alcoholic veterans who lived at the Veterans Administration, and low-rent hookers. I'd chosen it because I didn't think any of the other reporters who'd descended on the area would dare go in there.

I'd been in Pappy's twice in my life, both times to interview reluctant witnesses in criminal cases I was involved in. I hadn't run into any trouble, but from the look of the clientele, it didn't seem far-fetched that a person with a smart mouth or a bad attitude could easily get himself cut or bludgeoned, and it didn't help that Blaire Reed and I looked as out of place as a Jewish rabbi at a Newport cockfight. I wasn't wearing a tie, but the gray dress slacks, navy blue button-down, and black loafers didn't fit in with the jeans, Harley T-shirts, and work boots, and Blaire's low-cut, red silk blouse and high-cut, black skirt had drawn plenty of stares when she walked in. A fifty-something waitress wearing tight capri pants and a T-shirt that was tied into a knot above her fleshy navel asked us what we wanted to drink. I asked for a Budweiser and when Blaire asked for a Red Stripe, the woman rolled her eyes and said, "We ain't got none of that. We sell American beer."

"Coors," Blaire said with a catty smile. She looked me over like I was a piece of meat in a butcher's window and said, "So you're the infamous Joe Dillard."

"And you're the famous Blaire Reed."

"What was it like?"

"What was what like?"

"Killing those men. Did you get a rush from it?"

"Maybe I should go outside and come back in so we can start over."

"Ah, so we're a little touchy about it, are we?"

"It was a long time ago, and as far as I'm concerned, it didn't happen. Do you want to talk about Richard and Mary and Lindsay Monroe, or do you want to waste our time rehashing old news?"

"You're handsome, you know, especially for an older guy."

"That's what my wife tells me."

"How is your wife? I heard she went through some rough times."

"Beautiful as ever. Tough as nails."

"I hope you don't mind, but I did some research on you after you called."

"I thought you might."

She picked a smartphone up off the table, pushed a few buttons, and started to read.

"This is some of what I learned. Joseph Jackson Dillard, forty-five. Native of Johnson City, Tennessee, graduate of the University of Tennessee College of Law. Excellent criminal defense lawyer who became jaded and went to work for the district attorney. Excellent prosecutor who eventually wound up being appointed by the governor to fill the vacancy created when his boss was arrested. Lousy D.A. who resigned after what became a very public shoot-out with Colombian assassins at his house. Married to Caroline, who owns and operates a dance studio. Two children named Jack and Lilly, both early twenties and out of the nest. Two dogs. Honorable discharge from the army back in the day. Saw combat in Grenada, won a Silver Star. Pays taxes on time, no debt. Long on principle but sometimes short on emotional control. Lives on Lakeview Road near Boones Creek. How am I doing so far?"

"How did you find out about the dogs?"

She smirked and poured her Coors into a glass.

"And now you've been hired to represent the parents of a kidnapped child who are suspected of being involved. How much are they paying you?"

"A lot. Who were your sources for the story you wrote that came out this morning?"

"My sources are reliable and anonymous."

"It isn't true, if that matters to you. They didn't have anything to do with their daughter's kidnapping."

"Who cares? It's great entertainment."

"By printing something like that, all you're doing is putting pressure on the police to continue investigating a falsehood when they could be looking for a missing girl and a kidnapper."

"Is that why you wanted to meet with me? So you could give me a lecture on responsible journalism?"

Blaire glanced up and to her right as I became aware of a presence over my left shoulder. I turned my head and recognized the man immediately. He'd put on about twenty pounds since I'd last seen him five years earlier. His hair was longer and he'd grown a short beard, but there was no mistaking that leer.

"Who's your lady friend, Dillard?" he said. He was holding a half-empty mug of draft beer in his right hand and a pool cue in his left.

"Explain to me how that would be any of your business."

"Come on, now," he said. "Can't we let bygones be bygones? Introduce me."

I slid to my right a little so I could see him better. I wasn't about to take my eyes off him, especially with him carrying the mug and the pool cue.

"You want to be introduced? Fine. Blaire Reed, meet Phil Landers, a former TBI agent who was fired after I trapped him in a lie on the witness stand five years ago. He's an alcoholic, a hopeless womanizer, a prolific liar, and the worst cop I ever met."

Landers bowed dramatically. "It's always a pleasure to meet a beautiful woman, although I can't say much for your choice of company."

"We were in the middle of a conversation," I said.

"Is that right? What were you talking about?"

"The price of eggs in China. Feel free to slither back over to the pool table any time you like."

Landers took a couple steps forward so that he was right next to the booth. He looked down at Blaire.

"Old Dillard here thinks his dung is odorless," he said. His speech was slurred, and I noticed he was swaying slightly. "He's one of those hypocrite idealists. You know the type. One of those people who thinks he's better than everybody else, who thinks he knows what's right and wrong better than everybody else. But when it comes down to nut-cutting time, he can lie and cheat with the best of them. Has he been telling you stories about all the criminals he helped walk away from justice? He'd do anything to win a court case. If it was a crime for a lawyer to lie, he'd be serving a life sentence."

The slow boil that had started when I recognized Landers had turned to something bordering on rage. When Landers was still a TBI agent, I'd grown to despise him. I regarded him as the antithesis of everything a police officer should be, and when I finally got a clear shot at him, I took him out of the game. I hadn't heard a word about him since, but as I sat there looking at him, listening to his self-righteous sarcasm, smelling his foul breath from three feet away, I felt a strong urge to beat him to a bloody pulp. At the same time, I knew I should just get up and walk out of the bar, but I couldn't make myself do it. I looked across the table at Blaire.

"You should leave now," I said to her.

She smiled wickedly. "Not a chance."

"Seriously, you should leave before—"

I saw movement out of the corner of my eye and barely got my left arm up in time to keep the beer mug from hitting me in the head. I heard Blaire shriek as the mug shattered against the wall. The next thing I knew, Landers, who was a good-sized man, had stepped back and raised the pool cue over his head, intending to bring it down on me like a sledgehammer. I launched myself out of the booth and hit him in the chest with my right shoulder. I managed to get both my hands beneath his hips and lifted as I drove him backward. We smashed into a table and wound up on the floor among spilled beer and broken shards of glass. I rolled away from him, got to my feet, and was about to go after him again when I felt hands grabbing both my arms and shoulders. I struggled against them as I saw three more men grab Landers. A huge, bald man wearing an apron and carry-ing a blackjack stepped between us as the men who had grabbed me pulled me backward.

"Let us go!" Landers bellowed. "I've been waiting years for this!"

The man with the blackjack pointed it in my direction.

"Don't let me see you in my place of business again," he said.

He jerked his head toward the door, and I felt myself being half-carried, half-dragged in that direction. I kept an eye on Landers, who was being dragged in the opposite direction, back toward the pool tables. He was bellowing at the top of his lungs about the things he planned to do to me.

The three men who were dragging me shoved me through the front door into the parking lot. I turned and started walking toward my truck when I saw a flash of light. Blaire Reed was standing ten feet away, pointing a camera at me. I'd forgotten all about her.

"Thank you for a lovely evening," she said. "I can't wait to tell all the other kids about it."

CHAPTER EIGHTEEN

There was a red moon rising over Boone Lake as I pulled into the driveway just after ten o'clock. I stopped and got out of my truck and walked to the edge of the driveway about fifty feet from the garage, looking out over the bluff at the light reflecting off the water. I was reluctant to go inside because I knew Caroline would be disappointed in me. I wasn't injured other than a couple bruises and a small cut beneath my eye from a piece of shattered glass. My shirt was torn, though, and three buttons were missing. I felt like a kid coming home from school after getting into a fight on the playground and having to face his mother.

I heard the garage door opener buzz, and the door began to lift. Rio, our German shepherd, came streaking under it like a rocket with the yappy little poodle at his heels. Rio was five years old, a sleek, muscular, hundred-pound mass of frenetic energy. He buzzed my legs, swatting me with his tail as he passed, yelping his welcome. He stopped ten feet away, turned, and buzzed me again. The teacup poodle, Chico, started jumping up and down like he was on a pogo stick. So much for a quiet entrance.

"What are you doing out there?" Caroline called from inside the garage.

"I'm coming." I got back into the truck and pulled it in while the dogs circled at a dead run. Caroline was standing in the doorway that led from the garage into the kitchen. I knew she was waiting to kiss me and say hello.

"I ran into Phil Landers," I said as I stepped inside. "And before you start on me, it wasn't my fault."

Her hands were already on her hips. "You got into a fight with him?"

"Sort of. It was more of a brief wrestling match. Only lasted a few seconds."

"Where?"

"A bar in Johnson City. Pappy's."

"And what were you doing at Pappy's?"

"It gets worse. I was meeting a woman."

I walked past her, around the kitchen counter, down a short hallway into the bedroom. I could hear her footsteps right behind me.

"What woman?"

"A reporter from *The World*. You know *The World*? One of those supermarket tabloids? I had this half-baked notion that I could make a deal with her to try to keep the coverage about Mary Monroe balanced. Turned out to be a bad idea."

"And where does Phil Landers fit into this?"

"He was playing pool at the bar and he saw me." I started unbuttoning my shirt and turned to face her. I shrugged my shoulders. "I didn't know he hangs out there."

"And you started a fight with him?"

"No. He started a fight with me."

"How? What did he do?"

"Do you really want to hear all the gory details?"

"Did he insult the woman? Did you feel compelled to defend her honor?"

"Look, the guy tried to hit me in the head with a beer mug, okay?"

"Why didn't you just walk away as soon as you found out he was there?"

"I had as much right to be there as he did."

Her hands were no longer on her hips. Instead, her arms were folded across her chest and her face had taken on the demeanor of a block of ice.

"I know you're dying to lecture me," I said, "but there's something else we need to discuss. Something much more important."

"What could possibly be more important than you regaling me with tales of your manhood? I can't believe this, Joe. Out fighting in a bar like a common redneck."

"I like being common, and we've all got a little redneck in us. Let's go sit on the deck."

I finished changing into my grunge clothes, walked past her again, grabbed a beer from the refrigerator, went into the den, took the old photo of my father off the shelf, and went out on the deck. Caroline came out a few minutes later carrying a bottle of water.

"You're too old to fight," she said.

There wasn't any point in replying. She was going to have her say. She rattled on for a few minutes about the possibilities of injury, arrest, and embarrassment, about how such things would impact her and the kids, about how my temper had always been a burden to me and that at some point I was going to have to learn to control myself. I sipped the beer and looked out over the water while she talked, sort of half-listening. When she finally took a breath, I said, "Guess what? I met my father today."

"Don't change the subject. What?"

"I met my father today. Remember the guy at lunch yesterday? He came back this morning. He wanted to talk to Sarah and me. Turns out he's my father."

She stared at me for a bit, wide-eyed. "How is that possible?"

I told her about the ambush, the dog-tag switch, the desertion, the family in Malaysia, the identification, and the photographs. I told her about the body lying in his grave.

"He says he was too ashamed to face up to it," I said.

"Too ashamed? But ... but ... why now?"

"I think he's dying. He said he wants to be buried next to Ma."

By this time, her demeanor had changed completely. She'd moved around the table and taken my hand.

"How do you feel about that?" she asked.

"I'm not sure. I don't think Ma would want him there. She wasn't exactly the forgiving type."

"She loved him."

"She thought he was dead. She loved a ghost. If she'd known he abandoned us she would have hated him."

"How did Sarah take it?"

"Better than I thought she would, but I'm worried about her. I tried to call her on my way home and she didn't answer. I'd hate to see this push her off the wagon. She's been doing so well."

"How did you leave it with him?"

"Not great. I told him to get out. He gave me a phone number and a room number at the hotel where he's staying."

"Are you planning to contact him?"

"I was hoping you'd help me decide what to do."

"You're positive it's him?"

"As sure as I can be without a DNA test. When you think about it, it has to be him. I mean, besides all the identification and the fact that I'm a younger clone of him, why would he claim to be our father if he isn't? What would be in it for him? It just wouldn't make any sense for someone to run that kind of con on us."

Caroline stood and moved behind me. She wrapped her arms around my neck and kissed me gently on the ear.

"There's nothing we can do to change the past," she said. "All we can do is try to manage the present as best we can. So you have a father now. The children have a grandfather. I have a father-in-law. He's family, Joe, and I can understand a young man running away from certain death or capture in the jungle thousands of miles from home. I can understand the shame it must have caused him, especially if he's anything like you. I say we forgive him and open our hearts to him. Do you think you can do that?"

"I don't know, baby. I guess I can try."

CHAPTER NINETEEN

After Caroline went to bed at midnight, I went downstairs to my study, turned the computer on, and spent the next two hours doing research on people who had kidnapped, abused, and killed children. It turned out to be one of the most sickening experiences I'd ever put myself through. People like Albert Fish and Westley Allan Dodd and Robert Black and Wayne Williams committed acts so utterly void of humanity that I found myself thinking of them the same way they thought of their victims—as objects. How a human being could do such vile things to a child was beyond my understanding. I suppose I thought that by reading about them I might be able to gain some insight into the person who took Lindsay Monroe, but the more I read, the more I found myself simply hating them. I didn't want to understand them or their psyches or their sexual proclivities. I just wanted them out of the gene pool.

The worst of it, though, was the knowledge that while I was reading, Lindsay Monroe was most likely being held by someone like them. She was probably being kept in a closet or a trunk or a basement or a barn somewhere, terrified and alone, deprived of the basics of human dignity, while her captor fantasized about what he would do to her next. How long did she have? How long before his fantasies ran their course and he strangled her or stabbed her or beat her to death and then disposed of her like the weekend trash?

One name kept popping up on the searches, a Virginian named Ernest Shanks, who had terrorized the city of Norfolk from 2000 to 2002. Unlike many child predators that are caught, Shanks made a full confession to the police, and his descriptions of how he stalked and kidnapped young girls and what he did to them before he killed them made my stomach churn. Shanks killed sixteen girls, all between the ages of five and nine. He kept them chained to a pole in a soundproof room he'd built in the basement of his house. Thirteen lived for two weeks, two lived for three weeks, and one made it a month. When he tired of them, he strangled them and dumped their bodies into the bays, coves, inlets, rivers, and lakes around Norfolk. The police finally caught him the same way they caught Wayne Williams in Atlanta a couple decades earlier. They staked out the bridges and stopped his car after they saw him dump something into the water off a bridge. They found an eight-year-old girl who had been missing for two weeks the next morning about a mile downstream, and eventually Shanks confessed. He told the investigators that if they ever let him go, he'd do it again, and again, and again. They tried him and convicted him of all sixteen murders and sentenced him to death. He'd gone through the lengthy appeals process and was scheduled to be executed in two weeks.

As I sat there reading, an idea kept tugging at the fringes of my mind. It would wriggle its way into my consciousness and I'd push it away, only to have it return a few minutes later. Ernest Shanks was what Lindsay Monroe's kidnapper aspired to be. Ernest Shanks was the master while the unknown white male Tom Short had described was a neophyte. I reached for my cell phone and called Tom.

"Do you think you could get us in to see a convicted child killer who's on death row in Virginia?" I said when he answered.

"Are you familiar with the concept of sleep?"

"I can't sleep."

"I can. As a matter of fact, that's what I was doing until about ten seconds ago."

"Can you get us in? I want to talk to this guy."

"Who is it? Shanks?"

"So you've heard of him."

"Of course I've heard of him. Everyone in the field of forensic psychiatry who has studied pedophilia has heard of him."

"I'd like to see him tomorrow."

"I'm leaving for the Outer Banks tomorrow, Joe. I'll be gone for a week."

"Then I'll go alone."

"I don't think I can set it up that fast, and even if I could, he doesn't have to talk to you if he doesn't want to."

"Check into it, would you? There's a little girl out there somewhere. Maybe he can help us find her."

"I'll see what I can do."

"Call me back."

"In the morning. I'll call you in the morning. People in Virginia probably sleep sometimes too, you know."

CHAPTER TWENTY

Charles Russell called me at six the next morning and asked me to come to his hotel room. When I walked in, I noticed a large room-service tray covered with bagels and cream cheese and fruit and oatmeal and juice. Earl Botts was sitting at a table next to the tray staring at an iPad and sipping on a cup of coffee.

"Help yourself," Russell said.

I poured myself a cup of coffee and picked up an apple. Russell, who had taken a seat at the table next to Botts, motioned to a chair across from him and I sat down. There was an open laptop on the table in front of Russell. He glanced at it and back at me.

"I like to keep up with the news," he said. "Check it every morning, usually *The Washington Post, The New York Times* and *The Wall Street Journal.* I read the Nashville paper once in awhile if there's some local news I'm interested in. But since this happened with Lindsay, I've been forced to expand my horizons just a bit. What do you think of the tabloids, Mr. Dillard?"

"Probably about the same thing you think of them."

"This dumbing down of the American culture is a pity, isn't it? The print tabloids have been around for a long time, but now we have tabloid television and reality television and online news organizations. There seems to be an endless supply of meaninglessness and sensationalism that has turned out to be quite profitable for the purveyors. It doesn't say much for us as consumers, does it?"

"I suppose not."

"Some of the tabloid television shows are just a notch above snuff films, and truth seems to be more of an inconvenience than a goal for these tabloid journalists. Have you seen this morning's tabloids, Mr. Dillard?"

"I don't read them."

"There's one in particular I thought you might be interested in. There's a story written by a woman named Blaire Reed. Do you know her?"

I nearly choked on the apple I was chewing.

"I met her last night."

"Yes. You made quite an impression."

He turned the laptop around so I could see the screen. The headline screamed at me: "Suspect Parents Hire Brawling Lawyer." There was a grainy photograph of me being shoved out the front door of Pappy's by three large men. One of them was pointing his finger at me and saying something I'm certain was both unpleasant and profane. Beneath the headline was a story.

"Would you like me to read it to you?" Russell said.

"I was there. I know what happened."

"It isn't very flattering."

"Some things are ugly. Is this a deal breaker?"

"A deal breaker? Do you mean are you fired?"

"Am I?"

"That decision would be up to Mary and Richard, but I doubt they'll want to fire you. As for me, I admire your pluck. I will require an explanation, however."

"I don't usually make a habit of explaining myself to strangers."

"Surely you can set aside your principles for a moment. Humor me."

I looked over at Botts, who was stone-faced, then back at Russell. I silently cursed myself for being so stupid and gave Russell the nuts-and-bolts version of my history with Phil Landers and the altercation at the bar. He asked a few questions and I answered them honestly. When he was satisfied, he said, "There's another story in this particular tabloid that was written yesterday. One about Mary and Richard being suspects."

"I know. That story was the reason I met with her in the first place. I wanted to talk to her about how damaging those kinds of stories can be to defendants, how they can corrupt the judicial process, but Landers interrupted us and things went downhill from there."

"I have a question for you," Botts said without looking away from his computer. "How could you have failed to notice the false bottom in the trash can yesterday? Did you even bother to look inside the can before you dumped three million dollars of Mr. Russell's money into it?"

I took another bite of the apple and chewed it slowly while I looked at Botts.

"I know a lot about some things," I said, "but I have to confess that the appearance of the inside of garbage containers isn't one of my areas of expertise. I admit I didn't examine it carefully, but even if I had, I doubt I would have noticed anything. Are you trying to assign blame for your failure, Mr. Botts?"

He looked up and gazed at me with those strange, golden eyes.

"I don't fail," he said.

"So what happened yesterday was a success?"

"I'd advise you to mind your tone, Mr. Dillard."

"Gentlemen, please," Russell said. "Let's not lose sight of our ultimate goal, which is finding my grand-daughter and getting her back safely. Mr. Dillard, I asked you to come here this morning so we can formulate some kind of strategy for getting Lindsay back. I assume you've given the matter some thought. Mr. Botts and I have some experience—not a great deal, but some— dealing with kidnappers, which is why I was comfortable with leaving the police out of the equation. But we underestimated our adversary yesterday, which is something we've rarely done in the past and certainly don't intend to do again. You're from this area. You know the people here. You've dealt with the local criminal community, for lack of a better term, for two decades as both a defense attorney and as a prosecutor. I'd like to know what your thoughts are as far as who you think may have taken Lindsay and how we might best go about finding her."

I looked at Botts again. He was fiddling with a fork, twirling it between his fingers.

"Do you have any solid leads?" I said to him.

He switched the fork from his right hand to his left and kept twirling. He didn't even acknowledge the question.

"We have some ideas," Russell said, "but nothing concrete as yet."

"Richard and I went over a list of contacts from his cell phone yesterday."

"I know," Russell said. "I spoke to Richard after you met with him. He came here and we covered the same territory. Earl and his associates have already begun interviewing people."

"Good," I said. "How many have you talked to?"

"Thirty-two as of midnight last night, but we haven't found anything of particular interest. We'll start again at 8:00 a.m."

"Are you keeping a record of the interviews?"

"We are."

"Will you share them with me?"

"Of course."

"I spoke with a forensic psychiatrist yesterday evening, a man I've known for a long time and who has worked with pedophiles. He helped me narrow it down a bit."

"We're looking for a white male, early to mid-twenties, social misfit, probably narcissistic," Botts said in a monotone. "He's physically strong, relatively intelligent, and probably local. He most likely works some kind of trade that requires a ladder and a truck or a van. Probably dropped out of high school. He lives alone and he works alone. He has a substance-abuse problem, probably alcohol. He's keeping Lindsay in his home or an outbuilding on his property, and he's using her to satisfy his sexual fantasies. He'll kill her and dispose of her body if we don't find her soon."

"Did you find out I was going to see Tom Short and bug his office?"

"It isn't astrophysics," Botts said. "It's criminal profiling."

"I'm hoping to go to Virginia today to see a man named Ernest Shanks," I said. "He kidnapped and murdered more than a dozen girls, all of them around Lindsay's age. I know it's a long shot, but I might be able to get something from him that will help us."

"This isn't *Silence of the Lambs*," Botts said. "This is the real world. You'll be wasting your time."

"Maybe, but it seems a better use of time than sitting around this table twirling a fork or sitting in the woods all day while somebody steals three million dollars from under my nose."

I stood to leave while Botts gave me a look that would melt diamonds.

"You gentlemen have a nice day," I said. "Mr. Russell, I'll call you after I talk to Hannibal Lecter."

CHAPTER TWENTY-ONE

I've always hated the smell of penitentiaries. They all smell the same, a sickening mixture of fear, testosterone, and danger. It had taken Tom Short less than two hours to get me permission to talk to Ernest Shanks. He'd called me just before 10:00 a.m., but when I tried to book a commercial flight from the Tri-Cities airport to Richmond, Virginia, I found out I'd have to fly through either Charlotte or Atlanta, and I wouldn't be able to get back until the next day. So I got in my truck and started driving. It took me six hours to get to a speck of a town called Waverly, Virginia. Waverly was home to Sussex I prison, Sussex I was home to Virginia's death row, and death row was home to Ernest Shanks.

The warden, an overweight man named Ted Remine, gave me a quick tutorial on Shanks, but I'd already read most of everything he told me on the Internet.

"He'll probably sit there like a mute," Remine said as we walked out of his office door and started the journey to the belly of the prison. "He's done it before. Agrees to see people and then sits there and stares at them. Won't say a word. It unnerves them, which is exactly why he does it. He enjoys messing with people's minds."

We walked through a half-dozen checkpoints, past concrete walls and chain-link fence and concertina wire and through steel doors that clanked and moaned as though they were in pain. Death row was announced by a painted sign above a steel door that led to an enclosed block of cells. There were twelve men on Virginia's death row that day. Shanks was next in line for execution.

The room where we met was a small cube of concrete block painted gray with an unpainted concrete floor. There was one stainless steel stool and a Plexiglas partition framed by steel. In the middle of the partition was a round, perforated steel plate through which sound could pass. I stood there for about five minutes until I heard the whish of an air lock followed by a bolt sliding. Ernest Shanks shuffled into the room on the other side of the glass accompanied by the faint tinkle of the chains on his shackles and two oversized, uniformed guards.

His head was shaved, which made him look older than I'd expected. From what I'd read, I knew Ernest Shanks had started his killing spree at the ripe young age of twenty-two. It had gone on for two years. They caught him when he was twenty-four, and his appeal process had taken ten years. In the photos I'd seen of him, he had medium-length dark hair, a wispy mustache, pale skin, and looked slim. The man sitting on the other side of the glass was wearing blue denim and was clean-shaven and doughy. His cheeks were pink and puffy, and there were bags beneath his brown eyes. He didn't look fierce or cunning; he looked soft and pathetic. He regarded me with a bemused, scornful look, a half smile on his thin lips. The guards seated him on a steel stool, the same thing I was sitting on, and backed away. Shanks stared at me in silence, which, I admit, made me uneasy.

"Thank you for seeing me," I said.

"I had no choice in the matter, but I have to confess I don't mind. I have so little contact with people that I get lonely sometimes." His voice was high-pitched, and he spoke with a slight lisp. "They said you're a lawyer from Tennessee."

"That's right. Name's Joe Dillard."

"Are you writing a book?"

I shook my head. "Don't have the patience for it."

"I wrote a book after I was sentenced to death," Shanks said. "It took me two years. It was about a serial killer who specialized in young girls. I wrote in graphic detail about this killer's fantasies and how he made them become real."

"How did it end?"

"He captured three girls at the same time and died during an episode of sexual role-playing that was so exquisitely intense that his heart simply gave out. It was beautiful, but it was stolen from me by a guard. The entire manuscript, four hundred pages, gone just like that. I thought he was going to try to sell it to one of those sleazy smut magazines, but the next day he and a couple of his sadistic buddies brought a metal trash can into my cell. They cuffed me to a chair and forced me to watch while they burned my manuscript a page at a time."

"That's too bad."

"I detect sarcasm."

"Yes, you do."

"I don't think I care for you very much, Joe Dillard."

"That's a shame. I like you just fine."

He took a deep breath and rolled his head from side to side, stretching his neck.

"How do you like the haircut?" he asked. "It's a special haircut, reserved for those who have elected to be executed by electrocution. I could have opted for the lethal injection, but I think the electric chair is so much more dramatic. It allows me to leave an indelible image behind for the people who will witness the execution, especially the guards. They'll see me with the hood over my head, hear the current buzzing, smell my flesh cooking. I think they'll remember the smell for a long time to come."

"I'm sure they will."

"It's important to me to be remembered. How I'm remembered isn't important, just the fact that I'm remembered, that I made an impact. What about you, Joe Dillard? How do you hope to be remembered?"

"I don't know. Just as a good man, I guess."

"And what is your definition of a good man?"

"A man who values life, who values family and friends and hard work and dedication and honesty."

"So you value life?"

"Very much."

"As do I."

"But you've taken life," I said. "Sixteen times."

I looked down at the table in front of me, hoping he hadn't somehow heard of the shoot-out last year. If he had, he'd simply come back with, "So have you." I looked back into his eyes. They were like slate chalkboards, dark and dull and void.

"Can we talk about why I'm here?" I said.

Shanks shifted on the stool. "You're here because a young girl has gone missing in the town where you live. You've been hired by the girl's family to help find her, and you've come to me in an ill-conceived attempt to gather information that might be helpful in saving her life. You think because I'm about to be executed, I may attempt to atone for my sins by assisting you."

"You learned this from the guards?"

"Who learned it from the warden, who learned it from the Department of Corrections, who learned it from one of their shrinks, who learned it from the psychiatrist in Tennessee that requested this interview."

"Will you help me? Can you help me?"

"I probably could if I was so inclined, but I'm not."

"Why?"

"Because I understand him. I identify with him. I don't want him caught."

"Her name is Lindsay Monroe. She takes dance and plays the violin. She's just a child, an innocent."

"Pity, isn't it? You're mistaken to think of her in that way, though, if you truly want to understand him. He doesn't think of her as an innocent child. He thinks of her very much the way an adolescent boy thinks of the girl he's groping in the backseat of his mother's car. She's nothing more than a vehicle for the release of sexual tension. Admittedly, most teenage boys don't kill the girl after they achieve orgasm, but then, the boy isn't doing anything that is condemned by society, is he? He's just doing something that comes natural to him. It's accepted."

Shanks paused for a few seconds, still looking directly into my eyes. I held the gaze.

"This man you're looking for, this young man, he won't kill the girl because he wants to," Shanks continued. "He'll take no pleasure in the actual killing. It's merely a necessary step, something he has to do to avoid detection so he can move on to the next one, so he can evolve. This actually brings back such memories, memories of when I was first gathering my courage, making my plans. I envy him in so many ways. The urges he feels are more powerful than anything you can imagine. They drive him day and night. I liked to dress them up, you know. Pretty dresses, little nightclothes, sportswear, whatever caught my fancy at the time. It enhanced the experience for me."

I raised my hand and shook my head. "Stop. I didn't—"

"These urges he's feeling, these images he's seeing in his head, they consume him. He's *living*, don't you see? He's experiencing life at a level that few can fathom. Now that he has one, now that he's taken her, every fiber of his being is alive and tingling with anticipation of the things he'll do to her and, and, and, oh my God—"

"Enough!" I pounded my fist on the table and glared at him. "I didn't come here to give you some kind of vicarious thrill."

He stood up and looked down at himself. His pants were stained around the bulge of an erection. "Too late," he said. "I haven't been this hard in years."

I stood and pushed the button on the wall so the hacks that were monitoring the room would release the door lock and let me out. The guards on the other side of the partition had already flanked Shanks and were starting to guide him toward the exit. I could hear him laughing.

"Tick-tock, Joe Dillard," Shanks called. "Best get on back to Tennessee now. The rose bloom is wilting."

CHAPTER TWENTY-TWO

The drive back to Tennessee seemed interminable. I spent some time telling myself how stupid I'd been, wasting an entire day on such a hare-brained scheme. Botts had been right. How could I have thought that Ernest Shanks would help me, even if he could? The idea was even worse than the one I'd had the night before, meeting Blaire Reed at Pappy's bar hoping that she might somehow assist me in balancing the news coverage surrounding Lindsay Monroe's disappearance. Did what the reporters wrote or said really matter? I knew it did because what reporters wrote or said often swayed public opinion, and public opinion often swayed decision makers. If enough public pressure was brought to bear, even the feds, supposedly insulated by layer upon layer of bureaucracy, would react. I kept telling myself that I'd wanted to meet with Blaire Reed to try to convince her there were two sides of this story, not just the side the police were feeding her. But I'd blown the opportunity and gotten in a fistfight, now publicized to boot. I shook my head at the thought of it. Maybe I was losing my edge, or maybe I never had an edge. Thinking back, I knew I'd made a lot of decisions in my life based on anger, and most of them were bad decisions. Caroline was right. What was a forty-five-year-old man doing fighting in a honky-tonk? It was stupid, plain and simple. I should have just walked away.

After the session of mental self-flagellation, I started thinking again about the case I was working. All the evidence I was aware of pointed to an unknown intruder. The cut screen, the ransom note, the text messages and phone calls Richard had received. But the police apparently suspected Richard and Mary of being involved somehow. What could either or both of them possibly hope to gain by concocting a scheme to kidnap their own child? Had one of them killed Lindsay in a fit of rage or by accident and the other was covering? Was Lindsay in a shallow grave somewhere, placed there by her own parents who were now desperately trying to escape responsibility? Based upon the limited contact I'd had with them, the notion that either of them would harm or take the child seemed beyond reason, but was there something I didn't know? Something I couldn't know? The more I thought about it, the more I believed that the police were grasping at straws and that the only logical explanation for Lindsay's disappearance was that she'd been kidnapped by a stranger, and like Ernest Shanks said earlier, the clock was ticking.

I called Charles Russell and asked about the interviews Botts and his associates were conducting.

"We've been able to contact twenty-five more people," Russell said, "and we've eliminated every one of them as a suspect."

"That's fifty-five people in two days," I said. "How many people does he have working for him?"

"Enough. They'll work until midnight and then we'll start again in the morning. And how about your trip to Virginia? Any progress?"

"No. I'm on my way back."

"Mr. Shanks was uncooperative?"

"You might say that. I'll talk to you tomorrow."

I hung up and went back over the conversation with Shanks in my mind. There was one thing he said that kept surfacing: *"I liked to dress them up."* I dialed Caroline.

"How did it go?" she said.

"Not good."

"He won't help you?"

"Not intentionally, but he may have helped inadvertently. Would you consider it unusual for a man to buy little girls' clothing?"

"I've never really thought about it," Caroline said, "but yes, I guess it would be unusual. Did you ever buy clothes for Lilly?"

"A couple times when she was a teenager and she was with me telling me exactly what she wanted. But never when she was small. That was one of your departments."

"Why are you asking?"

"Something Shanks mentioned while he was going psychotic on me. He said he liked to dress up the girls he kidnapped in frilly dresses and different outfits. I was wondering where he might have gotten frilly dresses. He must have bought them himself. I don't see him risking having someone do it for him."

"And you think the man who took Lindsay might have done the same?"

"It's possible, isn't it? Right now, possible is about all I have. Where would a man go to buy little girls' clothing?"

"It depends. Expensive or inexpensive?"

"I don't know. The sick jerk would want the stuff to be nice, but probably not too expensive."

"He'd probably need some help picking things out, don't you think? If you go into one of the big box stores, you're pretty much on your own. But stores that specialize in clothing usually have clerks that will help you."

"How many stores like that in the area?"

"A bunch."

"Make me a list, would you? We'll go over it when I get back."

"What time will that be?"

"Around midnight."

"How much sleep did you get last night?"

"Not much, but I'm okay."

"I hate to worry you with this, but I got a call from the diner this morning. Sarah didn't make it in to work. I've tried to call her at least thirty times. I went by her house, but nobody was home. Maybe you should stop by there on your way in."

My hands tightened on the steering wheel. I knew Sarah was upset about meeting Jack Dillard, the man who called himself our father, but she seemed to have control of herself when she left the day before. Or maybe I just wanted to believe she was in control. Maybe I didn't want to be bothered.

"What about Grace?" I asked Caroline.

"Sarah dropped her off at Lilly's apartment last night and said she'd be back in an hour. Nobody's heard from her since. Grace is with me."

CHAPTER TWENTY-THREE

S arah has always had an affinity for Ford Mustangs. The one she owned was a five-year-old, red convertible with a black rag top. She'd bought a vanity plate that said "BADGIRL" several years earlier and had kept it. It wasn't exactly inconspicuous.

I started with the old drug haunts that I knew about—three crack houses in Johnson City—but they'd all either been abandoned by the dealers or shut down by the police. I was relieved they were closed, not so much because they were a plague to any community in which they operated, but because I knew if I found her at a crack house, I'd wind up doing something that would afford Caroline another opportunity to harangue me about judgment and self-control. After checking the old crack houses, I cruised through the parking lots of several bars with no luck and was about to give up and go home when I remembered a motel where I'd found her ten years earlier. It was called The Bradley Motel, an old, family-owned place that had evolved over the years into a seedy flop joint. It was located about halfway between Johnson City and Jonesborough on the 11-E highway. I saw the Mustang parked in front of the door to Room 6 as soon as I pulled in. I turned off the lights, shut down the engine, and sat in the cab of my truck for a few minutes, trying to anticipate what I was about to encounter. She would most likely be drunk, high, foul-mouthed, and irrational. I'd dealt with her in that state many times in the past. It was never pleasant.

I walked up to the door and knocked lightly at first, then harder. I finally found the sense to turn the doorknob and was surprised to find it unlocked. The door swung open.

Sarah was sitting on the bed with her knees pulled up to her chest, wearing the same clothes she'd been wearing when she left my office the day before, staring at the television screen. The television was turned on and was the only light in the room, but the sound was turned down completely. The room was rank with cigarette smoke, and on a table next to the bed I could see an ashtray full of butts and a full, 750-milliliter bottle of Ketel One vodka. I closed the door and walked to a chair that was in the corner a few feet from the bed. I sat down and leaned forward. She didn't move.

"Whatcha watching?" I said. It was an old war movie that I didn't recognize. Shells on the screen were silently exploding; soldiers were falling and dying in silence.

About ten seconds later, she said, "I quit smoking a long time ago, you know." Her voice was quiet, her eyes still on the screen. I listened for the telltale slur in her speech, but it wasn't there.

"Yeah, I know you did. People say it's one of the hardest things in the world to do."

"I knew you'd come. I don't know why, but you've always been there when I needed you, whether I wanted you or not."

"I'm sorry it took me so long. I had to go out of town today. It was—"

"I've been telling myself since around midnight last night that if I could just make it another hour without opening that bottle, you'd come and you'd talk me out of it."

I looked at the bottle again. "Doesn't look like it's been opened."

"It hasn't. Is Grace okay?"

"She's with Caroline. She's fine."

"I shouldn't have left her, but I know what I can be like when I get this way. She's better off without me."

A tear slid from her left eye and down her cheek.

"She'll never be better off without you, Sarah," I said. "She adores you. She loves you. We all love you. Nobody would be better off without you."

"Sometimes I'm glad Raymond raped me when we were little. If he hadn't, I don't think you would have come to my rescue so many times."

"If Raymond hadn't raped you, I wouldn't have had to rescue you."

"You'd think I'd get over it at some point, wouldn't you?"

I nodded toward the bottle. "Looks to me like you have."

"What's it like, Joe?"

"What's what like?"

She pointed with an index finger at the television screen. "What those men, those boys, are doing. Trying to blow each other up. Trying to kill each other. You've done that. What's it like?"

I got up and moved to the side of the bed. "Scoot over a little," I said, and I sat down next to her and pulled my knees up the same way she had.

"It's terrifying at first, at least it was for me. Different guys react to it in different ways. I've seen guys freeze up and not be able to move, I've seen guys curl up on the ground and cry, and I've seen guys strut around with their chests puffed out like it wasn't even happening. But for me, once the initial shock of the explosions and the gunfire and the screaming and yelling wore off, it just sort of became something I knew I had to do. I volunteered for it, if you can believe that. But we trained so much it became almost instinctive. Does that make any sense?"

"Were you angry when it was happening? Did you feel ... what do they call it? Bloodlust?"

"Not really. Full of adrenaline, but as far as bloodlust goes, that isn't really the way it works. You have a mission, you complete the mission. If the enemy gets in the way, you take him out."

"Did you ever run away? Like *he* did?"

There it was, the cause behind the effect. I knew this was about Jack Dillard. It was just a matter of time until she got to it.

"No, Sarah, I never ran away, but honestly, I can understand why he did it, especially when I think about some of the things he said about so many of his team members being killed and wounded and how his best friend was blown up right next to him."

"So you've forgiven him for abandoning us?"

"I don't think 'forgiven' is the right word. Who am I to judge or to forgive? I wasn't there. I don't know what I would have done under the same circumstances. Besides, he was what, nineteen years old? He was younger than Jack is now. And what he said about not knowing why he was there, why he was killing or trying to keep from being killed, I understand that to a certain extent. World War I and World War II, we needed to be there, I suppose. But all these little wars in between: Korea, Vietnam, twice in Iraq, Somalia, Bosnia, Afghanistan, even Grenada. Were those places we really needed to be? Old men keep sending young men off to kill or be killed in foreign lands while they spew their platitudes about duty and honor and freedom and loyalty, and all the while the gap between the rich and the poor in our own country continues to widen and jobs get shipped overseas and education continues to falter and it seems to me that all of this killing and being killed comes down to one thing. Greed. It's all about greed. It's ultimately meaningless for everyone except the ones who make money off the bloodshed."

She turned her head and looked at me, a slight smile forming at the corners of her mouth.

"Did you lubricate your jaw before you came in here?" she said. "I don't think I've ever heard you say that many words without stopping in my entire life."

"I take back everything I said about loving you. I don't even like you. You aren't worth all the worry you cause me."

She reached over and patted my knee with her left hand, but she quickly withdrew it and the melancholy look returned. "Let me rephrase the question, as you lawyers say. Are you willing to accept him?"

I shrugged my shoulders. "I don't think I can accept him as a father. He wasn't there. He's missed everything. But I can probably accept him as a sick, lonely old man who needs a friend right now."

"So many things could have been different," Sarah said, her eyes still misting. "If he'd been around, I mean. Ma would have been so much different, so much happier. We wouldn't have been alone all the time. We would have been—"

"You're torturing yourself. We can't change a thing. Besides, we're doing okay, aren't we? I have Caroline and the kids. You have Grace. We have each other. We're healthy. The diner is doing great, Caroline survived cancer and loves her dance school, and I'm still practicing law. Things could be a lot worse."

She gave me a sidelong glance and said, "I never took you for a Pollyanna."

"I know. I think this whole getting-old thing is affecting my brain. And speaking of old, I'm also exhausted. Since you're not going to go on a drinking binge, can we get out of this dump?"

She slid her legs off the side of the bed and put her shoes on. She picked her purse up off the table and said, "Okay, I'm ready."

I walked to the door and held it for her. The cigarettes and the bottle of vodka remained on the bedside table. As she was going out the door, I said, "That Ketel One is pretty good stuff. Mind if I take it with me?"

CHAPTER TWENTY-FOUR

A couple days later, we got a break.

Caroline had made a comprehensive list of stores that sold young girls' clothing in the Tri-Cities area, and over the next forty-eight hours, she and a group of mothers from her dancing school descended on the stores like locusts. It was an amazing effort, led and organized by my wife. The mothers went out in pairs and questioned sales clerks and managers about whether a man had come in anytime in the past few months and purchased clothing for a young girl. A woman at a store in Kingsport recalled a man in early August who came in and bought several items: outfits, undergarments, shoes, etc. He spent more than three hundred dollars and paid in cash. The clerk remembered that the man said he was buying the clothing for a first-grader. It was to be a gift, he said. She described him as young, mid-twenties to early thirties, white, medium-build. She couldn't remember any specifics about his appearance other than she thought he was wearing a baseball cap of some sort. She didn't remember the exact date he was in the store, but when I contacted the store manager, she said they had security cameras in the store and kept the video recordings for a year.

I met with the store manager and the clerk the next morning. They'd gone back over the security footage after the dance moms left and had found the man we were looking for. As I sat in the manager's office gazing at the computer monitor, I wondered whether I was looking at a kidnapper, a child rapist, an extortionist, and possibly a serial killer. There was nothing special about his appearance—he was medium height and build, wearing blue jeans, a short-sleeved, white shirt and work boots. He was also wearing a baseball cap with an Atlanta Braves logo on it. The cap was pulled low on his forehead, and the camera angles were such that they prevented me from getting a good look at his face. He walked with a limp though. I didn't know whether the condition that caused the limp was permanent or temporary, but at least it was something distinctive.

"Are there any cameras outside?" I asked the manager, who was middle-aged and wearing a pearl necklace.

"Yes," she said. "A real estate management firm based in New Jersey owns the shopping center, and they contract with a security consultant in Asheville, North Carolina, that operates and maintains the outside cameras."

Getting a look at those tapes was a bit more involved, but after contentious calls to both the real estate management firm and the security consulting firm, neither of which was accustomed to releasing security tapes to anyone other than the police, I hopped in my truck and drove to Asheville, which was only an hour away. The office was on the twelfth floor of a building a couple blocks from I-40. I was ushered into a private office by a balding young man wearing khakis and a yellow golf shirt. He sat me down at a monitor and told me to push play while he stood behind me. I watched the screen as the man in the Braves baseball cap walked out of the clothing store and climbed into a large, forest green panel van that was parked in the middle of the lot.

"How many cameras in the lot?" I said over my shoulder.

"Three."

"You've watched the video?"

"Yes."

"Can we get the license plate?"

He leaned over me and started pushing keys. The back of the van came into focus. He pushed more keys, isolated the license plate, and zoomed in on it. The tag number was clear.

"Have you made me a copy of this?" I said.

"I have."

"Gotcha," I said as I jotted the tag number down.

I was back in Johnson City and sitting across from Special Agent Dedrick before noon.

"I think I have a video of the kidnapper," I said, sliding a disc across his desk.

"You brought me a video of your clients?"

"Ever heard of Ernest Shanks?"

Dedrick looked at me deadpan. "Of course I've heard of Ernest Shanks."

"I went to see him."

"Good for you."

"He told me he liked to dress up the little girls he killed."

"Good for him."

"I thought maybe the guy who took Lindsay Monroe might do the same thing. All the profile information says he's probably a budding serial killer and has some sexual issues. Some friends and I canvassed stores in the area that sell little girls' clothing, hoping we might find one that remembered a man buying clothes for a little girl. That's unusual, don't you think? A man buying clothing for a little girl?"

"I think it's unusual that you'd go talk to a piece of garbage like Ernest Shanks."

"We found one, at a store in Kingsport. A man who bought three hundred dollars' worth of clothing for a first-grader. He paid in cash so I couldn't get you a credit card number, but the store had tapes. There's a video of him buying the clothes on that disc, along with video of him walking to his van and driving away. The tag number is clear if you enhance the video a little. I wrote it down for you though. As a courtesy."

I pushed one of my business cards that had the tag number written on the back across the desk.

"There's the tag number. Now all you have to do is find out where he lives and go get him. I'm guessing Lindsay will be there somewhere if he hasn't killed her."

Dedrick looked down at the disc and the card and then back up at me. He took a deep breath.

"Forgive me," he said, "but if I remember correctly, you gave me a lecture on search and seizure law just a few days ago. Something about probable cause, wasn't it?"

The comment didn't merit a response.

"The reason I point that out is that in case you don't know the law, or in case you've forgotten it, what the law says is that in order for me to 'go get him' I have to have a warrant of some kind. An arrest warrant, a search warrant, something like that. In order for me to *obtain* an arrest warrant or a search warrant, I have to draft an affidavit that lays out the reasons why a judge should sign the warrant and allow me to barge into this man's house and search it or barge into his house and arrest him. In this case, if I understand you correctly, my reason, my probable cause, will be that a man bought some clothing for a little girl."

"He fits the profile," I said. "Young, male, white, driving a panel van. After you run the tag number and find out who he is, you might find more. Maybe he has a criminal record. Maybe he's even a sex offender. Maybe he's worked for Richard and Mary Monroe in the past."

"And maybe he's just a guy who bought some clothes for a kid. Maybe he bought them for *his* kid."

"And maybe he bought them so he can dress up and photograph the little girls he's kidnapped and plans to kidnap in the future. Before he kills them, of course. Or maybe after he kills them."

"You're way out of line, counselor," Dedrick said. "We'll run our investigation. We don't need your help."

He slid the disc and the card back to me.

"You're not even going to look at it? Are you nuts? What if I'm right? What if this is the guy and he has Lindsay?"

"He isn't the guy and he doesn't have her."

"How can you be sure?"

"Because one of your clients killed her."

"Then why isn't one of my clients under arrest?"

"Very soon, counselor. Now get out."

CHAPTER TWENTY-FIVE

"**H**is name is Morelock. Dean Morelock. He's an electrician by trade, which explains the van. He works for himself, does jobs on an independent contract basis."

Earl Botts was speaking. After I left Dedrick's office, I called Charles Russell immediately, delivered a copy of the video I'd gotten in Asheville to him at his hotel, and Botts went to work. I didn't know how he did it so quickly, but by 5:00 p.m., Botts had already put together a dossier on Dean Morelock. I was back in Russell's hotel room to listen to what he had to say.

"Has he ever done a job for Richard and Mary?" I asked.

"Not that I know of," Botts said, "but it's possible. Bolton Electric has done a couple jobs at Richard's when they were remodeling sections of the house, and this Morelock guy has done some subcontracting work for Bolton Electric."

"How long ago?"

"The last time Bolton Electric worked for them was eighteen months ago."

"So Morelock could have been there."

"It's possible. We've made contact with Bolton, of course, and learned that they occasionally use independent contractors, but they're not being as cooperative as they might be. We're in the process of persuading the owner of the company to go back through his records to determine if Dean Morelock worked at Richard and Mary's house. Unfortunately, the owner of the company, a Mr. Robert Bolton, is scuba diving in the Cayman Islands right now. It will take a day or two to get the information we need."

"We might not have another day or two."

"We know that," Russell snapped. "We'll handle it."

"How?" I asked. "You'll handle it how?"

"We're going to pay Dean Morelock a visit."

"When?"

"Tonight."

"I want to be there," I said.

"I figured as much," Russell said. "Be back here in two hours."

Morelock lived in a mobile home in the South Central community not far from the Nolichuckey River. The Internet provided Botts with satellite photos, and he set about planning the raid from the hotel room with the precision of someone who had obviously spent a good deal of time in the military. I watched and listened with a mixture of fascination and anxiety as Botts summoned men into the suite. They arrived inconspicuously—individually or in pairs—over the course of the evening. Each man or pair of men retreated to a bedroom with Botts for a half hour or so and then left. A total of eight men, all of them stoic and hard-looking, came and went. Between visits, Botts talked on his cell phone and pored over a laptop computer. Russell, to my amazement, announced that he was going downstairs to the hotel bar and left the room. I asked him once whether he thought Richard and Mary should be apprised of what was going on. His answer was, "What if we're wrong? You want to kill them with false hope?"

Around 9:00 p.m., Botts asked me to come and sit at the table.

"We're going in at midnight," he said. "Two of my men are in the woods outside Morelock's home right now. They'll provide recon and intelligence. At eleven thirty, we'll leave here and drive to the river. You will stay with me. There will be clothing and protective gear for you in the van. What size boot do you wear?"

"Thirteen."

"You can change on the way. Once the house is secure and Morelock is neutralized, you and I will go into the house. Do you have any experience in interrogation?"

"Of course. I've been a lawyer all my adult life. Before that, I was a Ranger."

"If Lindsay is there, and she's alive, we'll secure her, remove her from the house, and take her directly to the hospital in Johnson City. Once she's safe, we'll call the police. In the meantime, we'll hold Morelock. If Lindsay isn't there, you'll question Morelock and attempt to find out whether he took her, and if he did, where she is. You can use whatever tactics you deem necessary. If he admits he took her and she isn't there, I'll expect him to lead us to her, dead or alive."

"And if he admits killing her and leads us to her body?"

"We'll call the police after we've found her and they can take it from there."

I studied Botts's face—especially his eyes—looking for some clue, some insight into the man. He betrayed nothing.

"Who are these men that have been coming and going?" I asked. "Who are *you*?"

"We're Mr. Russell's employees. We manage risk."

"What branch of the military were you with?"

"It doesn't matter."

"Is Botts your real name?"

"Botts is a name, and I answer to it, so I suppose the answer is yes. Just keep your eyes open and your mouth closed while we're conducting our business. I've seen your service record. You should know the drill."

"How did you get a hold of my service record?"

"The less you know about how we do things the better. To be perfectly honest, I'm uncomfortable with your presence here, and I'm certainly uncomfortable with you going along with us tonight. I told Charles as much, but he insists that you go, and he's the boss."

"Should I thank him or shoot him?"

"Ah, a little levity," Botts said, but he wasn't smiling. "I suppose it isn't entirely inappropriate at this moment, but when we walk out the door of this hotel room in a couple hours, I'll expect you to leave your sense of humor behind."

CHAPTER TWENTY-SIX

A black van was waiting in the hotel parking garage at 11:30 p.m. As soon as I climbed into the rear through the sliding door, one of the five men sitting on the floor—there were no seats—tossed a bundle of clothing at me, and I started changing into black utilities, black combat boots, and a black, close-quarter vest. The vest was far more high-tech than what I'd worn so many years ago in combat. It had both hard and soft protective panels in it and weighed only four or five pounds. The other men in the van were checking their weapons—submachine guns and pistols—and their communication devices. Botts had climbed into the passenger seat in the front alongside the driver. I felt like I'd suddenly been dropped onto the set of a Hollywood thriller, but the weapons were real, the ammunition was real, and the feelings of danger and anticipation were visceral.

We drove for about a half hour and pulled off Highway 107 onto Charlie Carson Road. From looking at the aerial views Botts had pulled up on his computer, I knew Morelock's trailer sat in a small clearing at the end of a gravel driveway that was approximately three hundred yards long. The driveway branched off another driveway that wound through flat farmland that belonged to Morelock's family. Botts had said the Morelocks had been farming the rich, river-bottom land for a hundred years, but the last two generations had been largely infertile, and the few males they had produced hadn't been interested in farming. The land the family owned was now leased to another farmer. Morelock's mother still lived on a small plot in the old family home. His father was dead. Morelock lived alone on a part of the property near the river that was subject to spring floods and had never been cleared. It was a perfect place to conceal a stolen child.

The driver turned off the van headlights as we pulled off Charlie Carson Road into the Morelocks' common driveway at midnight. The driveway that led to Dean Morelock's trailer forked off to the right about a hundred yards in. Botts was talking on his radio to the men who were concealed in the trees around the trailer. About ten seconds after we passed the fork in the driveway, the van stopped and the driver turned off the engine. Botts keyed the microphone on the headset he was wearing and said, "You know what to do. Go."

The five men in the rear of the van with me disappeared through the sliding door into the darkness without saying a word. I sat motionless for about thirty seconds before Botts said, "Let's go, Dillard."

I climbed out of the van and Botts handed me a small flashlight. We started walking at a brisk pace up the gravel driveway. The sky above was clear, the temperature around fifty, the moon a waning gibbous that provided enough light so that the driveway looked like a softly glowing tunnel through the trees and underbrush. When we were about a hundred feet from Morelock's trailer, we rounded a bend in the driveway and I could see beams from flashlights that were mounted on the submachine guns bouncing around inside. There had been no loud noises when the front and back doors were breached. There was no yelling, no cursing, none of the mass, macho confusion I associated with police executing a search warrant and breaking into a house. Botts's guys had gone in quickly and quietly.

Botts strode up the wooden steps of a small, rickety porch and entered the trailer. I was right on his heels. The smell of cat urine was so strong I almost gagged. One of Botts's men was just inside the front door. He motioned to his left, and Botts and I walked through Morelock's small living room, down a short hallway, and into a bedroom. Morelock was on the floor, face down, his wrists bound behind his back by plastic hand restraints. He was pale and scrawny, unclothed except for a pair of green boxer shorts, and he reeked of alcohol. Botts stood over him for a few seconds without saying anything. Two of his men were standing on either side of Morelock's bed, their weapons trained on his head.

"Search it," Botts said, and both of them left the room.

Botts was holding a small, high-powered flashlight in his right hand. He trained the beam on the back of Morelock's head, looked at me, and said, "He's all yours."

I stood over Morelock, unsure. Then I thought of Lindsay Monroe, the innocence in her eyes, the beauty and the simplicity of her. I thought of Ernest Shanks baiting me, of him standing and looking down at his erection, of the evil he represented, and how this man, this thing on the floor at my feet was just like him, a destroyer of beauty, a defiler of innocence.

I reached down, grabbed a handful of his thinning hair, and jerked him upward. He felt like a rag doll as the adrenaline began to pump through me. I lifted him off the floor and tossed him against the wall of cheap, wood paneling. I wrapped my right hand around his throat and flipped on the flashlight that I held in my left hand. I shined the beam directly into his eyes.

"Where is she?"

His eyes were wild with fear. Mucous was running from his nose, and I could smell the urine that had poured from him when Botts's men had rousted him from sleep. I let go of his throat and slapped him hard across the face.

"Where is she? Where is Lindsay Monroe?"

He stumbled forward a step and I grabbed his throat again. I slammed the back of his head into the wall.

"Lindsay Monroe! The little girl you took! Tell me where she is, *right now*, or I swear you'll be begging me to kill you in five minutes."

"I don't ... I don't ...."

I backhanded him this time, felt my knuckles smash his upper lip against his teeth. Blood began to seep from his mouth. He dropped his chin to his chest and started to cry.

"I don't know what you're talking about," he said.

Botts tapped me on the shoulder. When I turned, he jerked his head, signaling me to step aside. I backed off and he moved forward. He had a photograph of Lindsay in his hand. He shoved it in front of Morelock's eyes and illuminated it with the flashlight.

"We're looking for this little girl," Botts said. "She was kidnapped from her home. We think you took her."

Morelock began to shake his head furiously.

"I didn't! I didn't!"

"But you know who she is," Botts said. His tone was calm and measured. "You know who she is, don't you?"

"Everybody knows who she is," Morelock said, raising his head to look at Botts. The pronunciation was thick and slow. His lip was already swollen from the backhand. There was a lump the size of a grape at the corner of his mouth.

"I suppose you're right," Botts said, "but everybody doesn't have your ... oh, how should I put this? Your *proclivities*. You've been convicted of sexual assault twice, haven't you? Once as a juvenile and once as an adult?"

Botts hadn't shared that information with me before we left the hotel. It was probably a good thing. Morelock looked back at the floor and remained silent.

"We don't seem to be making much progress," Botts said. "Maybe I should turn you back over to my friend here."

I was seething after hearing about the sexual assaults. Morelock looked at me and must have seen something that frightened him.

"I pinched a girl's tit in high school and then my ex-girlfriend lied to the police when I was twenty," he blurted. "She said I raped her. It wasn't true, but they offered to drop it to a misdemeanor and my lawyer said I should take the deal. So I took it."

"And now you're a registered sex offender."

"It was better than taking a chance on spending twenty years in prison."

"Where is Lindsay, Mr. Morelock?" Botts said. "If you've already killed her, just say so, and I give you my word no harm will come to you. Lead us to her, and we'll make sure that you're treated fairly and with respect."

"I didn't kill anyone!" Morelock cried.

"Then you're still holding her somewhere. My men are searching your home now. We'll search the property next, your mother's home, the barns, the outbuildings. We'll find her, and when we do, if you haven't helped us, we're going to shoot you in the head, puncture your lungs, weigh you down with chains, and dump your body in that river over there. By the time you come up— if you come up—you'll be nothing but a skeleton."

"I don't have her," Morelock said. "I didn't take her. I don't know anything about it!"

"You bought a bunch of clothes at Little Princess in Kingsport!" I shouted. "For a first-grader! That's what you told the clerk. The clothes were for a first-grader!"

Morelock looked at me, then at Botts. I could see the realization come over his face. We had him, and he knew it.

"My niece," he said in a mournful voice. "I bought clothes for my niece."

"Stop lying!" I yelled.

Botts raised a hand to silence me. "Explain," he said to Morelock.

"My sister, her name is Brenda Stites. You can call her. I'll take you over there right now and you can see for yourselves. She has a daughter, Amanda. Brenda's going through a divorce and she's struggling. School was about to start back, and she told me she didn't have money to buy decent clothes for Amanda. I finished a job over in Kingsport and I went and bought the clothes. I took them and gave them to her—I swear it. I was just trying to do something nice. She's my sister ...." He broke into tears again and slid down the wall onto the floor. "I didn't kidnap that little girl. I swear it on my father's grave. I would never hurt a child."

Botts took a step back. "Stay with him," he said to me. "I'll be right back."

He was gone for less than thirty seconds. When he returned, one of his men was with him. He told the man to stay with Morelock.

"Let's go outside," he said to me.

We walked back through the trailer, out the front door, and down the steps into the yard. Botts spun on me suddenly and stuck his finger in my chest.

"I *told* Charles this was too good to be true," he said in a loud whisper. "I *told* him to keep you at arm's length, that you're nothing but a hayseed, a glory-seeker who acts on half-baked notions and is driven by some desperate need for recognition or validation. That stupid slob in there didn't have any more to do with Lindsay's kidnapping than I did, but you played on Charles's emotion and now look at us. We've invaded his home and assaulted him and what do we have to show for it? Nothing! Not a damned thing!"

"He could be lying," I said without conviction. "He fits the profile."

"Are you deaf and blind? Did you hear and see the same thing I saw and heard in there? I don't care what the profile is. He's not the guy that snuck into a house and stole a child. He's not the guy that manipulated all of us and took three million dollars of Charles Russell's money."

Drops of spit were flying from Botts's mouth as he spoke and landing on my face. As much as it angered me, as much as I wanted to show some bravado and tell him to go screw himself, as much as I wanted to punch him square in his beak-like nose, I knew he was right. Morelock wasn't sophisticated by any stretch of the imagination. He was pathetic, too pathetic to have engineered either the kidnapping or the theft of Charles Russell's money. I pushed Botts's hand away and backed up a few steps.

"So what do you suggest we do now?" I said. "This will come back on us. He'll call the police before we're out of the driveway."

Botts was pacing in a tight circle.

"No, he won't."

"What are you going to do? Kill him?"

"That will be up to him. I'll offer him a reasonable amount to forget this ever happened. If he opens his mouth after he's been paid, then I'll kill him."

CHAPTER TWENTY-SEVEN

I didn't know how much Botts—or Charles Russell—paid Morelock. I didn't know when they paid him or how they paid him. I didn't ask and I didn't care. I felt doomed on the ride back to the hotel. I felt like a miserable failure, like everything I'd done, every decision I'd made since Richard and Mary Monroe hired me, had been dead wrong. I felt like I'd let a little girl down, and I had no idea what I was going to do next.

I wanted to get away from Botts and Charles Russell and Botts's men. I wanted to get away from the Lindsay Monroe kidnapping for a little while. I wanted to forget about everything that happened that night, to go home and feel the warmth of my wife, attempt to regain some measure of strength and confidence, and go back at it the next day.

My spirits were lifted when I pulled into the driveway at two in the morning and saw my son Jack's Jeep parked near the garage. Jack had been playing professional baseball for two years and had made it to Double A. He'd been drafted by the Detroit Tigers after his junior year at Vanderbilt. Without any prodding from me or his mother, he'd finished his undergraduate degree by taking online classes. His baseball season had ended a couple weeks earlier, but he'd taken a vacation in California with three of his teammates. I knew he was on his way home, but wasn't expecting him until the next day. He was sitting at the kitchen table, shirtless, eating a sandwich when I walked in. He got up and gave me a bear hug.

"Man, it's good to see you," I said. "You look great."

Jack was the same height as me with thick, dark hair and his mother's brown eyes. He'd been training hard for nearly a decade, and the muscles he'd built over that time rippled with every move he made.

"You look like you've had a rough day," he said.

"You don't want to know."

"Mom said you're working a kidnapping case. What kept you out so late?"

"Like I said, you don't want to know. Speaking of your mom, where is she?"

"In bed. She went down around midnight. Said her old bones were hurting. Is she okay?"

It surprised me a bit that Caroline was asleep because she knew what I was doing, and she knew we were going to Morelock's that night. I expected her to be wide awake, full of worry and questions.

"I think she's fine," I said. "I've noticed over the past few weeks that she's been tired a lot, but I think it's probably because the dance school has started back. Teaching those kids takes a lot out of her, especially when she has to spot acrobatics."

"She said her back's been bothering her."

"Yeah, she's mentioned it a couple times, but you know how she is. She doesn't like to complain. So how was California?"

"Great. We started in San Diego and worked our way up the Pacific Coast Highway to San Francisco. We played some golf and did some hiking, swam in the ocean a few times. Hit a lot of bars. You should take Mom to Carmel and Monterey. They might be the most beautiful places I've ever been."

I went to the refrigerator and pulled out a couple bottles of beer. I handed one to Jack and we sat back down at the table.

"How long will you be home?" I said. "Do you have to go play in a fall league somewhere this year?"

He took a long pull off the beer and set it down slowly.

"I've decided not to go back," he said. "I'm going to retire and get on with my life. There are so many guys in the organization who are so good, I'll never make it to the bigs."

I sat there with my mouth open for a couple minutes, stunned.

"Just like that?" I said. "Without any discussion? You're going to quit?"

His eyes tightened just a tick, and he started running his finger around the top of the beer bottle.

"You can call it that if you want," he said, "but I don't look at it that way. I look at it as accepting the inevitable. My arm is good but it isn't great. I run okay but I'm not a speed burner. I can hit, but so can everybody else. They've moved me to first base, and first basemen are a dime a dozen. I hit twenty-one home runs this year. The first baseman in Triple-A hit thirty-five, and the Prince Fielder is playing first in the majors. There just isn't a spot for me."

"Maybe they'll trade you and you'll get a chance with another team," I said.

"The other teams are the same, Dad. They all have these freaks of nature, guys who are six foot five, two hundred and thirty pounds, who can run like deer, throw it through a wall, and hit it four hundred and fifty feet. I'm good, but I'm not great. I'm just not going to make it. I can hang around and make twelve hundred dollars a month for another few years if I want to, but I'd rather move on. I've been playing this game since I was a little kid. I've worked hard at it and it's been good for me. It paid for my undergrad degree and it'll pay for a graduate degree. So do me a favor, okay? Just tell me you're proud of what I've accomplished and that you're on my side no matter what."

I set my beer down on the table and looked him in the eye. "I'm proud of you, Jack," I said. "I love you and I'm proud of everything you've accomplished. I'm on your side no matter what."

"Thanks, Dad," he said.

"You're welcome. You said something about baseball paying for a graduate degree. Is that your plan?"

He took a deep breath and let it out slowly.

"I'm not sure how you'll feel about this either," he said, "but I've already been accepted to law school at Vanderbilt. I start next August."

"Wow," I said. "You've been busy. Why haven't you mentioned any of this to me or your mom?"

He smiled and shrugged his massive shoulders.

"Mom knows about it. We haven't said anything to you because we thought you might freak out. You've always had this weird love-hate relationship with the law and being a lawyer, but I've watched you all my life and I've learned from you and I don't think it will be that way for me."

I gulped down the rest of the beer and went to the refrigerator for another. He was right, of course, about my tenuous relationship with the law, but I was unaccustomed to members of my family withholding what I considered to be important information from me. I sat back down at the table and downed half the second beer.

"Freak out?" I said. "That's an interesting term. What does it mean in this context? What did you and your mother think I'd do if you told me you were considering going into law? Did you think I'd fall on my face and pound my fists on the floor like a two-year-old? Fall on my sword? Hang myself in the garage? Or did you think I'd march into the dean's office at the law school and tell him if they accepted you I'd go postal and start blowing people away? Maybe I'd set myself on fire on the front lawn in protest. Yeah, that's it. Self-immolation, like a monk protesting a war. Or better yet, maybe I would have grabbed one of your baseball bats out of your travel bag and beaten you to death with it. Is that what you mean when you say you were afraid I might freak out? I mean, I suppose I can understand it since I've always been such an unreasonable, violent, unstable jerk. I've been unapproachable, especially when it comes to my wife and kids. I'm working on it, Jack, but I guess I'll have to work harder. Thanks for reminding me."

"See?" he said. "See what I mean? What you're doing right now is exactly what I'm talking about. You're freaking out."

"What kind of law do you plan to practice?" I said. "Or have you and your mother decided that information might also be too sensitive for my fragile psyche?"

"I'm not going to talk to you if you're going to act this way," he said. "I think I'll just go on to bed."

"Okay. Go to bed. Get some sleep. Dream about your old man and what a jackass he's been your entire life."

I sat there fuming while Jack got up from the table, put his beer bottle in the recycle bin, and started out of the room.

"One more thing," I said. "You know the grand-father we've told you about, the one who was killed in Vietnam? The hero?"

"What about him?"

"He's apparently alive and well. Just thought you'd like to know."

CHAPTER TWENTY-EIGHT

"Where is Richard Monroe?"

The gruff voice on the other end of the phone belonged to Special Agent Dedrick. It was 7:30 a.m. I was at Sarah's diner eating breakfast after having managed to sleep for four hours following the disastrous raid on Dean Morelock's home.

"They're staying with friends," I said.

"I have a warrant for his cell phone, signed by a federal magistrate," he said. "I want it now."

"I'll call you," I said, and I hung up.

Richard and Mary had told me they were staying at a home in the Lake Meadows community in Boones Creek. I tried to call Richard's phone first, but I got nothing. No ring, no voice mail, nothing. I waited five minutes and tried again. Same result. Mary finally answered her phone the third time I called her.

"The police have a warrant for Richard's cell phone," I said. "I can file a motion to try to quash the warrant, but for now, we don't have any choice. He has to turn it over to them."

"Why do they want his phone?" Mary said in a thick, sleepy voice.

"I don't know. They must think there's something on it that will help them find Lindsay."

"There isn't," Mary said. "There can't be."

"Where is he? I've tried to call but his phone doesn't seem to be working."

"He must have gone to the office," she said. "I don't really know for sure. I've been asleep."

"I'll drive out there and talk to him."

At first, I thought it was odd that Richard would be at work, but as I drove toward the office complex in Gray where Richard's business was headquartered, I decided he probably needed something to focus on in order to keep from going insane. Mary was apparently dealing with the situation by medicating herself. Richard was dealing with the incredible stress and anxiety in a different way.

I was directed by a receptionist to his office and ushered in by a pretty young secretary. The room was mid-sized and tasteful. A bank of computers lined one wall. The second thing I noticed was a large photo of Richard, Mary, and Lindsay that had been framed and mounted on the wall behind Richard's desk. I sat down and looked at Richard's haggard face. He hadn't shaved in a couple days and dark circles had formed beneath his eyes.

"I got a call from Dedrick a little while ago," I said. "He has a warrant for your phone."

He leaned back in his chair and sighed. He laced his fingers behind his head and said, "It's gone."

"What? Your phone is gone?"

"I lost it yesterday afternoon."

"Lost it? How? Where?"

"I went out to Winged Deer Park and took a walk after I left your office. Mary called me just as I was getting back to the car. I noticed my shoe had come untied, and when I finished talking to Mary, I set the phone down on the roof of the car while I tied my shoe. When I straightened back up and got in the car, I forgot about the phone being on the roof. I drove away and was a couple miles down the road before I realized what I'd done. I went back and looked for it, but I couldn't find it. It must have slipped off the roof of the car. I called the cell phone company as soon as I got back to where Mary and I are staying, and they tried to track it, but there's no signal. Somebody probably ran over it."

"That isn't good, Richard."

"I'm sorry. I didn't do it on purpose."

"Dedrick is going to think you destroyed it."

"Screw Dedrick. I'm tired of his accusations and innuendo."

"Why do you think he wants your phone so badly?"

Richard shook his head and frowned. "I don't have a clue. Honestly. I have no idea."

"Is there anything you haven't told me? Anything I should know about?"

"Not a thing. I've told you everything you need to know."

"What about things I don't need to know? Are there any of those?"

"I'm not sure what you mean."

"Listen to me, Richard. I don't think you fully understand what you're up against. The FBI apparently thinks you've done something wrong. I need to know what it is. Is there anything you haven't told me about the interview? Anything they said or harped on that you haven't mentioned? Because if there is, I need to know about it right now. These guys are relentless. They'll take your entire life, put it on a slide, and look at it under a microscope if they think you're lying to them. They'll talk to your kindergarten teacher and your college professors, your high school buddies and old girlfriends. They'll find every enemy you've ever had and they'll talk to them too. They'll know what you eat for breakfast, your favorite color, what kind of music you listen to. You can't keep secrets from these guys, Richard."

"I don't have secrets! I've tried to cooperate with them from the beginning. Look right here." He pointed at a space on his desk. "I had a computer sitting right there. I let them take it! I let them search my homes, my vehicles! I gave them blood, for god's sake!"

It was the first time since I met him that I'd heard Richard raise his voice.

"Calm down," I said. "There has to be something you're not telling me. Why do they want the phone?"

"I don't know! Unless it's ... unless maybe ...."

"What? Spit it out."

"They think I lied to them about where I was the night before Lindsay was taken. I told them I went to the Peerless with a business colleague for dinner, and they said nobody at the restaurant remembered me being there. They looked at the security tapes and apparently I'm not on them."

"So where were you?"

"That's none of your business! It's none of their business! But I wasn't doing anything wrong and I didn't have anything to do with Lindsay's disappearance!"

He was yelling now. The veins in his neck and forehead were popping out, and his complexion had darkened.

"Are you having an affair?"

"Good god! You sound just like Dedrick!"

"Richard, talk to me. Are you having an affair?"

"No! And what if I was? What would that have to do with Lindsay being taken?"

At that moment, I heard a commotion behind me. Richard's eyes widened and his mouth dropped open. I turned to see what was going on just as Ross Dedrick walked past me. He was followed by three other men: Mike Norcross of the TBI, Mitchell Royston of the Jonesborough police, and Washington County Sheriff Leon Bates. Dedrick walked straight to Richard.

"Richard Monroe, you're under arrest for the murder of Lindsay Monroe," Dedrick said. He grabbed Richard's arms, pulled them behind his back, and slapped a pair of cuffs on him. He didn't acknowledge my presence and started pushing Richard toward the door. As they were walking out of the room, I heard Dedrick say, "You have the right to keep your mouth shut. Anything you say can and will be used against you in a court of law. You have the right to a scumbag lawyer."

The door slammed shut, and they were gone.

CHAPTER TWENTY-NINE

I waited a couple hours before I called Leon Bates. He and I had become close friends during my time at the district attorney's office and had worked several cases together, including the John Lipscomb case that culminated in the gun battle at my house. Leon saved my life that night, and he backed me up unfailingly during the brief but intense political and media firestorm that followed. He even hand-delivered my resignation as district attorney general to the governor of Tennessee.

I respected Leon. He was a decent human being, first and foremost, and beyond that, he was the best cop I'd ever met. He was astute and intelligent behind his charming, good-old-boy persona. He was an obsessive organizer and planner, and he lived by a complex, self-imposed code of morality that allowed him to walk the greasy tightrope between right and wrong and legal and illegal without ever seeming to slip. Leon was elected sheriff about the same time I started work as an assistant district attorney, so this was the first time he and I were on opposite sides of a case. As I drove to meet him, I wondered how it would play out.

He was sitting in a red Hummer in the cemetery behind Highland Church of Christ outside Jonesborough. It was a place we'd met several times before when we wanted our conversation to be private. Leon couldn't have a private conversation in a diner over a cup of coffee because everybody knew who he was and they wouldn't leave him alone. I'd even seen him sign an occasional autograph. He was wearing what he always wore, a khaki uniform with brown epaulets, a cowboy hat and cowboy boots.

"I see you got yourself a new vehicle," I said as I climbed into the passenger seat. "You get tired of the BMW?"

"I put a lot of miles on that Beemer," he said. "Thought it was time for a change. Took this off a coke dealer in Gray." He chuckled and shook his head. "Them boys just never learn. We took his house, his land, his livestock, his money, his vehicles, everything. He ain't got a pot left to piss in. Course he ain't gonna need his own pot for at least fifteen years. His living quarters are now provided and paid for by the great state of Tennessee."

I smiled and reached over to shake his hand.

"How you been, Leon?"

"Finer than frog hair, Brother Dillard. What's it like, defending the oppressed again?"

"It pays the bills."

"How's that pretty wife of yours?"

"She's good. Thanks for asking."

"What's it been, five years since the cancer hit her? No sign of it?"

"It's gone, knock on wood. She beat it."

"Good for her. Good for all of you. So what can I do for you? I reckon you'd like to know what's going on with your boy."

"I don't want to cross any lines, Leon, but I'd appreciate whatever you can tell me."

"No lines to cross. You'll get everything in discovery anyway."

"I assume you found a body."

Bates shook his head. "No sir, no body, but the arrest wasn't my call. That came straight from the United States Attorney in Knoxville. But we've got plenty of circumstantial evidence and we've got DNA evidence."

"DNA? How can you have DNA if you don't have a body?"

"Two days after Lindsay went missing, a TBI search team found her pajama bottoms and panties in a garbage bag in the bottom of a Dumpster out back of Richard's office. We sent it off to the FBI lab at Quantico. It took them a little longer than I thought it would, but it turns out they found two small blood stains and a large semen stain on the panties. They also found a couple pubic hairs. We got the results early this morning. The blood stains match Lindsay's DNA. The semen and the pubic hairs belong to Richard."

I felt as though I was deflating. Richard a murderer? Had he killed his own child to cover up a sexual assault? Had he killed her accidentally during a sexual assault and then staged an elaborate ruse to cover it up? It didn't seem possible. If it was true, it meant that once again, I had completely misread a client. Richard seemed gentle and easygoing. I just couldn't picture him raping and murdering anyone, let alone his own daughter.

"But the ransom, the kidnapper calling. I saw her picture on his phone, Leon. She was gagged, lying in a box."

"You sure it was her?"

"The money. The kidnapper took the money."

"We think Richard took the money."

"But I was with him that day when the texts and the calls came in. He couldn't have done it."

"He had help, Brother Dillard. Three million dollars can buy a little help. We don't know who helped him yet, but we'll figure it out eventually."

"Why would he steal three million dollars from his father-in-law?"

"Two possibilities. Number one is that they just don't like each other. We've talked to Charles Russell, and he doesn't have much good to say about Richard. Maybe Richard just wanted to stick it to him. The other possibility is that Richard is strapped for cash and might wind up losing his company. I don't know how much he's told you about this lawsuit he's involved in, but it could wind up costing him a fortune. The judge in the case held a hearing and listened to some of the proof, and he felt like the case was strong enough to put down an order freezing most all of Richard's corporate assets until they can get it all sorted out, which could take years. What we're thinking is that after Richard killed Lindsay, whether he killed her accidentally or on purpose, he decided to make it look like a kidnapping had occurred so he could extort money from his father-in-law. Either that or he planned the whole shebang from the beginning. He's an awful smart feller from everything we've been able to gather. Ruthless, too. You don't get as rich as he is and be as young as he is without being ruthless."

I folded my arms across my chest and started rocking back and forth in the seat. My mind felt like it was going numb, as though it had been injected with some type of anesthetic that would keep it from feeling pain.

"It gets worse," Bates said. "The ransom note was written on a computer we took out of Richard's office."

"Stop, Leon. You're killing me."

"We know he lied about where he was on the Friday evening Lindsay went missing. We just haven't been able to nail it down yet. I figure he met with his accomplice and made his final preparations. He might go a ways toward helping himself if he'd tell us who helped him."

"Helping himself? On a kidnapping and a murder? Not to mention extortion and theft and God knows what else. If you can prove all this stuff you're telling me, he's dead in the water. He might as well hang himself in his cell."

"Maybe he'll do that," Bates said. "It'd sure save us all a lot of time and trouble."

"What about the mother? What about Mary?"

"She's clean as far as we can tell. Don't believe she had a thing to do with it."

"Damn," I said. "I can't believe this."

"Do me a favor, would ya?"

"What's that?"

"Before Richard commits suicide, see if you can get him to tell us what he did with that little girl's body. She deserves a proper burial."

As soon as I got out of Bates's vehicle, I drove to Jonesborough to the jail. On the way, I kept telling myself not to judge, that it was simply too early to tell, that the things Bates had said to me weren't proof, they were merely statements. At the same time, I couldn't help thinking that by allowing myself to be deceived on the front end, I had wound up defending a man who had murdered his own child, covered up her death by staging a kidnapping, and then extorted millions of dollars from his father-in-law. If those things were true, then Richard Monroe was no different from Ernest Shanks. He was a monster, and I was his lawyer.

Richard had already taken on the look of a man who had been sentenced to death, which was something that had suddenly become a very real possibility. I'd been a staunch opponent of the death penalty early in my career, but as I'd aged, my attitude had changed, largely because I'd come to believe that some of the people I'd represented and prosecuted over the years were both incorrigible and unsalvageable. I'd seen so much violence, so much cruelty, and so little regard for basic human decency that I could no longer summon empathy for people like Ernest Shanks. They were like cancer—the only way to effectively deal with them was to eradicate them—and if Richard Monroe had done all the things he was now accused of doing, he deserved to die.

Richard had already been booked and issued his jail uniform, an orange, cotton jumpsuit that was far too large for him. He was now handcuffed, the cuffs were attached to a chain around his waist, and steel rings shackled his ankles. I stared at him in silence for a while, feeling as awkward as I'd felt the first day I met him, with one important difference. The awkwardness the first day was grounded in sympathy. Now it was grounded in anger and disbelief.

"I'm going to need for you to explain a few things to me, Richard," I finally said.

He'd been staring down at the table top. His eyes slowly came up to meet mine.

"There isn't any point in beating around the bush. You need to answer this question for me, right now, and you need to answer it truthfully. How in the hell did your sperm manage to find its way onto a pair of your daughter's panties?"

His answer was a silent look of confusion.

"Now is not the time to go stupid on me, Richard. This pair of panties I'm talking about? It was found in a Dumpster behind your office building along with the pajama bottoms Lindsay was wearing the night she disappeared."

He flinched slightly, and tears began to stream down both of his cheeks. Within seconds, his face morphed into an unrecognizable form and he began sobbing uncontrollably. I watched him without emotion, waiting for him to stop. If he'd done what they were accusing him of, the tears were nothing more than him feeling sorry for himself, remorse for having been caught and imprisoned. His head dropped onto the table and he started wailing in a loud, tortured cry.

"Get a hold of yourself," I said. "Richard! Richard!"

But he wouldn't, or couldn't, stop. It was unlike anything I'd ever heard or witnessed, a mournful lamentation worthy of a backwoods funeral procession. At one point he cried, "My baby's gone," but after that, he went back to moaning and wailing and crying. After almost twenty minutes, two guards came through the door. They pulled him up from the table and half-carried, half-dragged Richard out of the room.

I watched them without saying anything.

There simply wasn't anything to say.

CHAPTER THIRTY

After witnessing Richard's meltdown at the jail, I decided to drive to Johnson City and talk to the man who called himself Jack Dillard. Despite everything else that had been going on, I'd been unable to keep him from creeping into my thoughts. I had no idea what I would say to him, but I felt a strange sense of responsibility toward him now that he'd thrust himself into our lives. He was sick, he was old, and he was apparently my father. I couldn't just turn my back on him.

I heard the television through the door of the room number he'd left with me, so I knocked. It was a little after one in the afternoon. He opened it immediately and a broad smile came across his face.

"I'm so glad to see you, Joseph," he said. "Come in. Come in."

I walked in and looked around. It was a suite, clean and orderly, the bed made, clothes hanging neatly in a closet near the door.

"Have a seat," he said. "Just let me turn this off."

He motioned to a small couch and I sat down. He picked up a remote control, and the television went dark. Watching him move around the room was eerie. He was wearing what looked like a brand-new, orange hoodie with a University of Tennessee logo on the front and a pair of blue jeans. It was as though I was looking through a portal into the future, watching myself. He sat down in a chair across from me and rested his elbows on his knees.

"I've been watching the news and reading about your case," he said. "They've arrested the father? You must live an interesting and exciting life."

"Tell me again why you're here," I said.

"You're very direct, Joseph. I like that. Let me turn the question though. Why are *you* here? I've been hoping you'd come, but to be honest, I didn't think you would. Why did you?"

"Mostly because my wife is a kind and loving person, and she thinks it's the right thing for me to do."

"Her name is Caroline, right? How long have you been married?"

"A long time."

"Are you still in love with her?"

"Very much."

"That's wonderful. I think life is much more fulfilling when it's anchored by love."

"What's wrong with you?" I said.

"Beg your pardon?"

"You said you came here to die. You look sick. What's wrong with you?"

He started wringing his liver-spotted hands. "Started out as cirrhosis," he said. "Cancer now. In the liver."

"Caused by alcohol?"

He nodded.

"Still drink?"

He shook his head.

"How long's it been?"

"A couple months."

"So that's how you dealt with it? You medicated with alcohol?"

"It's how I slept," he said. "I worked every day, all my life. I took good care of my family. But at the end of the day, when night was coming on and I knew I'd have to lay down and close my eyes, I turned to the bottle. I'd drink myself into a stupor and pass out. I tried quitting a hundred times, but I couldn't sleep. I'd be awake for two, three days, or if I did manage to go to sleep, I had nightmares so terrible I can't even begin to describe them to you. So I always wound up going back to it. I knew it would catch up with me one day, and now it has."

"How did you make a living?"

"My wife's father owned a bar in downtown Kuala Lumpur," he said. "I bartended, cooked, bounced people out of the place, whatever he needed, for twenty years. He was good to me. He turned the bar over to me when he turned sixty—just gave it to me—and I ran it until last year when Adilah died."

"Adilah was your wife? How did she die?"

"She was killed in a car accident. Her sister was driving. They got sideswiped by a truck, went off the road down a small hill. The car rolled a couple times. Killed Adilah instantly."

"I'm sorry."

His eyes had become moist and his voice shaky at the mention of his wife, and I wondered again why he had come. He was ill and he was obviously still grieving, yet he'd traveled halfway around the world to find us. He'd mentioned that he had children in Malaysia, and I wondered why he hadn't remained there with them. Was there no comfort for him there? I thought briefly about how complex and difficult the relationships must have been, the American living in a foreign land, showing up out of nowhere, and carrying a pile of emotional baggage so heavy that the only way he could drag it through life was to numb himself with alcohol. He reminded me very much of Sarah in that regard.

"Tell me about your life, Joseph," he said. "Tell me what I've missed."

I was reluctant at first, but he seemed genuinely interested, and before I knew it an hour had passed. I told him about Caroline and Jack and Lilly and Sarah, about my time in the Rangers, about law school. He asked a lot of questions, and I answered most of them honestly but without revealing too much of myself. I wanted to treat him with respect and I wanted to get to know him at some level, but at the same time I found myself not being able to open myself to a man who had basically lived a lie his entire life. I did, however, invite him to lunch that Sunday at our house, and he accepted, saying he would be "honored."

Just as I was getting ready to walk out the door, he said, "Joseph, I want to ask a favor of you. Ever since the first day we spoke, I've been thinking about what you said about Lucas Venable's family and what you said about him lying in a grave marked with my name. I have to make that right."

I nodded, wondering what he wanted me to do.

"I know his parents are still alive and I know where they live," he said. "I need to go there, but I'd like you to go with me."

"Why?" I said. "It really isn't any of my—"

"I know it's a lot to ask and I'm sorry, but I'm afraid if I go alone I won't be able to do it. I don't think I'll be able to face them. Would you go with me, please? I'll pay for the plane tickets. I'll pay for everything. We could fly to Milwaukee, rent a car and drive to Fairfield, and then fly back the same night. Just one day. Would you consider it?"

"I'm in the middle of a case," I said. "I don't think I have time."

"One day, Joseph. Just one day. Please."

"When?"

"As soon as possible," he said. "I don't know how much time I have left."

I called Mary Monroe from my truck as soon as I left the old man's room. Her father answered her phone.

"I need to talk to Mary," I said. "Can we meet somewhere?"

"I don't think Mary should talk to you," Charles Russell said.

"Why not?"

"Because you now have a conflict of interest. It just wouldn't be appropriate."

His tone was cold and distant, almost robotic.

"That's exactly why I want to meet with her. Everything has changed. We need to decide how to go forward, whether I continue to represent Richard, whether I continue to represent Mary, or whether I should get out altogether."

"Mary has already spoken to another lawyer," he said.

"What? When?"

"This morning. As soon as we heard about her murderous, soon-to-be-ex-husband. The lawyer's name is Margaret Bain. I believe you know her."

Margaret Bain was a well-known divorce lawyer who represented only women and who handled criminal cases on occasion. She was educated at Cal Berkley, she was liberal to the point of being radical, she was openly lesbian, she was abrasive and prickly, and she had the reputation of being a man hater. I knew her only casually from her rare appearances in criminal court and her occasional lectures at bar association meetings, back when I used to attend them. I'd actually witnessed her pull a gun on another lawyer after a county bar association meeting that degenerated into a drunken melee at the country club in Johnson City a dozen years earlier. Margaret had gotten into a verbal altercation with a lawyer named Tom Munson and had eventually invited him to the parking lot for what she said would be "a well-deserved ass whipping." Like everybody else there that evening, I'd had too much to drink, and I couldn't resist following the crowd out the door to see what would happen. Margaret marched through the parking lot to a vehicle with Tom right on her heels. She unlocked the door, reached into the console, and came back out with a hand cannon that was worthy of Dirty Harry. She stuck the gun barrel into his forehead, pulled the hammer back, and said, "If you ever call me a dyke again, you better do it with respect."

Tom wet his pants, but he didn't call the cops. Nobody else did either. The only thing that came of it was that the attendance at bar meetings dwindled significantly for a couple years.

"Have you hired her?" I said.

"She's agreed to represent Mary."

"So she's filing for divorce?"

"What would you do if you found out that your spouse had murdered your child and stolen three million dollars of your father's money?"

"It sounds like you've tried and convicted him already. Are you familiar with the term 'presumption of innocence'?"

"Feel free to presume all you want, Mr. Dillard. As far as we're concerned, Richard can burn in hell for all eternity. We've spoken with the police. We know about the DNA, the clothing, the ransom note. We also know some other things. From this point forward, you can consider us witnesses for the prosecution."

"Slow down, Mr. Russell. Let's at least talk about this."

There was no response.

"Mr. Russell? Mr. Russell?"

I looked down at my phone. The call had ended. Charles Russell had hung up.

CHAPTER THIRTY-ONE

Early the next morning, I went back to the jail in Jonesborough to talk to Richard before his initial appearance in federal court in Greeneville, which was scheduled for one o'clock in the afternoon. The courthouse in Greeneville was less than thirty minutes away, but I knew the federal marshals would pick him up well before it was time to be in court. Nobody keeps a federal judge waiting.

I'd spent a great deal of time the previous evening thinking about Richard's behavior when I'd asked him about his sperm being found on Lindsay's pajamas. His reaction had been so forlorn that the more I thought about it, the more I accepted the possibility that it could have been genuine grief. It could have been the first moment that Richard knew, or perhaps accepted, that his daughter was dead. If he'd killed her, he would certainly have known she was dead, unless he'd gone temporarily insane and experienced some kind of episodic amnesia or psychological disassociation.

Richard looked washed out when the guards brought him in, even more so than the day before. Instead of the standard issue orange jumpsuit, he was wearing only a paper gown, open in the back, very similar to those worn by hospital patients. As soon as I saw the gown, I knew he'd been placed on suicide watch, which is probably the most humiliating form of incarceration the state has to offer. Suicide watch inmates are placed in a cell alone with no bed, sink, or toilet, clad only in the paper gown, and monitored closely by both male and female guards. Richard's eyes betrayed hopelessness above the dark bags that had formed, he was unshaven, and his hair was oily and unruly.

"Can you talk without losing control of yourself today?" I said.

My tone was matter-of-fact. I was still somewhat unnerved by the possibility that he had committed such an unspeakable crime, and it was a struggle to speak to him in a civil manner, but before I'd walked into the room, I'd told myself to put my emotions aside and try to offer him at least some modicum of respect. I tried to force myself to presume he was innocent, or at least fake it as well as I could.

"I can't get the image of her face out of my mind," he said softly. "She's smiling. She's beautiful."

"I don't usually ask my clients this question, Richard, but I guess I'm getting old and cantankerous. I just don't have the capacity to put up with some of the things I used to, so I'm just going to ask you flat out. Did you kill her?"

He clenched his cuffed hands into a tight ball and shook his head.

"No," he said, barely above a whisper. "I didn't. I didn't kill her. I didn't kidnap her or fake a kidnapping. I didn't steal Charles's money. I didn't do any of the things they're accusing me of."

"Look at me," I said. "Don't look at the table. Look me in the eye and explain to me how your sperm made its way onto her pajamas."

He continued shaking his head, but he lifted his eyes to meet mine.

"I don't know," he said. "I have no idea."

"Did you have sex with her? Did you try to have sex with her? Did you make her touch you? Did you masturbate and ejaculate on her?"

"No!" he said, his voice taking on some volume and authority. "I've never, ever, not once, even *thought* about doing anything of the kind, let alone *done* it. I'm not a child molester, I'm not a pervert, I'm not a murderer, and I'm not a thief. I loved Lindsay more than anything in this world. I've never done anything that would harm her."

"Just so you know," I said, "the police would very much like to find her body. If you snapped somehow, if you did something you didn't mean to do and you panicked, you could probably help yourself a little—and I mean very little—by telling them where she is."

"I don't know where she is."

"If I'm going to stay on this case, I want you to take a polygraph. We won't have to give the results to the police, which means that if you fail, then me, you, and the examiner will be the only three people who know it. I also want a doctor to do a forensic psychiatric examination of you. I want an independent expert to examine the DNA evidence, an independent expert to examine the computer files they say contain the ransom note, and independent experts to examine any other forensic evidence the police have developed. You'll have to pay for all of that, plus my fee. You're going to be locked up so you won't have access to anything. I'll need you to assign a power of attorney to someone of my choosing who can manage your business affairs until this is over so we can pay for everything. It'll cost a lot of money, Richard, and there are already two extremely difficult complications—the lawsuit you're involved in and your divorce proceeding."

He blinked several times, as though he couldn't process the information I'd just offered.

"Divorce? Mary wants a divorce?"

"I talked to her father. She's hiring a divorce lawyer and she's going to be a witness against you. I don't know what she's told the police or what she plans to tell the police, but she's apparently turned on you."

He took a deep breath and released it slowly.

"It's him," Richard said.

"What do you mean, 'him'?"

"Charles. He's behind this."

"Behind what?"

"All of this. He hates me. He's framing me."

"So you're saying that Charles Russell engineered a sham kidnapping of his own granddaughter, engineered the fake theft of his own money, has somehow managed to get a hold of some of your sperm, placed it on Lindsay's pajamas and planted them in a Dumpster at your place of business, broke into your office and used your computer to type out a ransom note, and is now trying to railroad you into the death penalty? Why, Richard? Why would he do that?"

"Because he hates me."

"Why does he hate you?"

"He's jealous of me."

"That's ridiculous. I wish I was recording this so I could play it back for you. This is what you want me to present as a defense? Ladies and gentlemen of the jury, my client's father-in-law is so jealous of him that he concocted this elaborate scheme to frame his son-in-law for murder, kidnapping, and theft? Do you think he killed Lindsay, Richard? Just to flesh out the scheme?"

"He wouldn't kill her."

"Then *where the hell is she?* Do we point the finger at Mary too? Mary must be involved somehow. Charles wouldn't steal Lindsay and torture his own daughter in the process just to frame you because he's jealous. They must be doing this together, right?"

"Are you enjoying this?" Richard said. "Are you enjoying the sarcasm?"

"No, Richard. I don't think enjoyment would be a word I'd use to describe what I'm feeling right now."

"Mary isn't involved. She loves me. She loves Lindsay. She just isn't that kind of person. But Botts, Botts would be right in the middle of it."

"Ah, the mysterious Mr. Botts. So your theory now is that Botts is Charles's accomplice and Mary is oblivious. That should be simple to prove."

"You don't know Charles. You don't understand him the way—"

"Enough, Richard," I said, holding up my hand like a traffic cop stopping a vehicle. "I've been doing this a long time, and I've heard this kind of thing before. Client commits a crime. Client gets caught. Client comes up with incredible explanation for evidence that is unexplainable. Then more evidence comes along so client starts tweaking things a little bit here and a little bit there. He weaves new explanations into his story. He bends and twists and molds his version of the facts until he has a version of the story that he thinks works for him, and before you know it, he's gone over the story in his mind so many times he actually starts believing his own lies. That's where we're headed. That's where you're going."

"But I'm not—"

"I said that's enough! Here's what's going to happen. I'm going to appear in federal court with you in a couple hours. I'm going to tell the judge that I'm there for the initial appearance only, that you haven't hired me to represent you at trial. And you haven't hired me, Richard. You understand that, don't you? Representing you on a first-degree murder is going to cost you a great deal more than the twenty grand you paid me a few weeks ago, but I don't want you to pay me yet. We'll enter a plea of not guilty at arraignment. As soon as it's over, I'm going to arrange for you to take a polygraph test here at the jail sometime in the next few days."

"I thought polygraph results aren't admissible in court."

"Admissible in court? You know the legal jargon, do you? I find that interesting. You're right though. They aren't admissible, but my experience has been that they're usually accurate. And if you fail, you won't have to pay me. I have no intention of representing a man who raped and murdered his own daughter. If you fail the polygraph, I'm out."

CHAPTER THIRTY-TWO

Richard's initial appearance went off without a hitch. I never cared much for practicing in federal court, but there was at least one thing I could say for the judges. They weren't grandstanders like so many of the state judges. They didn't have to run for election because they were appointed for life, and as a result, they were far more apt to simply tend to business. The courtroom was packed with media, and the steps and the sidewalk outside were covered with angry citizens chanting ugly mantras, but I walked past them as quickly as I could, eyes straight ahead, trying not to listen to the idiotic questions that were hurled at me like rotten eggs. I silently marveled at questions like, "Mr. Dillard! Mr. Dillard! Did your client kill his daughter?" Did the morons really think I would answer?

The proceeding was held in front of a federal magistrate named Denise Mingo. I entered a not-guilty plea on Richard's behalf while he stood silently beside me. There was a brief argument over bail, but I knew we'd lose. Richard was accused of first-degree murder in one of the highest profile cases the area had ever seen, and he had plenty of money. Judge Mingo wasn't about to let him out on bail so he could use his wealth to run. The entire hearing took less than ten minutes. As soon as it was over, I walked back out the door, back through the crowd, got into my truck, and drove away toward Johnson City.

Caroline had an appointment with her oncologist at 3:00 p.m. to get the results of a bone scan she'd been given a few days earlier. The pain in her back had become worse with each passing day, and she often complained of pain in her arms and legs. We'd both attributed the pain to her helping her students perform acrobatic tricks—she called it "spotting"—but it had persisted for so long that she finally went to see her oncologist to find out whether the cancer treatments she'd had could be causing problems in her bones. I arrived at the oncologist's office at 2:30 and found Caroline in the waiting room. I squeezed her hand, and we sat in silence until a nurse came out to retrieve us. We walked back into an exam room and had just gotten settled when a young, balding, Middle Eastern man walked in and introduced himself as Dr. Hamadi.

"Where's Dr. Jobe?" Caroline said. Jobe was her regular oncologist.

"He's with another patient right now," Hamadi said. "I'm sorry to be the bearer of bad tidings, but the results of your bone scan show thirteen different areas of concern."

I heard Caroline take a quick breath and looked over at her. Her lower lip was trembling, and a tear had already slipped from her left eye.

"Areas of concern?" I said. "What does that mean?"

"Unfortunately, when breast cancer metastasizes to other areas of the body, it goes to the bones about 80 percent of the time."

Caroline's fingernails were digging into the palm of my right hand. I was so shocked that I couldn't speak for a few seconds.

"Are you telling us it's back?" I said.

He nodded. "I'm afraid so. We have to do some more tests to be absolutely certain, but based on my experience with this sort of thing, the probability is almost 100 percent. I'm sorry."

Caroline let out a muffled sob, and then another, and another. It was one of the eeriest, most terrifying moments of my life. A little over five years earlier, we'd sat in a very similar room and received the news that the biopsy that had been performed on a lump in Caroline's breast revealed a malignant tumor called invasive ductal carcinoma. She'd been through months of chemotherapy, hours of radiation therapy, and more than twenty surgeries. She'd lost her hair twice. The area around her surgically removed breast had been radiated so thoroughly that it had turned black. She'd dealt with large open wounds that took months to heal after surgeons attempted unsuccessfully to transplant healthy tissue from her abdomen and her back to her chest in order to give her the appearance that she still had a breast. She'd endured more pain and anguish than any human deserves to endure, and now this man was telling us the insidious disease was back and it was now in her bones. For a moment, I thought I would vomit right there on the floor.

"Do you need a minute?" I heard the doctor say.

I nodded, and I'm sure Caroline did the same although I couldn't see her through the tears that had gathered in my eyes. We stood and embraced each other while Caroline cried openly and I tried desperately to keep from falling apart.

"I'm so sorry, baby," I whispered into her ear. "I'm so sorry."

She cried for a couple minutes more, and I held her in my arms, rocking gently back and forth. When she stopped, she looked at me and said, "I don't want to die."

"You're not going to die. Just put that thought out of your mind right now."

The doctor knocked and came back in a short time later. He talked about things I didn't understand, things I didn't want to understand. He mentioned life expectancy and pain management strategies and treatment plans. He said the tumors were now inoperable and incurable. Treatment for breast cancer had come a long way, he said. He'd seen patients live five, ten, even fifteen years. The last thing he told us was that he would be sending Caroline to another oncologist, a woman at Vanderbilt University.

"They have more bells and whistles than we do," he said.

Bells and whistles. My wife had just been handed a death sentence, and he was talking about bells and whistles. I wanted to choke him.

Caroline and I left shortly thereafter, she with a fistful of prescriptions for pain medications and sheets of paper with doctor's appointments listed on them and I with a heart so heavy I didn't know how far I could walk. When we got to the parking lot, I asked her to leave her car there and ride home with me.

I didn't want her to be alone.

I didn't want to be alone.

I lived the next couple days in a dense fog of emotions so powerful I haven't the words to describe them. My love was dying, and I was helpless to stop it. I was reminded of Prometheus, the mythical Titan who stole fire from the gods. Zeus punished him by chaining him to a rock on a mountain side. During the first night, an eagle came and ripped out Prometheus's liver. It grew back the next day, but the following night, and every night thereafter for eternity, the eagle would return and Prometheus would have to endure the terrible pain of having his liver torn from his body. The only difference between Prometheus and me was that my heart was being torn out instead of my liver.

Those first two days, as the family rallied around Caroline, I managed to remain calm and stoic in their presence, but late at night, after Caroline and Jack were asleep and everyone else had gone home, I would shut the dogs inside, walk out the back door and down the deck steps, stand on the bluff overlooking the lake, and cry. I cried alone because I was ashamed—ashamed of being weak, ashamed of being helpless, ashamed of feeling sorry for myself.

I'd never been a religious man, largely because my mother was an embittered atheist who constantly reminded me that anything that happened in this life was a product of circumstance, that self-sufficiency was important above all else, that there was no God, no grand plan, and that if something terrible happened, there was nowhere to turn but inward. She railed against those who worshipped God or blamed God or attributed anything to God, calling them weak fools who were unable or unwilling to accept that life is sometimes cruel and unfair. Prayer was nothing more than wishful thinking, she said, religion nothing more than a dogmatic form of social control. I came to regard her as an extremist in her bleak view of the world, but at the same time, I'd never been able to reconcile the notion that a kind, loving, and benevolent God would allow evil, cruelty, and disease to flourish so prevalently in a world He had created. I'd chosen the path of the agnostic, a man who made no claim of knowing what is on the other side of life but who, at the same time, chose not to examine the issue too closely, and as I stood there gazing over the bluff through watery eyes as my sweet Caroline lay suffering, I couldn't help but wonder whether my lack of faith had somehow contributed to her fate.

On that second night, after I'd been outside for ten minutes or so, I heard movement behind me and turned to see Jack walking in my direction. Like me, Jack's initial reaction to stress or frustration was often anger. The evening before, not long after Caroline and I had delivered the terrible news to him, I'd heard a steady banging in the basement and had gone down to check on him. He'd dragged an old, heavy punching bag that hadn't been used in years out of a storage closet, hung it up in the same place where I used to hang it, and was beating it viciously. I stopped in the doorway and watched for a short time. He was sweating profusely, breathing heavily, and cursing. I turned and walked away without saying anything to him, but I remember thinking that had the bag been a man, his ribs would have been reduced to sawdust.

Our tiff the night he returned from California had been forgotten as soon as it ended, and he and I had had several civil discussions about his future. He wanted to go to law school. He wanted to practice criminal law, most likely defense, and he wanted me to guide him. He was so much like me that it was frightening sometimes. He was kind and gentle and funny and had many excellent qualities, but he was sometimes competitive to the point of fanaticism, he wasn't above meeting violence with violence, his ego sometimes got in the way of reason, and nuance was a concept that usually escaped him. He was also often a walking contradiction—he would express a thought or an attitude far beyond his years, yet he wouldn't make a bed or clean a room or put a dirty plate in the dishwasher. He was a serious and excellent student and devoted to physical training, yet if you put him in a room full of his jock buddies, he could—and would—drink them all under the table. I'd decided his contradictory proclivities were typical of young men and had resolved to be patient with him.

He lumbered up next to me and wrapped an arm around my shoulders.

"Do you remember when she first got sick?" he said. "You took Lilly and me to breakfast out in Gray and gave us a speech."

"I did?"

"Yeah, you did. You told us that we weren't the ones who were sick and that you didn't want to see any self-pity. You told us to stay strong and to live well because that's what Mom would want us to do."

I nodded, vaguely remembering the conversation.

"This isn't your fault, Dad. I know you and I know what you're standing out here in the dark thinking. It isn't anybody's fault. I've been doing some research, and you wouldn't believe the number of women getting breast cancer these days. What's even more shocking is that it doesn't exist in some parts of the world, especially the Far East, which tells me it has to be diet based." "You've been researching it? What are the numbers on survival? How long is she going to be around?"

"The numbers aren't good." He dropped both his chin and his voice. "Ninety-five percent of the women who are diagnosed with metastatic breast cancer die within five years."

"She'll be in the five percent," I said immediately.

"I hope you're right. You know I hope you're right. But there's one thing I want you to keep in mind, Dad, because it's the only thing keeping me sane right now. Even if she isn't here in five years, she'll still *be here* for five years. That's almost two thousand days and nights. If we walked in there and asked her right now, she'd tell us that she wants us to make the best of every one of those days. She'd tell us not to sit around and cry, she wouldn't want us to stop living our lives and sit by her side, she wouldn't want us to treat her like an invalid. She'd want us to love, and she'd want us to work and play and laugh and cry and just *live*. Like we always have."

I stood quietly for a minute and then turned to face him full on. I placed my hands on his shoulders, my heart so full of love I felt like it would burst.

"You're quite a young man," I said.

He smiled, winked at me and said, "I had a good teacher. C'mon, let's go try to get some sleep."

CHAPTER THIRTY-THREE

After hours of research on polygraph examiners and a dozen phone calls, I decided to hire a retired FBI agent named David Trumble to administer Richard's lie detector test. Trumble had impeccable credentials. He had a law degree, he'd spent twenty-five years in the FBI, and he'd administered more than three thousand polygraphs. His Atlanta-based firm, Trumble and Associates, was one of the most respected private investigative agencies in the United States. He was expensive—ten thousand plus travel expenses—but I thought it would be worth it if Richard somehow managed to pass. Trumble's advertising was filled with endorsements from former FBI agents and U.S. attorneys, so I figured it would be difficult for the agents and lawyers handling Richard's case to simply ignore the results if they were favorable.

I'd thought a great deal about Richard's theory that his father-in-law was framing him for kidnap and murder. It didn't make any sense to me, but Richard was right about one thing: I didn't know Charles Russell. I didn't know the dynamics of the relationships between Charles and Richard and Mary.

The nagging question remained, however. Where was Lindsay? Sheriff Bates had told me Lindsay's blood was on the clothing they found. Blood and semen on the clothing of a missing child usually meant the child was dead, but the body had yet to be found despite one of the most intense searches I'd ever seen. And although Caroline had received devastating news regarding her cancer, she remained intensely interested in the case and continued to insist that Lindsay was still alive. I trusted Caroline's instincts and wanted to believe her, but the fact remained that I was confronted with evidence, and the evidence seemed to show that Richard wrote a ransom note, killed his daughter, staged a kidnapping scene, and topped it all off by stealing three million dollars in ransom money from his father-in-law.

David Trumble walked into my office at ten in the morning. He'd flown up from Atlanta the night before and had been at the jail with Richard Monroe since 7:00 a.m. I wasn't allowed to attend the session. Trumble was a short, slight, studious-looking man with salt-and-pepper hair and green eyes behind circular glasses. He wore a brown suit with a heavily starched, white shirt and a brown tie. I'd had dinner with him the previous evening, and he'd explained his particular methodology of conducting the polygraph exam. I already had a pretty clear understanding of how the test worked, but Trumble talked about it as though it were a form of art. He struck me as a mix between fastidious scientist and passionate artist. I'd never before heard anyone gush about respiratory rates and heart rates and blood pressure and electrodermal activity. If he hadn't been so genuinely serious, he would have been hilarious.

He sat down across from me and folded his hands in his lap.

"That was interesting," he said.

"For ten grand you better have something more than that," I said.

"Your client was cooperative," Trumble said. "I took my time in the pre-test phase and was able to establish a solid rapport with him. By the time we got into the meat of the test, I think he was as comfortable as one can be under these circumstances."

"So you think the results of the exam are reliable?"

He nodded. "In my professional opinion and based on my experience, the results of the test are indisputable. I went into every aspect of the case with him. I approached his involvement from every conceivable angle. I will, of course, provide you with a written report of the results and my conclusions based on those results."

"Thank you," I said. "What's the verdict? Did he kill her?"

"Not only did he not kill her, he has absolutely no idea what happened to her. He didn't write the ransom note. He didn't stage the kidnapping scene, and he didn't take the money. And he's never abused his child, sexually or otherwise."

"You're certain?"

"I'd stake my reputation on it. I'd stake my entire career on it."

I stood, shoved my hands deep into my pockets, and started rocking back and forth on my heels.

"Damn, David, this gets worse by the day. If what you're saying is true, then Richard is innocent. But the feds have already played their hand. You were an FBI agent for how long, twenty-five years? In all that time, how often did you see a federal prosecutor admit he'd made a mistake by jumping the gun on an arrest or an indictment? How often did you see a U.S. attorney stick his tail between his legs and dismiss a case, especially a case as high profile as this one?"

Trumble shook his head, but he didn't reply.

"That's what I thought," I said. "Never. The track has already been laid and the train has left the station. Richard Monroe is going to get railroaded."

CHAPTER THIRTY-FOUR

Two days later, I was back at the federal courthouse in Greeneville, this time in a conference room surrounded by the law enforcers who bore the primary responsibility of bringing Lindsay Monroe's kidnapper and murderer to justice. Seated at the head of the table was Assistant U.S. Attorney Rudy Zeller, the man in charge of the prosecution. He was flanked by Ross Dedrick, Leon Bates, Mike Norcross, Mitchell Royston, and two older men in suits who were introduced as senior FBI agents who were part of the Child Abduction Rapid Deployment (CARD) team that had been assigned to Lindsay's case. In my briefcase were ten copies of the report David Trumble had expedited for me along with a motion asking the trial judge to allow Trumble to offer expert testimony regarding the results of Richard Monroe's polygraph test. I hadn't yet filed the motion because I was hoping against hope that Zeller would do what the feds always refer to as "the right thing." I was hoping he would give credence to Trumble's test results and allow an FBI polygrapher of his choosing to examine Richard. Beyond that, provided Richard performed as well on the FBI's test, I entertained the hope that Zeller would rethink his case and his evidence and get back to work finding the real kidnapper.

"I appreciate you agreeing to meet," I said as I took my seat at the far end of the table, opposite Zeller.

"I assume you're here to talk about some kind of deal," he said. "Has your client decided to tell us where her body is?"

"Not exactly," I said as I started sliding copies of Trumble's report around the table. "Have any of you guys ever heard of David Trumble? My understanding is that he's pretty famous in law-enforcement circles. An expert in the field of polygraphy, consultant to law enforcement agencies all over the country, subject of a television series that didn't get past the pilot phase, a real credit to the FBI."

"Never heard of him," Zeller said, picking up the report and starting to read.

"I'll bet if David Trumble had you hooked up to his machine right now, the machine would show deception," I said. "How about you, Agent Dedrick? Heard of Trumble?"

"What difference does it make? Tell me you didn't ask to meet with us to talk about a retired glory hound."

"Glory hound? Do I detect a hint of jealousy?"

Dedrick snorted and started reading. I waited a few minutes while the men around me began to digest the contents of Trumble's report. Zeller was the first to toss it on the table.

"This is garbage," he said. "Voodoo science."

"Trumble is willing to stake his professional reputation on the accuracy of the test," I said. "He wants to testify, to break some new ground."

"There isn't a chance in hell Judge Wilson will let this in," Zeller said.

"He might if you stipulate," I said.

"And why would I do that?"

"Because it's the right thing to do. Listen, the reason Richard and Mary Monroe came to me in the first place was because you guys were pressuring them to take polygraphs. Well, Richard has now taken one, administered by one of the foremost experts in the field. The results say he didn't have anything to do with his child's disappearance."

"His DNA says otherwise," Dedrick said.

"Somebody could have planted that," I said. "Richard is an intelligent man. If he'd killed his daughter during a rape or after a rape, do you really think he'd be stupid enough to put her soiled panties and pajama bottoms in a Dumpster outside his own office? And would he be stupid enough to write a ransom note on his own computer? He makes his living writing computer code. Do you think he didn't know someone could retrieve the note from his computer?"

"Every person in this room would agree that criminals do stupid things," Zeller said. "They panic and they do stupid things. Then when they get caught, one of their first arguments is, 'Do you think I'd be that stupid?'"

"We're getting off track here," I said. "I want to talk about this polygraph. I'd like you to give him another one. You can use somebody of your own choosing, an FBI examiner. If he passes again, maybe you should reconsider trying him for this murder."

"Not a chance," Zeller said. "Juries are the lie detectors in a courtroom. You start introducing stuff like this during trials and you wind up transferring the most important function of a jury to a machine."

"That's an unusual attitude for a fed," I said. "You guys use polygraphs all the time. You use them to make decisions on probable cause, you use them to make decisions on whether to prosecute, you use them to eliminate suspects and to zero in on suspects. Hell, everybody in this room outside of Leon and Mitchell had to pass a polygraph before the FBI or the TBI or the U.S. attorney's office would give you a job."

"And your point would be?" Zeller said.

"My point is you're a hypocrite. If a polygraph result fits your purpose, you say it's indisputable and stand behind it 110 percent, but if it doesn't, you call it voodoo science."

Zeller slid the report back across the table and stood. The FBI agents stood at the same time, obeying his silent command. None of them picked up Trumble's report.

"The next time you ask for a meeting, it had better be something worth my time," Zeller said as he started for the door, followed dutifully by his minions. "We already have enough to bury your client, and I promise you by the time the trial comes around, we'll have a lot more."

CHAPTER THIRTY-FIVE

The envelope was taped to the door. "Joseph Dillard" was handwritten across the front.

I'd made good on my invitation, and my father had come out to the house for Sunday dinner. He showed up a little before one o'clock in the afternoon. Caroline and I, Jack, Lilly and Randy and their baby boy, Joey, Sarah and her daughter, Grace, were all there waiting for him. Caroline and I had stuffed and roasted a couple chickens, whipped up a bunch of veggies, and made a couple apple pies. Sarah brought biscuits and rolls, Lilly brought a gallon of tea, and Jack brought his usual hearty appetite. The weather was warm and sunny, so Jack and I set up card tables end-to-end, and we were able to eat on the deck overlooking the lake. Nobody was quite sure what to call him, but he took care of that quickly by announcing we should all call him J.D., and that worked just fine. He stayed for three hours. Caroline, true to her nature, made him feel as though he was a member of the family, and the kids regaled him with stories of their upbringing. Even Sarah seemed to enjoy him. She was witty and funny and, as usual, occasionally profane. He smiled a lot, didn't talk too much, and seemed to enjoy the afternoon.

When it was time for him to leave, I walked him to the rental car he'd parked in the driveway.

"I set it up," he said. "The trip to Wisconsin to talk to Lucas Venable's parents. We leave Wednesday morning at 7:00 a.m. from the Tri-Cities airport, and we'll be back at 10:30 the same night. You'll go with me, won't you, Joseph? I already paid for your ticket."

"I'd rather have every tooth in my head pulled out with a pair of pliers and no anesthesia," I said.

"So would I, but like you said, it needs to be done. I know it was presumptuous of me to make you a reservation and I apologize, but I can't do it alone. I just can't. Please, Joseph. If you go with me, I swear I'll never ask another thing of you."

I had agreed, albeit reluctantly, and was at the hotel to pick him up at 5:30 a.m. on Wednesday morning. I reached out and pulled the envelope off the door and tore it open. There was one sheet of typing paper, which I unfolded. A short note written in the same hand as the name on the outside of the envelope said:

> Dear Joseph,
>
> I have decided I cannot face going to Wisconsin. In fact, I have decided that coming here was a terrible and selfish decision. I am going back to Malaysia where I belong. I have lived my life there and I should die there. Once again, I hope you can forgive me.
>
> Jack Dillard
>
> P.S. You have a beautiful family. Cherish them.

Once a coward, always a coward.

I balled the paper up, dropped it on the floor, and walked back out to my truck.

I hadn't laid eyes on Mary Monroe since the day the ransom was delivered, but I wanted to speak to her, to see whether I could get some sense of what had changed with her, of why she had turned on Richard so quickly. If she had turned on him because of the arrest, because of the purported DNA evidence, I wanted her to know that Richard had passed the polygraph test, that there was at least a possibility that he could be falsely accused. I'd called her cell phone more than a dozen times, but it always went straight to voice mail.

I knew that before Richard's arrest, he and Mary were staying at the home of an elderly married couple in the Lake Meadow subdivision near Boones Creek. The couple, whom Richard and Mary knew from church, migrated to Arizona the first week of September each year and didn't return until late spring. Richard and Mary had used the house to hide out from the growing horde of reporters that had descended on Jonesborough during the early stages of the investigation. Now that Richard had been arrested, the majority of the reporters had moved on to the next sensational story. They would return for the trial, but in the meantime, the ever-present gaggle of newshounds that had milled around outside Richard and Mary's home in Jonesborough had disappeared. I wondered whether Mary had gone back.

It was six in the morning, and I was still fuming after finding the note that Jack Dillard had taped to the door of his motel room. I wasn't looking forward to breaking the news to everyone in the family that their long-lost father, father-in-law, and grandfather had run away again, and I was angry for allowing myself to think that maybe, just maybe, I could have formed some kind of meaningful relationship with him. I was also upset because I knew that eventually my conscience would drive me to Wisconsin where I would have to face the parents of the young man named Lucas Venable who was lying in a grave marked with my father's name. Their son had been killed on the battlefield in Vietnam, and they deserved to know that. They would probably want to move his remains home to Wisconsin. I knew I wouldn't be able to just let it be.

I circled the block around the Monroe home a couple times to make sure there wasn't anyone hanging around or watching. When I was satisfied, I pulled into the driveway, which led to a garage behind the house. I got out of my truck and looked up. The screen covering the window in Lindsay's room hadn't been replaced. I'd seen it once before when I looked around before I went to talk to Tom Short the first time, but looking at it again gave me an uneasy feeling. In spite of everything that had happened, the possibility remained that the child had been taken by a stranger. An image of a man climbing down a ladder in the darkness with a child draped over his shoulder flashed through my mind. Once again, I wondered whether Lindsay was still alive. I wanted her to be alive, but I couldn't make myself believe it. The voodoo science, as Rudy Zeller had termed it, suggested to me that Richard didn't kill her. But the evidence said otherwise, and there was no stronger evidence than DNA.

I walked over to the garage and peered inside. The red Mercedes was there, along with a Lincoln Navigator. The morning was clear and quiet, the sun just beginning to peek over the mountains to the east. I followed a brick walkway to a door just off the back patio, climbed a couple steps, and looked inside. Mary Monroe was sitting at a table in the kitchen with her back to me. As she lifted a cup to her lips, I knocked softly on the door. She froze for a few seconds before setting the cup slowly back down on the table. She rose from the chair and turned toward me. She was wearing a pink bathrobe that appeared to be made of silk. The look on her face was calm, almost serene. A slight smile crossed her face and she moved in tiny steps—like a Japanese geisha girl—toward the door.

"Can I help you?" she said when she opened the door a crack. There seemed to be a vague hint of recognition on her face, but the question took me by surprise.

"I'd like to talk to you, Mrs. Monroe," I said. "Can I come in?"

She stepped back from the door and I looked closely at her. She was still a beautiful woman, but she was a mess. Her hair was matted and dirty, her skin tight and pale. She looked as though she hadn't slept in days, and she smelled like she hadn't bathed for the same amount of time. I noticed that her eyes were twitching—tiny, rapid movements from side to side. It was as though her eyes were vibrating involuntarily.

"Mrs. Monroe?" I said. "Are you all right?"

At that moment, I heard a door close and heavy footsteps descending a set of stairs. Charles Russell walked around the corner, already dressed for the day. He stopped short when he saw me.

"How did you get in here?" he said.

"She let me in."

He looked at Mary and his face softened.

"What are you doing up, Mary?" he said as he walked over and took her elbow. "Come. Let me help you back to bed."

I stood there, unsure of what to do, as they disappeared. I listened as they climbed the steps slowly, their footfalls growing fainter. He hadn't demanded that I leave, but I was more than a little uncomfortable standing in the Monroe kitchen listening to the steady tick, tick, tick of what must have been a grandfather clock near the base of the stairs. A few minutes passed before I heard Charles coming back down. I expected an angry exchange, but when he came back into the kitchen, he wore a look that conveyed resignation.

"You might as well sit," he said. "You don't strike me as the type who is just going to go away."

I sat at the table while he surprised me even more by pouring two cups of coffee.

"What's wrong with her?" I said as he sat down across from me.

"She's sleeping. It's the Ambien. She takes too much of it and she does things while she's sleeping. She won't even remember that you were here."

"So that's how she's dealing with everything? By drugging herself?"

He nodded. "I've thought about doing the same. I mean, who can blame her? Her daughter is dead, but nobody knows where her body is and her husband murdered her. Her entire world has exploded around her, and the only way she can deal with it right now is to numb herself completely."

"I can understand it," I said. "I have a sister who's done the same kind of thing. She was raped when she was very young, and she spent a lot of time medicating herself with drugs and alcohol. But this, what Mary is dealing with, I don't know what I'd do."

I looked across the table at him, at a face etched by age and worry. His granddaughter was gone. Three million dollars of his money was gone. His daughter was, for all intents and purposes, gone. His son-in-law stood accused of one of the most heinous crimes imaginable. Yet here he was, in his daughter's home at six fifteen in the morning, dressed as though he were going to work that day, still upright, still functioning at some level, still trying to manage whatever fragments that were left of his life. I felt a twinge of admiration for him although the admiration was diluted by pity. I thought again about how cruel life can be for some, how fate can be so unfair and so utterly arbitrary. What had he done to deserve this? What had Mary done? And Lindsay? Had her body been defiled and buried in some shallow grave, thrown down some abandoned mine shaft in the nearby mountains, burned to ash and tossed to the wind? Why did such things happen?

"What do you want, Mr. Dillard?" Charles said.

"I'm not sure, to be honest. I think I just wanted to talk to Mary."

"Are you here in a professional capacity, as Richard's defense lawyer?"

"I suppose I am."

"I thought maybe you'd quit and wanted to come over to our side."

"I don't quit in the middle of a case because things turn bad, Mr. Russell. I'm not wired that way."

"Again then, what do you want?"

"I guess I'm just searching for the truth, just trying to get some sense of what's going on. The last time I saw Mary, she was passed out on the floor of the hotel room the day we ... the day the kidnapper called and I delivered the money. She and Richard seemed to be so strong together, so *tight*. They were in a horrific situation, but they were dealing with it together. And now everything has changed. She's divorcing him from what you told me on the phone. She's going to be a witness for the prosecution. I guess I just wanted to ask her what changed."

He pushed his coffee cup—which he hadn't touched to that point—away from him with both hands. He laced his fingers together, leaned forward on his elbows, and looked directly into my eyes.

"I know your history, Mr. Dillard," he said. "When all of this happened, when Lindsay disappeared, I came to help look for her immediately, of course. But then Mary told me the police were accusing her and Richard of being involved, so I started reaching out to people I've known for years, people I trust. I asked them who they would call on for help if they were in a similar situation. These are people of means, people who have power, people who have education and contacts. We talked about lawyers in Nashville and Atlanta and Charlotte and even Miami. We talked about big firms, firms with political ties and money. We talked about mavericks, about lawyers that specialize in criminal defense, big names who have been able to get favorable results for their clients after the media had already tried and convicted them. One name kept popping up. They'd say, 'Have you heard of this local guy named Joe Dillard? He's done this and this and that and that.'

"I have to confess I'd never heard of you. I've always been much too busy, too preoccupied with what was going on in my own life to pay much attention to others. But after your name kept popping up, I asked Earl Botts to check you out. I know you and Earl haven't been on the best of terms, but I trust him completely. He compiled a dossier on you. He actually recommended that we not hire you. He said he had concerns about some things, primarily what he called your 'lack of respect for institutional logic.' Earl is a great believer in institutions, legal and otherwise. He said you were a loose cannon, a man governed only by his own conscience. He said you weren't above committing violent acts if it suited your—"

"Where are you going with this?" I said.

"I'm trying to tell you that in spite of what Earl Botts thinks, I respect you. I don't envy you by any means, but I respect you. That's why I didn't toss you out on your ear when you showed up here uninvited. But there are things you don't know about Richard, things I didn't know until recently."

"What things? What are you talking about?"

"Terrible things. Don't ask me again what they are because I can't tell you. I won't tell you. They'll come out at the trial."

"Do you really think Richard killed Lindsay?"

"I have no doubt he killed her. Richard has secrets, Mr. Dillard, the kind of secrets that eat away at a man's soul. They'll come out at the trial, though, and when they do, the jury will see what kind of man he is. Richard is going to get what he deserves. He's going to be convicted of murdering my granddaughter, he's going to get the death penalty, and after the government kills him, he's going to hell where he belongs."

CHAPTER THIRTY-SIX

Margaret Bain looked like a cross between a nose tackle and a porcupine. She was almost as tall as I was—over six feet—and she had to weigh in the neighborhood of two fifty. Her short, silver hair shot from her head like flame from a sparkler, and she always seemed to wear the dour expression of a woman who hated everything and everyone around her. She'd just taken a seat behind her desk, and her head was now framed by her law degree from Cal Berkeley, her law license, and a photo of a woman I didn't recognize.

"Who's that?" I said, pointing at the picture.

She turned and looked at it as though she didn't know whose photo was framed on the wall behind her.

"Susan B. Anthony," she said.

"Ah, women's suffrage. I haven't seen a picture of her since junior high."

"I'm a big fan," Margaret said. "So what can I do for you?"

"You can take your foot off Richard Monroe's throat."

Margaret Bain had been hired to represent Mary Monroe in a divorce proceeding. True to form for most divorce lawyers, she'd gone straight for the jugular by getting an order from the circuit court judge tying up what was left of Richard's assets. He couldn't spend a penny. I wasn't representing Richard in the divorce. I hadn't taken a divorce case in twenty years, and I wasn't about to start with Richard. I'd made some calls on his behalf, though, trying to find someone who would take his case.

"And why would I do that?" Margaret said.

"He can't even hire a lawyer," I said. "Nobody will touch him without a big retainer, and he can't pay a big retainer because you've tied up his money. On top of that, he hasn't paid me. I was planning to get him to sign a power of attorney so we could get access to some money to pay for his defense, but I haven't gotten around to it yet. I had to pay a polygraph expert eleven thousand dollars out of my own pocket, and now you've tied everything up and I can't get it back. He hasn't even paid me to represent him at trial yet."

She opened a desk drawer and pulled out a box of tissue.

"The poor thing," she said. "Do you think I'll need this? You already have me feeling so sorry for him I might cry."

"C'mon, Margaret," I said. "He needs money to defend himself. He needs to hire experts to examine the evidence the government has in the criminal case. All I'm asking for is a couple hundred grand. You got the judge to tie up what, a million and a half? Even if you fleece him in the divorce, he'll still be entitled to at least 40 percent of that money. There's plenty to go around."

"Ain't gonna happen," she said.

"Be reasonable, will you? Please? The guy is going on trial for his life. He has a right to the best defense I can give him."

"Go ahead. I guess the key word in that sentence would be *give*."

"Really? Are you serious? You've done some criminal defense work. You know it takes money to do it right."

"Are you saying that you'll be less than zealous if you're unable to collect a big fee from him? I believe that would be unethical, wouldn't it? That would be fodder for the lawyer police in Nashville. You could lose your license over something like that."

I'd screwed up by not insisting that Richard pay me immediately to represent him at trial. A first-degree murder case in federal court was worth at least a hundred thousand dollars to any experienced trial lawyer. Richard and Mary had given me a twenty-thousand-dollar retainer when they first hired me, but at the time, I didn't believe either of them would wind up being charged with murdering Lindsay. I'd already spent more than a hundred hours on the case and was looking at twice that getting ready for trial. If I couldn't get Margaret to agree to allow Richard access to at least some of his money, not only would I be unable to hire any more experts, I'd also wind up trying a murder case in federal court essentially for free.

"What do you want me to say, Margaret? I know you have him by the short hairs. I know he's charged with one of the most terrible crimes imaginable, but there's a strong possibility that he's innocent. Before you tied up his money, I hired one of the most respected polygraph experts in the country and he passed. He passed a polygraph. Put yourself in his place for a second. You're arrested for murdering your own daughter. You didn't do it, but your wife has bought into the police version of what happened and has filed for divorce. She hires a lawyer who ties up all your money so you can't adequately defend yourself against a federal government that has more money and resources than Bill freaking Gates. How would you feel?"

She picked the box of tissue up and opened the desk drawer again. She placed the box in the drawer, fiddled around for a second, and when her hand reappeared it held a long, thick cigar and a cigar cutter. She spent a couple minutes trimming the end off before picking up a large, silver lighter that was sitting on her desk.

"Don't mind if I smoke, do you?" she said.

"It's your office."

"These are Cuban," she said as she sucked and puffed. "You can get them if you know the right people and don't mind spending the money. I don't mind spending the money because I have plenty. The reason I have plenty is because I step on the throats of men like your client and I don't take my foot off until I've choked the life out of them."

"Good for you, Margaret."

"Ironic, isn't it?"

"What's that?"

"An old dyke like me sucking on something that looks like this."

I couldn't help smiling as the room began to fill with thick smoke.

"Let me just ask you to do the same thing you asked of me a minute ago, with one small variation," she said. "I want you to put yourself in *my* position. You're an experienced divorce lawyer who has built her practice advocating the interests of women who have been betrayed or psychologically or physically abused by men. You're aware of a sensational kidnapping case that has happened in the same area where you practice. You follow it because it's horrific, it's sensational, it's fascinating. It's appealing in a prurient sort of way. And then, out of the blue, you get a phone call from a gentleman one morning who tells you that his son-in-law has been arrested for killing his granddaughter. He tells you that his daughter—the mother of the child and the wife of the accused—is terribly distraught and that she wants to divorce this monster who has killed her baby, stolen her father's money, and destroyed her life. You meet with the grandfather and the mother. The mother is inconsolable, maybe a little high, but she's determined. She wants to rain fire and brimstone down on this ... this *thing*. She wants to see him burn in hell, but before he burns in hell, she wants to make him suffer as much as he's made her suffer. There's a ton of money involved, which means you're going to be paid handsomely. It's also a huge media case, which means you're going to get a ton of free publicity. It's a divorce lawyer's dream.

"So you do your thing. You zealously represent your client. You get the divorce court to agree that the monster shouldn't be able to hide or spend or otherwise deplete his financial resources, and the court puts down an order freezing the assets that haven't already been frozen. And then Joe Dillard waltzes into your office asking for mercy because he needs money to help defend the monster. He needs money for himself, he needs money for experts that he plans to hire to come to court and confuse the jury, confuse the issues. He wants you to show some compassion for his client. You respect Joe Dillard because he's been around awhile, he's been in the trenches, but you have this incredibly strong urge to tell him to go screw himself. Now, having put yourself in my position, counselor, let me ask you: what would you do?"

I shook my head slowly and rose from the chair.

"I guess I'd tell me to go screw myself."

She blew a long stream of gray smoke in my direction.

"Yeah," she said. "I guess you would."

CHAPTER THIRTY-SEVEN

The paperwork had arrived via a courier from Assistant United States Attorney Rudy Zeller's office three days earlier. It was a "Motion to Disqualify Counsel," a request by Zeller to the federal court judge to kick me off Richard Monroe's case. It was one thirty on a Thursday afternoon, and I was sitting on the witness stand in federal court in front of Judge Donnie Wilson, a man who had spent his entire adult life sucking up to his powerful friends, waiting for the previous judge to retire so he could get the coveted lifetime appointment to the federal bench. It had finally happened for Wilson five years earlier. I'd never appeared in front of Judge Wilson, had never had any dealings with him at all. I knew him by reputation only, and the things I'd heard weren't flattering.

"Raise your right hand," Judge Wilson said to me. "Do you swear or affirm that the testimony you are about to give will be the truth, the whole truth, and nothing but the truth?"

"I do."

"For the record," the judge said, "we are here on a motion to disqualify Mr. Dillard from representing

Richard Monroe in case number six-five-three-three-one, *United States of America versus Richard Monroe.* The motion was filed by the United States Attorney's office and alleges that Mr. Dillard has a conflict of interest that requires him to be removed from the case. The motion also states that Mr. Dillard will be subpoenaed as a witness for the prosecution in the upcoming trial. In response, Mr. Dillard has filed a motion to sever the counts and try the murder case and the theft case separately. Mr. Zeller is here representing the United States and Mr. Dillard is representing Mr. Monroe and, for the purposes of this hearing, himself. Proceed, Mr. Zeller."

Rudy Zeller got up from the prosecution table and moved to the lectern. Richard Monroe, cuffed and shackled and wearing the bright-orange jumpsuit issued by the jail, was sitting at the defense table. There were about a dozen reporters in the gallery.

"State your name for the record, please," Zeller said.

"Joe Dillard."

"Mr. Dillard, when were you hired to represent Richard Monroe?"

"I was first hired to represent both him and his wife, Mary Monroe. They came to my office a few days after their daughter, Lindsay Monroe, was kidnapped. They were concerned that the police were targeting them in the investigation and asked me to represent them."

"Isn't there an inherent conflict of interest in representing two people in a criminal proceeding?"

"There was no criminal proceeding at that point, but yes, I realized there was at least a potential for a conflict of interest, and I discussed it with both Mr. and Mrs.

Monroe during that first meeting. I explained that if one or both of them wound up being charged with a crime, there could be problems because they could wind up being witnesses against each other. Both of them were adamant about being innocent of any wrongdoing whatsoever and wanted me to represent them. I drafted a consent form that laid out the potential for a conflict of interest and both of them signed it."

"You just said they wanted you to represent them, but at that point, neither of them had been charged with anything. What exactly did they want you to do?"

"The police were accusing them of being involved. They had both been interrogated. They'd both given blood and hair samples and had consented to searches of their property. When the police asked them to take polygraph examinations, they felt like they needed a lawyer. They wanted to continue to cooperate with the police, but they wanted a lawyer to act as an intermediary on their behalf, to protect their rights under the Constitution."

"Why didn't you suggest that they each hire separate counsel?"

"I did. Like I said a minute ago, we discussed the conflict, and we discussed all the options. At that point in time, they didn't feel as though they needed separate lawyers. They insisted that they hadn't done anything wrong."

"Were they distraught?" Zeller said.

"Distraught? Of course they were distraught. They were terribly upset. Their child had disappeared and the police were accusing them."

"Do you think they were capable of making sound decisions under those circumstances?"

"As capable as anyone could be, I suppose. As I remember it, they were lucid and coherent, very articulate. They were emotional, which was certainly understandable, but they seemed to be reasonable, intelligent people who found themselves in a desperate situation. They wanted some help. They *needed* some help, so I agreed to represent them."

"For a fee, of course."

"I'm a lawyer, Mr. Zeller. It's how I make my living."

"And did your fee include delivering ransom money to the purported kidnapper?"

"I didn't know it at the time, but yes, it eventually came to that."

"How much was it? Three million dollars?"

"I believe so. That was the demand made by the kidnapper, but I didn't count the money."

"It must have been quite an adventure. Tell the court about it, Mr. Dillard."

I turned and faced the judge, who was looking at me over a pair of black-rimmed reading glasses. His face betrayed nothing.

"It happened very quickly," I said. "The Monroes and I had been talking for over an hour, maybe two, when Mr. Monroe got a text message on his phone that said—and I'm paraphrasing here because I don't remember the exact wording of the text—but it said something along the lines of if Richard wanted his child back, it was time to pay the ransom. A note had been left on Lindsay's pillow that demanded three million dollars in ransom. The note also said that if the police were involved in any way or if the kidnapper or anyone who worked with him was apprehended by the police, then Lindsay would be killed. Like I said before, I don't remember the conversation word for word, but we had a brief discussion about the police. The Monroes insisted that the police be excluded from the negotiations and from the ransom drop. They wanted to follow the kidnapper's instructions, deliver the money, and get their daughter back."

"Excuse me, Mr. Dillard," Zeller said, "but Richard Monroe didn't just happen to have three million dollars with him, did he?"

"Richard didn't have the money," I said. "He was involved in some type of litigation that had resulted in a court freezing most of his corporation's assets. But Mary's father, Charles Russell, is a wealthy man, and he had raised the three million dollars. I was told that Mr. Russell had the money at the Carnegie Hotel in Johnson City, that we could get our hands on it quickly. The kidnapper was pressing us for time. He wanted the money delivered in one hour. I remember telling Richard to ask the kidnapper to prove that he had Lindsay and that she was alive. Richard sent him a text, and a few seconds later he received a media message that was a photograph of Lindsay. She was lying on her side in what appeared to be a wooden box, and it appeared that she'd been bound and gagged. It was an incredibly intense situation. We discussed what we should do for a little while longer, and then we made a decision to go to the Carnegie Hotel and pick up the money. A few minutes after we arrived at the Carnegie, the kidnapper called Richard's phone.

His voice was altered somehow, like it was being run through some kind of electronic device. He sounded like an alien. I remember he threatened to cut Lindsay's head off and at that point, Mrs. Monroe fainted and fell to the floor. During the confusion, I wound up with Richard's phone and a suitcase full of money, and the next thing I knew I was driving my vehicle north on I-26. I kept getting periodic text messages from the kidnapper that directed me where to go. Eventually, I ended up at Steele Creek Park in Bristol."

"How did the money come into your possession?"

"Mr. Russell gave it to me while I was at the hotel. It was in a suitcase."

"What did you do with it?"

"When I got to Steele Creek, I was told to follow a trail that ran through the woods near the lake. After I'd walked a half mile, maybe three-quarters of a mile, the kidnapper called me and told me to dump the money from the suitcase into a metal trash can that was about fifty yards in front of me and then turn around, walk back to my vehicle, and leave. That's exactly what I did."

"And you did all of this without notifying the police?" Zeller said.

"That's correct. My clients didn't want them notified, and I honored their wishes."

"And to make this long, fascinating story just a bit shorter, the upshot of all this is that the alleged kidnapper somehow managed to take the money and didn't return the child, isn't that correct?"

"There was apparently a false bottom in the trash can and beneath that a tunnel leading to a drain culvert. I didn't see it myself, but I was told by Mr. Russell that the kidnapper used the drain culvert to conceal himself and took the money from the can. Mr. Russell had employees in the woods watching, but—"

"That's enough," Judge Wilson said. "I'm ready to rule on your motion, Mr. Zeller."

I started to say something else, but I'd practiced law long enough to know that once a judge made up his mind—and judging from the tone of his voice and the look on his face, this one obviously had—there was absolutely no point in arguing.

"After hearing Mr. Dillard's testimony and after having reviewed the indictment in this case," Judge Wilson said, "I find that Mr. Dillard has a clear conflict of interest that precludes him from further representing the defendant, Richard Monroe. By his own admission and by his own actions, he has become a witness. And while I don't condone Mr. Dillard's conduct, I can understand it to some degree. He found himself in a terribly difficult position and was under intense pressure. Having the luxury of hindsight, I suppose we can all second-guess the things he did, especially his decision to exclude the authorities, but I believe him when he says he was following his clients' wishes. What he did may have been ill-advised, but it wasn't illegal. However, there is no getting around the fact that he delivered money that was eventually stolen and is the basis for the theft charge against Mr. Monroe. The prosecution's theory, if I am not mistaken, is that Mr. Monroe killed his daughter and then staged a kidnapping in order to extort money from his father-in-law. In response to Mr. Zeller's motion, Mr.

Dillard has filed a motion to sever the theft case from the murder case in which he argues that even if the court finds he has a conflict in the theft case, he could still represent Mr. Monroe in the murder. The court finds that the offenses charged in the indictment are based on a series of acts connected together or constituting parts of a single scheme or plan, and therefore severance is not warranted."

The judge turned his head toward me and removed his glasses.

"You have a glaring conflict of interest, Mr. Dillard," he said, "and there is no legal basis for severing the offenses. Bottom line? You're sitting this one out, counselor. Court's adjourned."

PART III

CHAPTER THIRTY-EIGHT

The leaves on the mountains were starting to turn, the green quilt slowly transforming to gold, orange, and red. I was driving Caroline home from her radiation treatment the day after Judge Wilson booted me from the Richard Monroe case. We'd learned from the doctor at Vanderbilt that the cancer inside her was aggressive and farther along than the doctors first thought. A scan had revealed that her spine had already been invaded so thoroughly that three vertebrae were fractured. The radiation treatments, which were being administered in Johnson City, were intended to kill the cancer cells, but they were doing far more than that. The radiation burned her throat and made it painful to swallow. It also made her nauseous. The combination of nausea and the pain in her throat made her spurn food, and because she wasn't taking in any calories, she was losing weight quickly and had very little energy. She spent long hours in bed, reserving the little strength she had so she could continue teaching at her beloved dance school, and when she walked through the door at home after teaching, all she wanted to do was sleep. She ate pain medication like candy and was taking weekly intravenous drips to strengthen her bones and shut down her ovaries. She was halfway through the radiation, and as soon as that was finished, she would have to begin chemotherapy.

I'd been spending a lot of time at night listening to her breathe, terrified by the thought that she might suddenly stop. It was the loneliest I'd ever been. The thought that she might not be there in a year or two years or, at best from everything I'd read on the internet, five years made me sick with sorrow and anger and frustration. I found myself talking about it less and less but thinking about it more and more. What would I do without her? How would I possibly go on?

"I'm worried about you," she said from the passenger seat.

I smiled and looked over. Other than the weight loss, you couldn't tell by looking at her that there was anything wrong. She was as beautiful as ever.

"You're worried about me?" I said. "I'm fine. You're the one who glows in the dark. I don't even need a light to read when you're asleep."

"I'm serious," she said. "You look terrible, you're not eating, you've stopped working out, and I *know* you're not sleeping."

"Sleep is overrated."

"I know how hard this is on you, Joe. I can see in your eyes how worried you are, and then when you add what happened with your father and what's been going on with this case into the mix, I'm afraid you're pushing yourself a little too far. I know you're tough. I know you pride yourself on being able to take anything the world dishes out, but I think you need to slow down a little right now, maybe find a support group and talk about how you're feeling."

"I'm not going to a support group, Caroline. I'm not going to go in and listen to a bunch of people whine about their problems."

"Lilly is going to one."

"I know. She told me, and good for her. If it helps, good for her. But I'm not going. I have a support group. I have you and Jack and Lilly and Sarah. That's all I need."

"You know what the statistics are, don't you? With metastatic breast cancer? You know there's a good chance I won't be around much longer."

"Don't," I said. "I'm not up for this conversation right now. I don't want to think about ... I can't, Caroline. I can't think about it."

She reached across and took my hand.

"You know I'll fight," she said. "I'll fight to my last breath. But if it happens, when it happens, you're going to have to be stronger than ever. The kids will need you more than ever. You can't ... you can't quit."

I pulled the truck to the side of the road and stopped. I hadn't really spoken with anyone about Caroline's illness since the night Jack came outside and talked to me. People had mentioned it, of course. Lilly had posted the news of Caroline's diagnosis on Facebook, which was something that angered me so much I had to force myself to keep quiet about it. Had I mentioned it to her, I would have said things I regretted, and she would have wound up in tears, so I kept my mouth shut. But the news spread quickly, and people felt obligated to inquire about her, to convey their best wishes, to let me know they'd put Caroline on prayer lists at their churches. My response was always a polite, "She's fine, thank you for asking," and either a quick escape or an awkward change of subject.

I slammed the truck into park and looked at her. I felt my eyes filling with tears.

"I don't think I can do it, baby," I said. "Please don't ask me to go on without you. We've been through so much together. I just can't imagine ... I just don't know how I can ...."

And then I lost it. She scooted across the seat and wrapped her arms around my neck, and I cried like I'd never cried in my life. My macho façade melted away, and I let grief pour from my soul while she held me and whispered in my ear. I don't know how long we sat there by the side of the road, but it was a long while. I wasn't accustomed to sobbing uncontrollably, and the worst part of it was that as I finally began to regain some control over myself, I realized it probably wouldn't be the last time it would happen.

"I'm sorry," I said when I composed myself enough to speak. "The last thing you need right now is a weak husband."

She put a finger under my chin and raised it.

"Don't apologize," she said, her eyes glistening. "And don't ever call yourself weak again. You're the strongest man I've ever met."

"I don't feel so strong right now."

"I know, but you have to keep going. You have to keep doing what you've always done. Let your heart be your guide and keep going."

I took a deep breath and wiped my nose on my sleeve.

"I feel like you're being punished for something I've done," I said. "I've made so many mistakes. I've been so arrogant, running around acting like I could save the world or something, like I know better than everyone else what's right and what's wrong. I'm such a fool."

"You're not a fool, and you're not done saving the world. I want you to do something for me, Joe. I want you to stop feeling sorry for me and worrying about me and worrying about what might or might not happen. Can you do that for me? Please?"

"Probably not, but I can try."

"Good. There's one other thing."

"What's that?"

She slid away from me a little and her eyes took on some intensity.

"You made a promise to me a little while back, and I expect you to keep it."

"Promise? What promise?"

"You promised me you'd find Lindsay Monroe."

"No, I didn't. I said I'd do my best, and I have. But she's gone, Caroline. She's dead. She'll probably never be found."

"She isn't dead. I told you before she isn't dead and now I'm telling you again. She's still out there, Joe. She's still alive. The judge may have kicked you out of the courtroom, but he didn't kick you out of the fight altogether. Go out and find Lindsay Monroe. Bring her back home where she belongs and put an end to all this madness."

CHAPTER THIRTY-NINE

Richard Monroe had continued to disintegrate day by day, bit by bit. His hair was greasy and unkempt, his skin paler, the bags under his eyes bigger and darker. Like my wife, he was losing weight quickly, although the disease that had attacked Richard was eating away at his soul rather than his body.

A young guard had given me some trouble when I came in. He'd heard about the judge kicking me off the murder case, and as jail guards tend to do, he tried to exercise what he perceived as his power by telling me I couldn't talk to Richard. It didn't go well for him though. A quick phone call to Leon Bates adjusted his attitude.

Because Richard's assets had been tied up by a gaggle of lawyers and judges, he couldn't afford to hire someone to replace me. Judge Wilson had appointed the federal defender's office, which is exactly what it sounds like—the feds' equivalent to the public defender. Richard didn't complain or offer any kind of resistance; as a matter of fact, he didn't say a word. It was as though he'd already been tried and convicted and sentenced to death.

He looked at me without a sign of recognition or acknowledgement when the guards brought him in. I knew he continued to live in isolation—they called it administrative segregation—because he was considered to be a suicide threat. They'd stopped making him wear the paper robe, but he spent all day, every day alone. He was also an accused child killer, so putting him in the general population at the jail would have had serious consequences. He plopped down heavily in the chair across from me after the guard walked out and stared at the table top.

"When you and Mary hired me, you asked me to do three things," I said. "Protect you from the media, protect you from the police, and help you find your daughter. I've failed at all three."

"So why are you here?" he said without looking up.

"Because I'm not finished. The judge says I can't represent you in court, but that doesn't mean I have to stop looking for Lindsay."

"Lindsay's dead."

"I don't believe that. I think she's alive, and I think you can help me find her."

"Why? Why do you think she's alive? What proof do you have?"

"I don't have any, but I don't have any proof that she's dead either."

"Have you forgotten that she was taken in the middle of the night? That her clothing was found with her blood on it and my semen?"

"Did you rape her and kill her, Richard?"

"No."

"Then someone is framing you, and if someone is framing you, there's a chance she's still alive. Help me find out who it is."

His eyes came up and he smiled sarcastically.

"We've been through this, remember? I told you I was being framed and you said I was being ... what was the word you used? Ridiculous. You said I was being ridiculous. You said you wanted to play it back for me. You said I was lying to myself."

"That was before you passed the polygraph."

The sarcastic smile disappeared from his face.

"You guys are all alike, aren't you? No wonder everybody hates lawyers. You call me a liar, you ridicule me to my face, but then you hire a whore. The whore hooks me up to a machine that says I'm telling the truth, so now you're back down here wanting what? More money? So you can go on a knight's quest to find my long-lost daughter? So you can be a hero? Tough luck, counselor. I'm all tapped out."

"I'm not here for money. I'm here for the truth."

"The truth," he snorted. "You don't want the truth. You can't bill me for the truth."

"Then give it to me for free. Tell me where you were for those three missing hours the night Lindsay was taken. It's the key to this whole thing. Do you know why, Richard? Do you know why it's the key? Because wherever you were during those three hours, you left some of yourself behind, and whoever you left it with used it to frame you for kidnapping, murder, extortion, and theft."

"You're wrong. You don't know what you're talking about."

"Then straighten me out. Tell me where you were. Who were you with?"

"She's just a kid. She doesn't have the brains to pull off something like that."

Finally. An admission. He was with a woman.

"Who is she? What's her name? Where does she live?"

He shook his head, and his eyes went blank again.

"What the hell is the *matter* with you, Richard?" I said. "What are you afraid of? That your wife will find out and file for divorce? Or is she under age? Are you looking at a statutory rape charge? Afraid you might ruin your reputation? We're a little past all that, don't you think? C'mon, Richard. Now is the time."

"She wouldn't have," Richard said. "She couldn't have."

"Who is she?"

"There's no point in dragging anyone else into this."

"Did you have sex with her that night before you went home? Did you leave some of yourself there? Because if you did, and if the polygraph is right and you're telling the truth about not being involved in Lindsay's kidnapping, then she needs to be dragged into it. Give me a chance, Richard. Give yourself a chance. Give *Lindsay* a chance."

He lifted his cuffed hands behind his head, laced his fingers around the back of his neck, and started rocking back and forth on the edge of the chair.

"After Lindsay was born and Mary had the problems, she lost all interest in sex," he said. "She didn't want me anymore, at least not that way. I tried to understand it, to accept it, you know? But I'm young. I'm too young to be celibate for the rest of my life. I wasn't trying to hurt anyone. I didn't do it very often. I didn't mean to ... didn't mean to—"

"Her name," I said.

"Kayla. Her name is Kayla Robbins."

CHAPTER FORTY

Kayla Robbins lived alone in an apartment in Johnson City a few blocks from East Tennessee State University. I'd waited until early the next morning, using a tactic I'd seen used by the police on many occasions. The police liked to catch suspects or witnesses who might be difficult just as they're getting out of bed, before their heads were clear. The combination of surprise and pressure loosened tongues, and I needed Kayla Robbins to talk to me.

A cold, steady drizzle was falling as I walked through the parking lot to her apartment. I knocked twice, waited a few seconds, and knocked again, this time louder. I was surprised when she opened the door. She was frumpy and had obviously been asleep, but she was every bit as beautiful as Mary Monroe. She was also much younger. Her hair was long, wavy, and blonde, her eyes large and cobalt blue. Her skin was smooth and tanned, her lips full. She was about five seven and wearing a fuzzy, pink robe tied with a belt at the waist.

"Kayla Robbins?" I said.

"Who are you and what do you want?"

Her accent wasn't east Tennessee, and her demeanor wasn't that of a pretty young college girl.

"Name's Dillard. I need to talk to you about Richard Monroe."

"You a cop?"

"Lawyer. Can I come in?"

"You can say whatever you have to say from right there."

"Fine," I said, raising my voice. "What I have to say involves you being an accessory to kidnapping, extortion, and murder, and if you're going to make me stand out here, I'm going to say it loud enough so every one of your neighbors can hear me."

She stared at me in silence for a few seconds before she stepped back and pulled the door open wider. I walked in and she motioned to a couch in a small living room. I looked around and noticed the place was pure college kid. It was sparsely furnished, hardly anything on the walls, an empty pizza box and a couple empty Coors Light bottles sat on a coffee table, and there was a faint smell of marijuana lingering in the air. I sat down on the couch, and she took a seat in an overstuffed chair about ten feet away.

"I'm not an accessory to anything," she said.

"But you know exactly what I'm talking about, don't you?"

"I assume you're talking about Richard's little girl being kidnapped. I didn't have anything to do with that."

"You were with him a few hours before she was taken."

"So? I was with him lots of nights."

"How long have you been seeing him?"

"Why don't you ask him?"

"I already have. I just want to see if you lie to me."

She crossed her legs—which were long, tan, and exquisite—and folded her arms across her chest.

"Four months," she said.

"How did you meet?"

"He answered an ad. It isn't illegal, you know. What I'm doing. It isn't illegal. I talked to a lawyer about it. I'm just trying to get by."

"What exactly are you doing?"

"Richard didn't tell you?"

"Like I said a second ago, I need to make sure you tell me the same story Richard has told me. Don't worry about what you think he may or may not have said. Just tell me the truth. His life could depend on it. Now tell me about you and Richard."

"I want some kind of deal," she said. "I want you to sign something that says I won't get into any trouble."

I stood up and started walking around the room.

"This is what I can offer you," I said. "If you tell me the truth about you and Richard, and especially about the night Lindsay went missing, then I won't spend a considerable amount of time making your life a living hell. Richard Monroe is about to go on trial for a terrible crime that I don't think he committed, and I think you have information that can help him. If you choose to withhold that information or if you lie to me, the first thing I'll do is sue you. I don't know what I'll sue you for right now, but you know how lawyers are. I'll come up with something. I'll drag you into the court system and keep you there for the next three years. The next thing I'll do is go to my good friend Leon Bates. He's the sheriff here and he hates drugs. I smell pot, and there are a couple roaches in that ashtray on the table. If you use it so much that you can't hide it from a stranger, then I figure there's a pretty good chance you do some other things too. And since you mentioned that you advertise, I have to assume you're a prostitute. You might not like to think of it that way, but that's probably what you are. And if I take a really close look, I don't doubt that I'm going to find a pile of skeletons in your closet from the floor to the ceiling.

"Now, on the other hand, if you help me, if you're truthful with me, then I'll become your best friend. I was the district attorney here for a while, and I have a lot of friends who are cops and lawyers and DAs. In the line of work you seem to have chosen, you might need a favor someday. I'll be the guy you call when you need that favor."

I crossed the room and stood over her. I had no idea what she knew or what she might be hiding, but the look on her face told me I'd struck a nerve. Her bottom lip was quivering. The bravado she'd shown earlier had dissolved.

"Talk to me!" I said it with such force that she jerked involuntarily.

"About six months ago, a girlfriend of mine told me about this website," she said. "It's sort of a dating service, only a little bit different. Girls are looking for guys to take care of them, and guys are looking for girls to take care of."

"So it's a sugar daddy service," I said.

"Whatever. I moved down here from Pittsburgh to be near my mom because she's sick and all. She and my dad got divorced when I was ten, and she had a pretty bad drug problem so I wound up with my dad. But she stayed in touch and she's sick, so when I graduated from high school, I came here and I'm in college and I'm trying to get by but it's expensive, you know? The only jobs out there are crappy, minimum-wage jobs, so when this girlfriend told me about this website I decided to give it a try. I know I'm pretty and all that, I mean guys have been hitting on me since I was twelve. And she said I could get a man to totally take care of me, you know? So I paid the money, and I put a profile on there and right away I got a message through the service from Richard. We went back and forth a few times and finally I agreed to meet him for dinner over in Kingsport. We hit it off pretty good, and we met a few more times and it sort of went from there. At least he's not some *old* dude, you know? He's handsome and all and he treats me good."

"How much does he pay you?"

"Twenty-five hundred a month."

"And he's been doing that for four months?"

"Yeah, and he buys me gifts, too. He bought me a really nice necklace and a bunch of clothes, and he's taken me to some nice restaurants in Asheville and Charlotte and Knoxville."

"And in return for this money and these gifts and meals, you have sex with him."

"He said his wife wouldn't pay any attention to him, that all she cared about was their daughter. He said he's lonely, so yeah, we had sex sometimes. Not every time we were together, but sometimes."

"Have you seen him since Lindsay was taken?"

"No. I haven't heard anything from him, and I haven't tried to get in touch with him."

"Why? Don't you need your money?"

"I just thought ... I just ... I don't know. I mean, he was in the newspaper and on television and all this stuff was going on and I didn't think it would be such a good idea."

Up until that point, I believed everything she said, but when I asked her why she hadn't tried to get in touch with Richard, the tone of her voice changed and her right foot started to rock up and down. There was a small kitchen with a breakfast nook about ten feet from where I was standing, and I walked over and picked up a chair. I carried it back to where she was sitting, turned it around backward, and plopped myself down right in front of her. I put my elbows on the back of the chair and leaned forward.

"When was the last time you had sex with Richard?" I said.

"That night. That Friday. He came over after he got off work and stayed for a couple of hours."

"How long had it been before that?"

"I don't know. A couple weeks maybe. It wasn't like he was obsessed with me or anything."

"Did Richard use a condom?"

"I'm on the pill. He doesn't need to."

"Did he climax that night?"

"What? What's wrong with you? Why would you ask me—"

"Answer the question! Did he ejaculate?"

"Probably, I mean, he always did."

"So what happened that night?"

"What do you mean?"

"After Richard left. What happened? He left pretty early, right? What'd you do the rest of the night?"

"I don't know. I probably just watched a movie or something."

"Did you go out?"

"No."

"Did anybody come over? Did you talk to anybody?"

"I don't think so."

"What did you do with his sperm, Kayla? Did you take a shower and wash it down the drain? Flush it down the toilet? Maybe put some in a little cup or a vial or a syringe and give it to somebody?"

"I don't know what you're—"

"Did you go down to Richard's and steal his little girl? Maybe take some of the sperm he left behind and plant it on her clothes? What'd you do with her?"

"I didn't. I swear to God I didn't have anything to do with that."

"But you know who did, don't you?"

"No! I don't ... I mean ... I didn't ...."

She sniffled, a tear slipped down her right cheek, and I knew I was close.

"You didn't *what*?"

"I didn't *know* what he was going to do with it, okay? He paid me five thousand dollars for it, but I didn't know what he was going to do!"

"*Who*? You didn't know what *who* was going to do?"

"I don't know his name, okay? He said he was some kind of investigator."

"What did he look like?"

"I don't know. About as tall as you, I guess, but younger. Real sharp nose, like a bird. You can't say anything to him. The last thing he said to me before he left was that he'd kill me if I ever told anyone, and I believed him."

Sharp nose. Like a raptor. Paying for silence and then threatening to kill her if she talked. It was too familiar.

It had to be Botts.

CHAPTER FORTY-ONE

"You're not gonna believe this," I said when I climbed into Leon Bates's Hummer. I'd called him as soon as I left Kayla Robbins' apartment. He was in Johnson City, he said, and suggested we meet in a crowded parking lot on the East Tennessee State University campus. I told him about my conversation with Kayla and her revelations about her "arrangement" with Richard and her sale of a sample of Richard's sperm to Botts while the rain pelted against the windshield.

"So if this little filly is telling the truth," Bates said, "it changes things a bunch. I reckon that explains why your former client passed the polygraph."

"He's still my client, Leon. Maybe not in the courtroom, but I have unfinished business."

Leon shook his head slowly.

"So what are you gonna do now?" he said. "Go after Botts, find that little girl, bring her home, and make the feds look like fools?"

"That's exactly what I'm going to do, and you're going to help me."

"Hold on now, brother. I ain't on your side anymore, remember? I'm the lawman and you're the defense lawyer. We already got an indictment, made an arrest. We're getting ready for trial."

"*They* got an indictment and made an arrest. The feds. *They're* getting ready for trial. I'll bet they won't even call you as a witness. They came into your county, took the case from you, and they got it wrong."

"I ain't so sure they got it wrong, but I'm tickled to death they came in and took it," Bates said. "This case has stunk to high heaven from the get-go. We've had a little girl missing, the media all over us, you running around delivering ransom money, the girl's daddy lying about this and that, and her momma so messed up on drugs now we can't even interview her. We've had the granddaddy and that Botts feller second-guessing every move we've made, and now here you come telling me that you think Botts is behind the whole thing."

"That about sums it up. How closely have you looked at Botts?"

"We didn't look at him. Had no reason to. Botts didn't even show up until after the girl was taken, and everything we found led us straight to Richard Monroe. Tell me something, Brother Dillard. What about motive? If Botts is involved in this, why would he go to all this trouble? Why would he set all this up, take the girl, steal the money, and frame the father?"

"I was hoping you'd ask him when you arrest him."

"You realize you ain't got a smidgen of proof, don't you? All you've got is the word of a trollop."

"Doesn't matter. We find Lindsay, it's game over."

"And how do you propose we find her?"

"We find Botts and follow him until he leads us to her."

"You got any idea where he is?"

"Charles Russell's company is based out of Nashville. Charles and Botts live in Nashville. Charles is still here, taking care of Mary, but I haven't seen Botts since Richard was arrested. I assume he went back to Nashville."

"I can't go snooping around Nashville without notifying the sheriff and the chief of police, and with everything that's gone on up here with this case, neither one of them will be happy to see me coming."

"Don't tell them, Leon. Look, you check out Botts and gather up a few of your high-tech toys. We go to Nashville, we follow Botts for a few days, maybe a week. If we don't find anything, we turn around and come home and nobody's hurt. But if we find her, if Botts has her hidden somewhere, then you can call the cavalry and get us some help getting her back."

"I don't know," Bates said. "Sounds like a wild goose chase to me."

"Yeah, well, we've chased a goose or two before."

"We have, haven't we? Cooked a few of 'em, too."

"I'm going, Leon. With you or without you, I'm going to Nashville. I'd rather it be with you."

"Dad gum it, Brother Dillard, you beat all I've ever seen. You know that? You beat *all* I've ever seen."

CHAPTER FORTY-TWO

It was difficult to leave Caroline, but Jack and Lilly were there to look after her and she wanted me to go. Bates and I left for Nashville at three o'clock that afternoon on a jet Leon somehow chartered on short notice. When I asked him how he did it, all he said was, "I do favors for people sometimes, Brother Dillard. And sometimes people do favors for me." Because Nashville was in the central time zone and the Tri-Cities was in the eastern time zone, we were on the ground and in our rental cars by 3:30 p.m. We rented two innocuous-looking sedans in the event we had to follow Botts, but as Leon explained to me on the flight, he had other things in mind.

Leon had spent the late morning and early afternoon checking out Earl Botts, and while he didn't learn anything that would explain a motive for Botts to kidnap Lindsay Monroe, he learned enough to realize that we were dealing with a potentially dangerous man. Botts, who was raised by Charles Russell and his wife after Botts's mother was killed, had followed in Charles Russell's footsteps and joined the Marine Corps right out of high school. He'd volunteered for their elite Force Reconnaissance unit and had wound up in the thick of the action in Iraq. He'd been captured when his recon team crossed into Syria while attempting to ambush Iraqi leaders who were fleeing the country. The Syrians held him for three weeks—and tortured him in the process—before releasing him and two British SAS soldiers in a deal brokered by the British government. He was discharged from the Marines after serving five years and three tours in the Middle East, and he immediately went to work for Charles Russell's "risk management" firm. There wasn't much information available on Russell's firm, but I knew from my conversations with Charles Russell that they specialized in executive and diplomatic protection, primarily in Central and South America. With the combination of his Marine Corps training and his security work, we knew that Botts would be an expert in such things as weapons, communications, surveillance, counterintelligence and hand-to-hand combat, and we knew that if it came to violence, we could have our hands full no matter how many cops we brought to the party.

Bates said the public records showed Botts's permanent address as a condominium in a gated community in Belle Meade, but Leon didn't want to go anywhere near the place. He wanted to get a GPS tracker on Botts's vehicle so we could follow his movements from a distance and remove the risk of being spotted. The Tennessee Department of Motor Vehicles showed that Botts owned a car and an SUV, but we had no way of knowing whether he'd be driving a personal vehicle or a company vehicle. In order to get the tracker in place, we had to get our eyes on him at Russell Risk Management.

We checked into adjoining rooms in a hotel off Briley Parkway, just a few miles from the airport, and left the hotel in Leon's rental. We rode north on Briley and then east on Lebanon Pike for several miles until we came to an isolated compound near the Stones River. The two-story, block building was painted white and surrounded by an eight-foot high chain-link fence. An awning over the front entrance identified the place as Russell Risk Management, Inc. There was a guardhouse at the only entrance to the parking lot manned by two uniformed guards. Bates rolled past without slowing.

"Looks like Russell's company is pretty serious about security," I said.

"Yep. Nothing we can't handle though," Bates said.

He continued driving for another hour, making wider and wider circles around the neighborhood where Russell Risk Management was located.

"High ground?" I said.

"You got it," Bates said. He pointed to his right. "That spot over there looks pretty promising." He was pointing to a tree-covered hill. "Let's go check it out."

We arrived back at the hotel just as darkness was beginning to fall. I unpacked some of the things Leon had suggested I bring—things like boots and warm, dark-colored clothing and gloves—before I knocked on the door that adjoined the rooms. Leon opened it and I walked in. He was wearing blue jeans and a green shirt with a button-down collar.

"This is the first time I've ever seen you without your uniform and your cowboy hat," I said.

He winked and smiled. "I generally only take that uniform and hat off for one thing," he said.

"Yeah? What's that?"

"Sleep, Brother Dillard. Get your mind out of the gutter. Lookie here. I got something to show you."

He unzipped a large bag that was sitting on his bed.

"You mentioned high-tech toys," Leon said. "I got high-tech toys."

He showed me a high-powered spotter's scope, a pair of thousand-dollar binoculars, a smartphone, two laptop computers, a palm-sized GPS tracking device attached to a set of three magnets that Leon said were so powerful they could be removed only with a pry bar, and a couple of prepaid cell phones.

"Wow," I said. "This is real spook stuff."

"Them FBI boys got nothing on ol' Leon," he said.

The next things he pulled out of the bag were two MP5 submachine guns.

"If we wind up in a gunfight, we ain't goin' in with no peashooters," he said.

I shook my head and said, "I'm not here to kill any-body, Leon. I had my fill of it last year."

"I figured as much," Leon said, "but I can't have you thinking about what happened last year, Brother Dillard. This Botts is a bad hombre and you know it. If he has that little girl and we get onto him, I don't think he'll want to give her up without a fight. I know you know how to use that weapon. When we go out tomorrow morning, I want you to strap it on."

I shrugged and picked up the gun. It was very much like the weapons I'd used in the military, although it was more compact. The feel of it sent tingles through my hands.

Leon opened the laptop and started banging keys. I knew from past experience that he loved technology and was highly proficient at using it. I smiled as his fingers whizzed across the keyboard. Leon Bates, redneck techie.

"Pull that chair over here," Leon said. "I need to show you a few things."

For the next hour, we discussed possibilities and plans and what might or might not happen while Bates clicked and panned and zoomed in and zoomed out. Finally he looked at his watch.

"We need to be out the door at 3:00 a.m., rain or shine," he said. "I reckon we ought to try to get a little shut-eye. Tomorrow could be an awful long day."

CHAPTER FORTY-THREE

Botts showed up at Russell Risk Management at 5:45 a.m., after Leon and I had sat beneath ponchos in the freezing rain for more than two hours. Despite the fact that we were more than a quarter mile away and two hundred feet above him, the spotter's scope I was looking through, combined with the lights in the parking lot, left no doubt that it was him. When he got out of his SUV, I was surprised to see him wearing what appeared to be a suit and tie beneath a long dress coat. Maybe he was running the company in Charles Russell's absence and had to dress the part.

We'd decided to wait out the morning and see if he left the building at lunchtime. If not, we had an alternate plan, but our hope was that he'd leave the building, and we'd be able to follow him in the heavy Nashville traffic and then get the tracking device onto his vehicle while he was inside a building eating lunch. I'd left my rental car in a parking lot a couple blocks away, and as soon as we were sure Botts was in the building, Leon dropped me off at my car and both of us drove to spots we'd picked the night before. Both of us could see the Russell Risk Management parking lot and front gate clearly, and both of us could easily get into traffic. We'd take turns keeping him in sight and stay in touch with each other on our cell phones.

Botts walked out of the building in the company of two other men just before noon. All three of them got into his SUV, and they pulled out of the front gate. Bates took the lead and I followed about a block behind. Lebanon Pike was crowded, and Botts stayed on it for twenty minutes, heading west, before he turned onto Hermitage Avenue and then onto Korean Veterans Boulevard. He made one more turn before he wound up turning into the parking lot of a garish orange, block building. The name "Arnold's" was painted on the side of the building. People were standing in line outside beneath umbrellas. I didn't know what they served in there, but I told myself that if people were willing to stand outside in the cold rain, I'd have to make it a point to bring Caroline to Nashville when this was over.

My phone buzzed.

"Wait for him to get inside the building," Bates said, "and make the call."

I saw Bates turn left ahead of me. He was circling the block and getting himself into position to slap the magnetic GPS transmitter onto the undercarriage of Botts's SUV. I turned right and circled from the other direction. There was a parking lot a block away that gave me a view of the front of Arnold's, and I waited until I saw Botts and his companions get inside. I called Leon back.

"You ready?" I said.

"I'm ten feet from his vehicle but there are people standing outside and people coming and going. Is he inside?"

"Just got in."

"Give it five minutes."

I Googled our exact location on my phone to double-check the address, waited five minutes, picked up the prepaid cell Bates had given me, and dialed 9–1–1.

"Nine-one-one, what's your emergency?" the dispatcher said.

"I'm driving on South Eighth near Arnold's Diner!" I yelled into the phone. "There's a man with an assault rifle walking across the railroad tracks toward downtown. I don't know what he's going to do!"

"Calm down, sir. Did you say there's a man with an assault rifle?"

"Send the police! He looks crazy! Hurry!"

"Would you repeat the location?"

I hung up. I knew it was enough. Bates and I had talked about what would make the biggest splash with the police, and in this day of mass shootings and rabid debate about gun control, we decided a report of a crazy-looking man carrying an assault rifle would do the trick. I'd just committed a crime, but we needed the diversion. It worked like a charm. Within two minutes, sirens were screaming, and everyone at Arnold's Diner was looking down the street away from the parking lot. Leon was able to get out of his car, slide beneath Botts's SUV, slap the GPS device into place, and drive off unnoticed.

Botts left Arnold's a half hour after he walked in the door and started back toward Russell Risk Management. Leon called me as soon as Botts pulled out of the parking lot and said, "Have you looked at the app?"

"We're on him," I said. "It's working."

We spent the rest of the afternoon in our cars, driving aimlessly within a half-mile radius of Russell Risk Management. The laptop with the precious GPS signal stayed open on the passenger seat beside me. Leon and I wanted to stay mobile in case Botts left the building and we wanted to stay close. I put over a hundred miles on the rental car that afternoon doing between twenty and thirty miles an hour. I called Caroline twice. I called Jack and Lilly. I ate the first Big Mac I'd eaten in years and it was delicious. I parked the car in random lots and got out and walked around the block a couple times, carrying the laptop with me. There were many anxious moments wondering whether Botts would walk out and catch a cab to the airport, whether he'd leave with a friend or with another employee or with a woman, but at 6:21 p.m., the signal started flashing.

Botts was on the move.

Instead of driving west toward Nashville and Belle Meade, however, he drove to Interstate 40 and headed west all the way to Highway 109. Bates and I, still in separate cars, stayed a mile behind him. The cold rain of the morning and evening had given way to full-out thunderstorms, and the rain pounded against the windshield as I drove along. When he got off the interstate, Botts turned north toward Lebanon and wound up pulling into the parking lot of a place called Cherokee Steakhouse on Old Hickory Lake. He was there for an hour and then stopped at a grocery store in Lebanon before going back across the lake and turning onto a narrow road called Potter's Lane that led to the lake. Bates and I pulled into a convenience store parking lot, and I got into Leon's car.

"He's here," Leon said, pointing at a satellite image from Google Maps of an isolated house that sat fewer than fifty feet from the shoreline of Old Hickory Lake. We talked for a few minutes about the best way to get a look inside the house without being detected and decided to go back across the South Water Street bridge and see if we could get a look from the other side of the narrow channel. There was a road that led to a water treatment plant directly across from the house where Botts had parked. It took us about fifteen minutes to get to the plant and another ten to find a spot that provided both cover and a clear view of the house. Bates and I settled in beneath a huge beech tree and trained our optics on the house.

Darkness had fallen, the wind was howling, and the rain was falling diagonally. Both of us were wearing ponchos that Leon had brought with him, and as I looked through the scope, I was grateful for Leon's foresight and for his toys. The scope was incredibly powerful. The images I was seeing were illuminated and crisp even in the driving rainstorm.

"There's a woman," Bates said over the wind. "Do you see her?"

The side of the house that faced the water was almost all windows. The lot surrounding the house was covered in trees, but the yard between the house and the water had been cleared, and I could easily make out the image of a dark-haired woman moving around in the kitchen. She appeared to be cooking supper. I knew Botts was there somewhere, but I couldn't see him. Less than ten minutes later, I saw movement coming down a set of stairs to the woman's left. An image came into focus that nearly took my breath away. It was a little girl.

"Leon?" I said.

"Is it her?"

She looked to be the right age. Shoulder-length, dark hair. I waited until she walked into the kitchen where the light was better. I turned a button on the scope I was holding and zoomed in on her face. I'd looked at her photograph a hundred times. There was no doubt in my mind.

"It's her, Leon," I said. "It's Lindsay Monroe."

CHAPTER FORTY-FOUR

"**D**id I ever tell you how much I hate it when you're right?" Leon said as he gazed through the binoculars. The wind had picked up even more, and he had to yell in order for me to hear him.

"What now?" I yelled back.

"I ain't exactly sure. I'm playing this by ear."

"I know one thing that isn't going to happen," I said. "I'm not letting that child out of my sight until I have my hands on her."

"What are you gonna do? Swim across this channel?"

"If I have to. I'm not going to give Botts a chance of disappearing with her again."

"He ain't going anywhere, Brother Dillard. Let's call the good guys, get the cars, drive back around there, and go in from the other side."

"In order to get the police to go in quiet, we'll have to find the sheriff or the chief of police or the TBI or whoever and tell them what's going on. It'll take all night for them to gather everybody up, make a plan, and execute it. If we just call 9–1–1, they'll come fast but they'll come loud. He'll hear them and he'll either take off or worse. He might kill her if he thinks he's about to go down."

Bates was silent for a long while. Finally, he said, "Stay here and keep her in sight. I'll be back as soon as I can."

"Where are you going?"

"To find something that floats. I've got my phone. Call if anything happens."

Leon disappeared, and I was left alone in the dark a thousand feet from the house that contained little Lindsay Monroe. I could see her sitting at a small table in the kitchen and watched as the dark-haired woman served her supper. She didn't appear to be injured or in any kind of distress, and I wondered what Botts had told her about why she was there or what had happened to her parents.

I kept panning the house looking for a sign of Botts but saw nothing. After nearly half an hour, I heard the words, "Brother Dillard," come across the wind and I looked to my left. Leon was paddling along the shoreline in a canoe.

I came out from under the tree and climbed into the canoe. The submachine gun was hanging from a strap across Leon's right shoulder. I'd done as he requested— the weapon he'd given me was hanging from a strap across my shoulder as well. Leon handed me a paddle, and we started toward the house.

We beached the canoe about fifty yards from the small house and clambered up a steep, muddy bank. Botts's SUV was parked in the gravel driveway. It appeared to be an old fishing cabin to which someone had added an upper story. It was constructed primarily of concrete block and painted gray. We made our way slowly all the way around it, using the trees for cover. There were only two doors, one at each end of the house. The lot was severe, covered with exposed rock and steep. There were no dogs in sight, and we hadn't noticed any pets in the house.

The woman and Lindsay Monroe had moved to a couch where Lindsay appeared to be reading a book. Leon and I made our way back to the spot where we'd first climbed the bank, and we each took a knee.

"What do you think?" Leon said.

"You take this door, I'll take the one on the other side," I said. "Botts must be upstairs. Let's go in quiet and try to get them out before he knows what's happened."

"I'm thinking it would be a good idea to call 9–1–1 about now," Leon said.

"Sounds like a plan. I'll see you inside."

I broke off from Leon and headed to the far side of the house as he pulled his phone from beneath his poncho. There was a set of steps leading to a stone patio, and I climbed the steps and looked through the door. I could see all the way through the house to the other door. Lindsay and the woman were still on the couch. As soon as I saw Leon's shadow looming through the window of the door on the far side, I reached down and turned the doorknob. It was unlocked, but the door squealed when I opened it, and both Lindsay and the woman looked up immediately. I put a finger to my lips and waved my left hand. The MP5 was hanging loosely, pointing downward, because I didn't want to terrify them. Bates came through the door and flashed a badge at the woman. He motioned for her and Lindsay to walk toward me. Just as the woman stood, there was a loud roar that came from the top of the steps and Leon went flying backward through the doorway. The woman and the girl both screamed and dived to the floor as I brought the MP5 up to my shoulder. There was a huge, stone fireplace just inside the door, about ten feet from me, and I took cover beside it. I couldn't see who was at the top of the steps and I had no idea whether he'd seen me. I assumed it was Botts, but there was a sheetrock wall between us. What I *could* see were the soles of Leon's boots. He'd gone over on his back and his feet were pointing straight up. I needed to get to him quickly.

The thought of Botts ambushing Leon infuriated me, and my field of vision began to narrow. There was an innocent little girl lying on the floor not twenty feet away and a psychopath with a shotgun either coming down the stairs or hiding at the top. The only sound in the room was the whistling of the wind and a muffled whimper coming from Lindsay. I'd told myself after the gunfight with the Colombians a year earlier that I would never again take up arms in anger, but at that moment, my promise to myself was the farthest thing from my mind. I flicked the selector switch on the MP5 to full auto and came off the wall.

Earl Botts must not have known we were coming. He must not even have suspected that we *might* come, otherwise he would have armed himself with something more substantial than a shotgun. A fully automatic weapon like the MP5 is capable of firing eight hundred rounds in a minute, more than thirteen in a second, and when I came off that wall I had no intention of giving

Botts any quarter. I opened up with the weapon, firing short bursts, and rushed the stairs. With that many bullets flying around him, Botts immediately retreated. I saw him dive into a room and slam the door. I cut loose a burst into the door that tore it from the frame and emptied the rest of the clip through the walls. As I was replacing the empty clip with a fresh one, I heard him yell, "Stop! Please, God, stop! Don't kill me! Please don't kill me!" The shotgun clattered across the floor through the doorway.

"Crawl out on your hands and knees!" I yelled. "Do it now!"

"I'm wounded," he cried.

"Crawl out now or you'll be dead!"

I heard him before I saw him. He was whimpering like the child downstairs. He came through the door on his hands and knees. When he looked up, there was a trail of mucous hanging from his nose and blood was seeping from a wound on his forehead. I felt no compassion for him as I slapped the cuffs Leon had given me on his wrists and dragged him down the stairs. I shoved him onto the floor in the small kitchen and hurried over to where Leon lay. To my great relief, he was breathing and his eyes were open.

"Leon?" I said. "Leon! Where are you hit?"

He looked at me quizzically for a second, but then his eyes took on a glint of recognition and he smiled slightly. In the darkness just beyond the door, I heard, "Drop the weapon! Drop it now! Get on the ground!"

I dropped the machine gun that had been my savior, raised my hands, and lowered myself onto my chest. The cavalry had arrived, albeit a bit late. I turned my head and looked at Leon.

"God bless Kevlar," he said, and he closed his eyes and drifted off again.

CHAPTER FORTY-FIVE

The twelve-gauge slug that lifted Leon off his feet and sent him flying out the door failed to penetrate the Kevlar vest he was wearing, but his head landed on the concrete patio and he wound up with a concussion that had him talking in circles for an entire night. I stayed in Lebanon with him and between sessions of listening to him ask the same five or six questions over and over, I made the necessary telephone calls to get the process of releasing Richard Monroe from jail started.

Lindsay was taken straight to the hospital. I didn't get to say a word to her. She was given a clean bill of health by the doctors, interviewed by the FBI, and released to her mother and her grandfather, both of whom had hurried to Lebanon as soon as they heard the news. I was relieved that we'd found her and that she was all right, but I knew that Earl Botts had done a tremendous amount of damage to the Monroe family, and I didn't know whether it could ever be repaired.

The dark-haired woman turned out to be a Mexican who was in the country illegally. Botts had found her through his company contacts and had brought her to Tennessee for the sole purpose of caring for Lindsay. She didn't speak a word of English, but through an interpreter she told the police that Botts hadn't mistreated her in any way. He told her Lindsay was the daughter of a wealthy corporate executive who had been threatened by Mexican drug lords and that the executive's wife had already been kidnapped and killed by the cartel. Lindsay, he said, was being hidden until some kind of deal could be struck. Botts kept them both in complete isolation. He delivered food and toys and books and music and whatever else they needed and spent most nights at the cabin where there was no phone, no computer, no cable, and no television. Lindsay was allowed to play in the yard for one hour a day under the direct supervision of the woman, but contact with anyone was strictly forbidden.

When the police searched the cabin, they found a safe in the basement. Inside the safe, they found three million dollars in cash. The serial numbers matched those recorded by Charles Russell's bank when he took possession of the ransom money. Even if the testimony of Kayla Robbins—the trollop, as Bates called her—was suspect, there was no getting around the fact that Botts was holding Lindsay Monroe prisoner and he had the ransom money. He was dead in the water on kidnapping and theft, and he was going to prison for a long, long time.

As soon as Leon recovered—it took two days before the doctors would release him—and we got back home, he went straight to the jail to interview Botts. That evening, he came out to my house, and over a couple of beers, he told Caroline and Jack and I what everyone had been wondering.

"You want to know why he did it?" Leon said. "Jealousy. Well, jealousy and resentment and revenge and rage. That's a lot of 'r' words, ain't it?"

"I thought Charles Russell raised Botts," I said.

"He did. Charles's wife was Botts's third-grade teacher, and along about Thanksgiving time that year, Botts and his momma were riding to school one day when they got T-boned. Botts's momma didn't make it and Botts himself wound up in the hospital for three months. Botts doesn't even know who his daddy is and apparently nobody else in the family wanted him, so Mrs. Russell, Charles's wife, got things arranged so he could live with them. They took him in. It was a selfless act, a beautiful thing to do, but ol' Earl didn't quite see it that way. As he got older, he felt like he didn't belong, like nothing he did was good enough. He was madly in love with Mary—he said he went so far as to ask her to marry him—but she wasn't interested. Said she thought of him as a brother, not a lover. When Charles's wife killed herself, Charles resigned his commission in the Marine Corps and started his company in Nashville. He hired a nanny to help with Earl and Mary, but by that time they were both sixteen and pretty much looked after themselves.

"When Earl graduated from high school, he went straight into the Marines. I reckon he was trying to get Charles to love him. He told me he thought Charles should have formally adopted him, but Charles said he never really gave it any consideration. Charles said he thought things were fine the way they were. Earl did good in the Marines except for that one incident when he got himself captured, and when he got out Charles put him to work for the company. Worked him hard, too. Sent him all over the world. Paid him real well, but Earl still thought he was getting the short end of the stick. After ten years of working there, he thought he'd paid his dues and that it was time for Charles to step aside and let him take over the company, but Charles had just turned sixty and he had no plans to retire."

"What about Richard?" I said. "How does Richard fit into all this?"

"Richard was the catalyst," Bates said, "the particle that split the atom and caused the whole explosion. You're gonna love this, Brother Dillard. Well, maybe you won't *love* it, but you'll sure find it interesting. When Richard started fooling around with that little ol' Robbins girl, Mary got suspicious, but instead of just confronting him, she called her daddy and asked for advice. And what does Daddy do? He sends his boy Earl Botts to investigate. Botts tails Richard for a little while, finds out what's going on, and realizes that he has a perfect opportunity to give all of them a great big what for. He loves Mary, but at the same time, he hates her because she rejected him. He hates Charles because he thinks Charles doesn't love him and respect him enough, and he hates Richard because Richard is cheating on the woman he believes he should have had all along. So he cooks up this idea to take care of all of them at the same time. When he goes back to Nashville, he tells Charles that Richard isn't fooling around with a woman, but that he *might* be fooling around with a man. He knows Charles is a bit on the homophobic side, and he knows Charles and Richard don't get along all that well. Then he makes his deal with the trollop and sets his plan into action. He crushes Mary by taking her daughter, the thing she loves the most. He frames Richard for it and turns Charles and Mary against him. He destroys the entire family and steals three million dollars of the old man's money to boot."

"What about Lindsay?" Caroline said. "What was he planning to do with her?"

"The crazy son of a gun was so delusional that he thought he could hide Lindsay for six months or a year—long enough to make sure Richard was gone for good and that Mary got all his money—and then he was gonna tell Mary that he knew where Lindsay was and she could have her back on one condition. The condition was that Mary run away with him. He had the place picked out and everything. He actually believed Mary would go for it, that they'd live happily ever after on some isolated island in the South Pacific."

Caroline sighed deeply. "And now he's going to spend the next thirty years in prison."

"And that's right where he belongs, Miss Caroline," Bates said, "because I'm telling you, that man is as cold as a mother-in-law's kiss. There ain't an ounce of remorse in him, and there's no telling what he would have done if your husband hadn't figured out what was going on and put a stop to it."

Caroline smiled and reached out for my hand.

"I knew you'd get her back," she said. "I knew it from the very beginning."

CHAPTER FORTY-SIX

L ife isn't fair sometimes.

As I stood holding my wife's hand beneath a fast-moving sky at the Veterans Administration cemetery at Mountain Home in Johnson City, I thought about what I'd said to Howard French at the jail just a few days before Lindsay Monroe went missing. It had certainly turned out to be true.

The headstone with my father's name on it had already been removed and the backhoe had scraped the top of the casket containing the body of Lucas Venable. There were three nameless men in green uniforms doing the work. One of them lowered himself into the hole and began to dig out the red tinted clay around the casket.

Standing just a few feet away were Lucas Venable's parents, Robert and Vanessa Venable of Fairfield, Wisconsin, eighty-three and eighty-two years old. They were kind and gentle people, and my heart ached for them as they stood silently and watched the men go about their thankless task. Caroline had accompanied me to Fairfield a week earlier. The visit had been difficult and emotional, but now, finally, after four and a half decades of uncertainty, the Venables had come to collect their son and take him home to his final resting place. As gut-wrenching as it had been to explain to them what my father had done, I took at least a bit of comfort in knowing they didn't go to their own graves wondering what had happened to Lucas.

Caroline squeezed my hand as the casket was lifted from the hole and the men began to clean away the mud and clay. A hearse was waiting to take the casket and the body to the airport. The Venables told me they planned to have Lucas's remains transferred to a casket of their choosing once they got him back to Fairfield. There would be a memorial service, and he would be buried in a family plot right next to the spots that were already reserved for them.

The thought of my standing in a similar place, watching as my wife was lowered into the ground, kept creeping into my mind. I would push it away, but it continued to gnaw away at my consciousness like a rat gnawing its way through a wall. How long would it be? Six months? Two years? Six years? She was fighting, but the cancer was relentless. I could see it taking bits of her day by day.

The men loaded the casket into the hearse and the driver closed the door. We said our goodbyes to the Venables and wished them well. As they walked away, I lingered by the grave site, thinking about all the times I had visited what I thought was a fallen hero. I'd been enamored by the idea, and I couldn't help but feel cheated.

An opening appeared in the clouds above and a burst of sunlight brought me out of my melancholy. Caroline stood on her tiptoes, cupped my face in her hand, and kissed me on the cheek.

"What does my hero want to do now?" she said.

I took her in my arms and squeezed gently.

"I want to do what you said the other day, baby," I said softly. "I want us to follow our hearts and keep on going. That's about all we *can* do, isn't it?"

CHAPTER FORTY-SEVEN

The wind outside was howling and bits of snow were flying around like swarms of white bees, but inside the darkened auditorium the air was calm and still and the mood as warm as a summer sun. I was sitting in the middle of the back row as the lights and the music came up, having slipped in just a few minutes earlier.

The past couple months had been difficult, but Caroline had made yet another determined run at recovery and she seemed to have stabilized. The brutal side effects of the radiation treatments on her spine had finally passed. She was eating again; she looked healthy and had more energy. The hormone treatments she was receiving had slowed the cancer down. We didn't talk about it often and tried not to think about it, but all of us knew the disease was still lurking like an assassin in the dark.

Caroline hadn't organized a dance recital at Christmastime in ten years, but this year she had decided she wanted her students to perform. Jack was backstage helping with props, Lilly was handling the lighting, and Sarah was in the dressing room helping the girls and the mothers with costumes. I usually handled the music, but

I'd begged off this time because I wanted to sit in the audience and enjoy the performance. It was a rare indulgence for me, an opportunity to shut out the brutality I dealt with on a regular basis and appreciate the beauty of dance.

There was one girl in particular that everyone was looking forward to watching. Little Lindsay Monroe had come back to Caroline's dance school two weeks after Bates and I had managed to get her away from Earl Botts. Richard had come to my office the day after he was released from jail, and we'd talked for a short while. He said he was planning to ask Mary to forgive him and try to reestablish the trust he'd violated. He wanted to somehow put his marriage and his life back together. I didn't know whether he'd be able to do it, but I respected his attitude and wished him the best. Things seemed to be working out, though, because Richard and Mary were sitting together four rows in front of me. I looked at them and thought about all the terrible things that had been said and written about them in the media and how much courage it took for them to be sitting in the middle of hundreds of people with their heads high, moving on with their lives. I thought about the capacity people have to forgive, and how powerful a force love can be if people will just let it into their lives.

A smile crossed my face as the first of the fairies, toy soldiers, and elves began to dance across the stage beneath the pastel-colored lights, and it stayed there for the rest of the evening. For that brief stretch of time, the evils of the world vanished like morning mist, and it felt good to feel good.

It felt good to be alive.

Thank you for reading, and I sincerely hope you enjoyed *Conflict of Interest*. As an independently published author, I rely on you, the reader, to spread the word. So if you enjoyed the book, please tell your friends and family, and if it isn't too much trouble, I would appreciate a brief review on Amazon. Thanks again. My best to you and yours.

Scott

ABOUT THE AUTHOR

Scott Pratt was born in South Haven, Michigan, and moved to Tennessee when he was thirteen years old. He is a veteran of the United States Air Force and holds a Bachelor of Arts degree in English from East Tennessee State University and a Doctor of Jurisprudence from the University of Tennessee College of Law. He lives in Northeast Tennessee with his wife, their dogs, and a parrot named JoJo.

www.scottprattfiction.com

ALSO BY SCOTT PRATT

BLOOD MONEY

By

SCOTT PRATT

This book, along with every book I've written and every book I'll write, is dedicated to my darling Kristy, to her unconquerable spirit and her inspirational courage. I loved her before I was born and I'll love her after I'm long gone.

PROLOGUE

1931
Carter County, Tennessee

The moon was full, a liquid, orange ball rising steadily over the mountains to the east, when Hack Barnes heard the first rumblings of the trucks coming toward him. He gazed upward and wondered about the omen. His coon hound had howled earlier, before the moon appeared. Hack was smart but uneducated; he believed in many of the suspicions handed down by his ancestors. One of them was: *"If a dog howls before the moon rises, someone is going to die."*

As he sat waiting, listening to the sounds of the forest that surrounded him – the yelp of a coyote, the screech of an owl, the breath of the wind – Hack couldn't shake the feeling that he was about to become a part of something mysterious, something dangerous. He was no stranger to lawlessness, no stranger to the dark side of life, but something was making him uneasy. Hack ran a calloused hand across his thick beard, leaned his Winchester rifle against the side of the barn, spit out a long stream of tobacco juice and stretched his neck toward the sound of the trucks. Through the leaves, he could make out the dappled beams of headlights coming over the ridge to the southeast, less than half-a-mile away. The beams bounced wildly as the trucks made their way across the potholes and washed out crevices in what passed for a county road that led to Hack's place – five hundred acres of rugged, East Tennessee mountain land that had been handed down through three generations.

A few minutes later, the trucks rattled up near him and the engines went silent. Hack could make out the figures of two men in the first truck. One of them was familiar. Carmine Russo, head of the Russo family and the most notorious gangster in Philadelphia, was in the passenger seat, while the other was a stranger, most likely a bodyguard. The passenger door opened and Russo stepped out. He was wearing suspenders over a long-sleeved white shirt that was rolled up to the elbows, dark slacks and dress shoes. A black fedora sat at an angle atop his head. A leather shoulder holster was wrapped around his thick torso, the butt of a pistol visible beneath his arm.

"Hack," Russo said, extending a beefy hand. The gangster was a couple of inches taller than Hack and at least fifty pounds heavier. His face was as round as the full moon above, his eyes like black, shiny marbles.

"Mr. Russo."

The bodyguard climbed out of the other side of the truck and positioned himself at the back. Another man Hack had never seen got out from behind the wheel of the second truck and stood next to the bed. Both of them were carrying Thompson sub-machine guns. Introductions were neither offered nor desired.

"Ready?" Russo asked.

"I reckon," Hack said.

"Anybody else know?"

"Nobody."

"Good man." Russo clapped Hack on the shoulder. "I knew I could count on you. Let's get it unloaded."

The trucks were Ford Model AA flatbeds. Large, canvas tarps had been tied down over the beds, and the two bodyguards set about untying knots and pulling rope through grommets. Each truck carried five stacks of thin, wooden crates, five to a stack. Twenty-five crates on each truck, fifty in all.

"Where do you want it, Hack?" Russo asked.

"In the barn."

Hack and the bodyguards began unloading the crates. Each had two rope handles. They were heavy. Russo stood by and watched, chewing on a cigar and surveying the surrounding darkness. The crates were carried into an empty stall in the barn and stacked neatly. It took them nearly an hour. When the last crate was in the stall, Hack began to re-cover them with the canvas.

"What are you going to do with them?" Russo asked. He was standing inside the stall now. Two hanging oil lanterns cast flickering shadows across his face.

"I'll load them on the mules and start hauling them up the mountain at first light," Hack said. "Looks like it's going to take me a couple of days."

"You've got a good place to hide them?"

"Won't nobody bother 'em."

"Would you like to see what you're keeping for me? Hey boys! Come on in here. Let's show Hack what we brought."

"Don't much care what it is," Hack said. "You asked me for a favor and I said I'd do it. I'll keep my word."

"Did ya hear that?" Russo turned to his bodyguards. "Now *that's* a man I can trust. How long we been doing business, Hack? Ten years?"

"A while, I reckon."

"Ten years," Russo said. The bodyguards had retrieved their Thompsons. They were holding them loosely, the barrels pointing at the barn floor. "Hack and me have moved thousands of gallons of liquor up the roads and the rails. Never a disagreement over a single dime. We could have moved a lot more, too, but Hack cares about quality. And he cares about secrecy. This is a man who knows how to keep his mouth shut."

Hack saw Russo's right hand move in a blur. He saw the pistol, heard the sound of the hammer cocking.

"It's a shame I can't say the same about you," Russo said. The stall exploded with noise and light. Two shots. The bodyguards fell to the ground in a heap. Hack didn't move. The night had gone silent, save for the sound of Russo's breathing. The acrid smell of gunpowder filled the stall. Russo turned his face slowly toward Hack. Hack looked into the dark eyes, uncertain of whether he would take another breath.

"My trial starts in two weeks, which means I might be back in a couple of months," Russo said. "But if I end up going to prison, it might be five years or more. When I get out, my business in Philly will be gone, but with the help of what's in these crates, I'll get it back in a hurry. If it isn't here when I get out ..."

Hack held Russo's cold gaze. "It'll be here," he said. "All of it."

"It better be, my friend. Because somebody will always be watching. Remember that. Somebody will always be watching."

PART I
PRESENT DAY

CHAPTER ONE

My name is Joe Dillard, and the young woman sitting across from me was lovely. Her name was Charleston Story, but everyone called her Charlie. Her hair was long and auburn, her eyes sapphire-blue and intelligent. Her skin was smooth and tanned, her smile perfect and easy. She was around twenty-five, fresh out of law school. I'd known her – not well, but casually – since she was a small child because I'd unsuccessfully defended her father on a marijuana production charge after the feds raided his farm over in Carter County more than twenty years earlier. It was one of my first cases as a defense lawyer in federal court and left me with a sour taste in my mouth. The girl's father, a young man named Luke Story, had been drafted into the army, sent to Vietnam, and had lost a part of an arm to a Viet Cong grenade before he was eventually caught growing dope. The federal judge who sentenced him was unsympathetic regarding the military service. He sentenced Luke to twenty-five years in prison for growing fifty marijuana plants.

"So what can I do for you?" I said after Charlie and I finished the obligatory small talk.

"I need a job," she said with a slight Tennessee lilt. "I finished at the top of my class in law school and interviewed with some of the best firms in the state, but as soon as they found out about Daddy being in prison, they all thanked me politely and showed me the door. I have to work under the supervision of a licensed attorney until I pass the bar and nobody else seems to want to give me a chance. I hate to spring this on you, Mr. Dillard, because I've heard about your wife and I know you don't take a lot of cases these days. It's probably asking too much, but is there any way you could help me out?"

"How is your dad?" I said, taken off guard by her directness and needing a moment to think. "How much longer are they going to keep him?"

"He gets out in a couple of months," Charlie said. "He has to spend six months in a halfway house in Knoxville after that, which means he won't be home for good until early spring, but at least we can finally see the light at the end of the tunnel."

I'd always admired people who were direct and got right to the point, but what Charlie was asking of me was something I'd never considered. With the exception of a few years I spent in the district attorney's office prosecuting criminal cases, I'd always practiced law alone. I'd never had an associate or a partner and didn't want one now. My wife was battling metastatic breast cancer and I was spending as much time with her as possible. My case load was light; I turned down far more cases than I accepted. I was renting a space in Jonesborough near the courthouse that consisted of a tiny waiting room, a half-bathroom, my office and two other rooms, one of which occasionally served as a conference room and another that was empty. I had no secretary, no paralegal, and no investigator, although I did have my son, Jack, who was home for the summer following his first year of law school at Vanderbilt. He'd set up shop in the conference room and was calling himself my law clerk, although I had no real need for a law clerk. Just as I was about to explain all of those things to Charlie, Jack's muscular frame materialized in the doorway.

"I'm sorry to interrupt," he said, "but can I speak to you in private for just a minute? It's important."

"Excuse me," I said to Charlie, "I'll be right back."

I got up and walked out of the office and down the short hallway to the conference room. Jack closed the door.

"You have to help that girl out," he said in a whisper.

"What? You were eavesdropping?"

"The walls are thin. But yeah, I was eavesdropping. You have to say yes."

"Why?"

"Because she's obviously bright. She said she finished at the top of her class. And it isn't fair that she's being blackballed because of her father. You're all about justice, Dad. It's unjust, an injustice, a travesty of justice, that that tremendously beautiful young lady in there can't break into the legal profession because her father is in jail."

"'Tremendously beautiful' being the key phrase, I suppose."

"I could learn a lot from her," he said. "We're about the same age. I think we'll become good friends."

"Inter-office romances are unhealthy and unwise—"

"Who said anything about romance?"

"So you're not planning to ask her out?"

"Of course not. Well, it might have crossed my mind, but maybe she already has a boyfriend."

"Do you want me to ask her for you? Better yet, why don't you go in there and ask her yourself?"

"Come on, Dad, *please*. She's a freakin' knockout. Even if we don't wind up dating, she's so easy on the eyes it'll make my summer much more pleasant. But don't do it for me, do it for her, or better yet, do it for justice. Nah, never mind that. Do it for me."

"You're a pain in the butt sometimes, you know that?" I said, and I turned and walked out.

"Sorry," I said as I sat back down behind my desk. "Do you have a boyfriend, Charlie?"

She blinked a few times. "What? Why?"

"Because my son seems to be quite enamored withyou."

She smiled and her eyes twinkled.

"He's cute," she said.

"Great," I said. "He thinks you're cute and you think he's cute. A perfect basis on which to make a sound decision and go forward in building a professional relationship."

"Wait," she said, "I didn't mean to—"

I held up my hand. "I was kidding, Charlie, but I can't give you a job. It doesn't have anything to do with your father. I just don't have a job to give. I don't take in enough work these days to be able to pay you a salary, and I don't have room for another lawyer here."

"You don't have to pay me a salary," she said. "I already have someone who is willing to pay me five thousand dollars to represent him. That should be enough to get me through until I pass the bar. I still live at home on Buck Mountain with my uncle so I don't have a lot of expenses. And as far as having a place to work, I have a cell phone and a laptop so I don't really need an office. I can work anywhere."

"You need somewhere to meet with clients," I said.

"What I need is someone to show me the ropes. The one thing they don't teach you in law school is how to actually practice law."

"You're right about that," I said, remembering how utterly helpless I often felt when I got out of law school and hung out my shingle. "If it hadn't been for the older lawyers around here when I was getting started, I would have wound up getting sued for malpractice every time I turned around. They really helped me out."

"Maybe it's your turn," she said as the smile returned to her face. "A little karma. What goes around comes around."

"Let me tell you a little about how this profession works," I said. "You start at the bottom of the totem pole. You have to take cases no one else will take, chase windmills no one else will chase. In a town this size, if you manage to stay with it, work hard, find a niche, and avoid all the pitfalls of substance abuse and greed that seem to plague lawyers, after ten years or so you'll be able to make a decent living. After twenty years, if you've managed to live within your means, you'll become somewhat comfortable, at least financially. After thirty years, you can start thinking about retirement, but you won't want to retire because you've worked so hard to achieve and maintain your station in the profession. After forty years, you'll be managing the health and personal problems created by constant stress and emotional turmoil. Sometime after that, you'll drop dead of a heart attack or a stroke and will soon be forgotten."

"I'll go ahead and slit my wrists now if you'd like," she said. "Do you have a razor I can borrow?"

I leaned back in my chair and couldn't help smiling back at her. She was so pleasant, and Jack was right about her being easy on the eyes.

"Where did you live in Knoxville while you were in school?" I said. "I spent three years down there. Both of my kids were born there."

"I didn't live in Knoxville. I commuted."

"You what? From Buck Mountain?"

"Five days a week for three years," she said. "I have a 75,000-mile law degree. My grandmother was sick and I didn't want to leave her alone, so I decided to make the drive every day. I'd leave at five-thirty in the morning and get back around six in the evening."

"And you still managed to finish at the top of the class?"

"I wasn't the valedictorian, but I was close."

The fact that she was so determined to become a lawyer that she was willing to drive roughly two-hundred and fifty miles round-trip every day to earn her degree impressed me. I changed my mind and decided right then to take her on board.

"What's the case?" I said. "The one that involves someone paying you five thousand dollars. Is it a criminal case?"

"No, it's civil. The client is a neighbor of mine named Roscoe Barnes. He's an elderly man and his son is trying to have him involuntarily committed to a mental institution. Roscoe is old, but he isn't crazy and he's in pretty good health."

"Is Roscoe wealthy?"

"I don't think so. He taught English at Cloudland High School for thirty-five years and his wife was a math teacher before she died fifteen years ago. He owns several hundred acres of land up on the mountain, but a lot of it is exposed rock. I don't see how it could be worth a lot of money, but Roscoe mentioned that his son – his name is Zane – wants his land. I get the sense that Roscoe isn't telling me everything, but he's mentally competent and he isn't a danger to himself or anyone else. That's the legal standard for involuntary commitment, isn't it?"

I nodded and said, "Has the son hired a lawyer?"

"Nathaniel Mitchell. They've already served the petition on Roscoe."

"Then the son has money. Mitchell is the most expensive lawyer in Northeast Tennessee."

"Zane is a developer," Charlie said. "Builds big houses in the mountains for the *nouveaux riche*. Maybe he's struggling because of the economic downturn in the housing industry, but I still don't understand why he would go after his own father's property."

"You should get an affidavit from an expert that says Roscoe is competent and file a motion to have the petition dismissed," I said. "Try to take them out of the game before it gets started. Once the discovery process gets underway, Mitchell will try to bury you in paper and he'll make things as expensive as possible hoping your client will run out of money and give them what they want."

"Roscoe won't give them anything. He's a stubborn old bird."

"I want to meet him and talk to him," I said. "If I'm going to help you out on a case, I want to know our client. Early Monday morning would be best for me."

Her eyes brightened.

"You'll do it, then? You'll supervise me?"

I nodded again. "We'll work something out as far as finding some space for you here."

"How much of the five thousand do you want?"

"Keep it. You need it more than I do."

Before I could say another word, she was on her feet and around the desk.

"Please let me hug your neck," she said.

I stood, bent over, and opened my arms. She squeezed me so tightly and for so long I started to feel light-headed.

"Whoa, whoa," I said. "I can't help you if you strangle me to death."

"Thank you, Mr. Dillard," she said when she finally let me go. "You won't regret this."

A minute later, she'd picked up her pocketbook and was walking toward the door. Just before she walked out she turned.

"By the way," she said. "The answer is no."

"I beg your pardon?"

"Tell Jack I said no. I don't have a boyfriend."

CHAPTER TWO

Later that afternoon, my cell phone rang. I looked down at the caller ID and smiled. It was my wife, Caroline, probably calling about where she wanted to eat for lunch.

"You need to go over to the Sullivan County jail," she said when I answered, "and talk to a young man named Jordan Scott. I just got off the phone with his father. He's been arrested for murder."

"Murder? What murder?"

"It apparently happened this morning," she said.

"I don't want to get involved in a murder case, Caroline. I thought we talked about—"

"I know, I know," she said, "but this one is different. You need to get over there right away. He needs help."

The tone of her voice was urgent, which was uncharacteristic.

"Who did he supposedly murder?" I asked.

"A cop. He's black, Joe. Just a kid, and he shot a white police officer. I think it's going to be a bad one."

"Then why do you want me to get involved?"

"Trust me," she said. "I've been talking to his father for the past forty minutes. He's a good kid from a good family. There are circumstances, Joe. This is something you need to do."

"What circumstances?"

"I heard them from his father. If I tell you, then you'll be getting your information third-hand. It's better if you get it straight from him. If you aren't comfortable representing him after you talk to him, then fine, don't do it. But if half of what his father told me is true, you'll take the case."

"Which means I'll probably get caught up in another firestorm."

"Firestorms are what you do best, baby."

The door buzzed and clanged, and I walked into a small interview room walled by concrete blocks of gunmetal gray and floored in gray linoleum. The sights, sounds and smells of county jails were routine to me, but the nagging feeling of claustrophobia never quite left me once I walked through the first, locked door.

The young man sitting at the round, steel table was wiry and strong, with a long neck and a pair of the biggest hands I'd ever seen. His ebony skin seemed to have been stretched tightly over his body like shiny, black cellophane. His kinky hair was thick and cropped close, his jaws square, sturdy and muscled. His physical presence reminded me of my son – all muscle and sinew, nothing extraneous. His eyes were the brown of chocolate syrup and he had deep dimples in his cheeks. He was handcuffed, shackled and waist-chained, wearing the green and white, striped jumpsuit and rubber flip flops that were standard issue at the Sullivan County Jail. Of the many jails I'd visited over the years, Sullivan County was one of the worst. It was overcrowded and filthy. Toilets and showers were stopped up, wiring was corroded and exposed, and the guards were cynical and abusive. If you believed what Winston Churchill once wrote – that you could judge a society by the way it treats its prisoners – then Sullivan County was a cruel and unforgiving place.

I set my briefcase down on the table and took out a legal pad and a pen.

"My name is Joe Dillard," I said. "I'm a lawyer. Your father called and asked me to talk to you. Anything you say to me is strictly confidential, but I want you to know up front that I'm not your lawyer, at least not yet. I want to hear what you have to say before I decide whether I'm going to represent you. Are you okay with that?"

He nodded.

"Your name is Jordan Scott?"

"Yes, sir."

"Do you know what you're charged with, Jordan?"

"Murder."

"Did you kill someone?"

"Yes, sir."

"Do you know who you killed?"

"His name was Todd Raleigh. He was a deputy for the Sullivan County Sheriff's Department."

"Do you want to tell me why you killed him?"

"Because he deserved to die."

CHAPTER THREE

This is what I learned during my first conversation with Jordan Scott, who was well-mannered, articulate and intelligent:

Jordan had grown up in a middle-class home in Kingsport. His father worked as a machinist at Tennessee Eastman in Kingsport and his mother was a speech pathologist in the Sullivan County school system. Jordan had a sister named Della who was one year older and a brother named David who was three years younger and who suffered enough brain damage during a traumatic birth to be classified by those who make such determinations as "borderline mentally incapacitated."

Jordan said he was a straight-A student at Dobyns-Bennett High School and an all-state athlete. He was an all-state running back in football, an all-state shooting guard in basketball, and won the state championship in the two-hundred meter hurdles in track his senior year. He had athletic and academic scholarship offers from Division I college programs all over the country, including the University of Tennessee, Kentucky, Georgia, North Carolina and Duke.

But Jordan decided to stay close to home. He didn't want to leave David, and although he was big, strong and fast enough to compete at the Division I level, he knew he wasn't – and never would be – quite big enough, quite strong enough, or quite fast enough to compete with the freaks of nature in the NBA or the NFL. East Tennessee State University in Johnson City was only a thirty-minute drive from home. It was a Division I school with a decent basketball team, and it offered something else that appealed to Jordan – a medical school. There were only a handful of African-American doctors in the region, and Jordan believed he could be of some value to his community in that regard, so he chose ETSU over all the others and enrolled. His parents bought him a used car when he graduated from high school, and between the academic and athletic scholarship money he received, he was able to pay all of his school expenses, split an apartment with a teammate, and stick some money in his pocket each semester. Life was good.

During his freshman year, Jordan maintained a 4.0 grade point average and led the basketball team in scoring and assists. He was named to the Atlantic Sun All-Conference team and was selected as Freshman of the Year. He also fell in love with a green-eyed, brown-skinned, Tara Banks look-alike named Holly Ross. Holly was from Ooltewah, a small town near Chattanooga. She was a volleyball player, a long, lean, reserved beauty who was studying biology and believed she was destined to help save the planet.

In May of Jordan's sophomore year, after a season in which Jordan struggled with hamstring and ankle injuries and still put up even better numbers than his freshman year, Holly went out for a jog alone. As she ran along a path through a stretch of woods at the Mountain Home Veterans Administration Center across the street from the ETSU campus, she was attacked, brutally beaten and raped at knifepoint, thus becoming the third victim of a serial rapist who terrorized the region for the next several months. The police had not released information about the first two rapes to the public, hoping to catch the rapist without causing a panic, but after Holly was attacked, they changed their plan and sounded the public alarm. Three women had been raped in three different counties: one in Sullivan County, one in Carter County, and Holly in Washington County. Over the summer, three more women, all younger than twenty-five, suffered the same fate as Holly. A multi-county task force was formed as the police searched desperately for the rapist.

Holly spent two weeks in the hospital following the rape, and Jordan was there every day and night. She went home for the summer and fell into a deep depression. Jordan drove to Ooltewah twice a week to offer whatever love, care and support that Holly would accept. He went with her to some of her rape counseling sessions, and, little by little, she seemed to come back from the abyss. By the end of August, when classes at ETSU resumed, she'd decided to go back to school and rejoin her teammates on the volleyball team, despite the fact that the rapist was still on the loose and still attacking young women. Jordan was inspired by her courage. He proposed to her on the fifth day of September and gave her a ring. It would be a long engagement – they planned to marry the day after they graduated – but Jordan said he knew he'd found his soul mate.

Nine months later, with the rapist still on the loose and still committing rapes, Jordan was stopped for speeding in Sullivan County as he and Holly were returning to ETSU from dinner at his parents' home. A Sullivan County deputy named Todd Raleigh walked up to the passenger window and leaned down. He recognized Jordan, and after giving him a short lecture on careless behavior, let him go. But as Raleigh spoke through the window, Jordan watched in horror as Holly broke down. Tears began to stream down her face and mucous ran from her nose. Her jaw muscles started to spasm involuntarily. She looked as though she'd come face-to-face with death. As soon as Raleigh went back to his cruiser, Jordan noticed the smell of urine. Holly had wet herself.

It took Jordan an hour to calm her down enough to speak. *It was him*, she said. *The voice, the eyes, the smell.* She was certain. Todd Raleigh was the man who had raped her.

What followed was a nightmare worthy of Dante. They called Holly's parents, and the four of them went to the sheriff's department together. They spoke to an investigator who immediately bumped them to the head of the investigative division, who bumped them to the chief deputy. What they were insinuating was ridiculous, they were told. Todd Raleigh was a dedicated officer with an impeccable service record. Holly's attacker had worn a ski mask, so she'd been unable to provide police with a detailed description. She knew he was white, she knew approximately how tall he was and approximately how much he weighed. He'd left semen in her, though. Why didn't they just get a DNA sample from Raleigh and either arrest him or eliminate him based on the results?

Not possible, she was told. To request a DNA sample from Raleigh would be akin to accusing him of rape. Besides, he had the same rights as anyone else. Without more evidence, they couldn't force him to give a sample. In fact, if it came down to it, they would advise him *against* giving a voluntary sample. The chief deputy, a fat, red-faced, bellicose, belligerent individual named Matthew Bacon, blatantly accused Holly of lying. Quite the lawsuit she'd have, he said, if a white cop was accused of raping a young black woman. A college woman, at that. Sensational lawsuit. Was she trying to get rich at this innocent officer's expense?

Jordan left the police department angry and frustrated. Holly was a mess. She retreated somewhere inside herself, into a psychological bunker where no one was allowed. He couldn't even get her to speak. That night, while Jordan lay on the couch in Holly's apartment, she went into the bathroom and slit her wrists with a razor blade. On the day she was buried, another young woman was raped.

Jordan became filled with a simmering rage. He also became obsessed with Todd Raleigh. He stopped going to class, didn't take his finals, and stopped going to basketball workouts. He believed what Holly had said about Raleigh and was consumed with the idea of making Raleigh pay for what he'd done. But he did so in a measured, calculating fashion. He began stalking Raleigh the way a lion stalks a wildebeest, patiently, hiding in the shadows. He borrowed cars from friends and teammates who were too concerned about his well-being to question. The cars served as both camouflage and shelter during long hours of surveillance. He bought a pair of binoculars, took a shotgun from his father's closet and kept it with him every time he followed or watched Raleigh. Within a week, he knew Raleigh's routines, and on the fourth day of the second week, he got what he wanted.

Raleigh left his apartment at 5:30 a.m. and appeared to be going for a run. Nothing unusual. Raleigh went for a run every day, but he never ran at the same place and the times varied depending on the shift he was working. On this day, he drove to the parking lot of an abandoned bakery about a mile from a park near the Holston River just outside the Kingsport city limits. The morning was gray and misty, the sun not yet up. Jordan hung back, watching as Raleigh got out of his car and jogged off toward the park. He waited ten minutes and drove past the park. He didn't see Raleigh, so he parked a couple of hundred yards down the road. He retrieved the shotgun from the trunk and slipped into a field adjacent to the park, moving low and slowly through the tall fescue. Jordan knew the park well – he'd run there many times in high school – so he worked his way to fence line on a rise that overlooked the southern end. Raleigh was nowhere in sight, and neither was anyone else. Jordan put his back against a poplar tree, laid the shotgun across his thighs, and waited. Just as the sun began to peek over the trees behind him, Jordan saw a small car pull into the parking lot. A solitary figure got out, walked to the rear of the car, and pulled a bicycle off a rack. It appeared to be a woman, though Jordan couldn't quite tell from where he was. The rider guided the bike onto the asphalt path that wound through the park and started pedaling.

The attack happened in an instant.

The biker had circled the far end of the park and had just started along the western border when a figure emerged, seemingly from nowhere, throwing a shoulder into the biker like a linebacker. The biker went flying, and a second later was being dragged toward the bushes. Jordan sprinted from his hiding place to the spot where he saw the biker disappear. He listened, and above his own breathing, could hear muffled sounds of struggle among the leaves and the underbrush. He flipped the shotgun's safety off and moved toward the sound.

The first thing Jordan saw were two sets of feet. Raleigh was grunting and cursing.

"Stop!" Jordan yelled, aiming the shotgun at the back of Raleigh's head. "Get off of her!"

The ski-masked man turned and locked predatory eyes onto Jordan, who was less than ten feet away. The girl – Jordan didn't even know her name – was bleeding from the nose and appeared to be half-conscious. Raleigh jumped up and tried to run, but the double-ought buckshot Jordan fired from the twelve-gauge blew half of his head off before he got ten feet.

Raleigh was dead.

Holly was avenged.

Jordan called the police and calmly waited for them to arrive.

After listening to what he had to say, I sat back and folded my arms.

"How much of this did you tell the police?" I asked.

"I didn't tell them anything other than I shot the man because he was raping the girl."

"They didn't question you?"

"They tried. I told them I wanted to speak to a lawyer."

"Do they have the gun?"

"Yes."

"Did the girl say anything to you before the police got there?"

"She was crying. I asked her if she was all right but she seemed to be afraid of me. I guess I can't blame her since she saw me shoot the man. Am I going to spend the rest of my life in jail?"

"I don't know, Jordan. It's possible. I have a pretty good idea how they'll come at you. They'll say you went vigilante, and there's no place for vigilantes in a civilized society. They'll say Raleigh was running away when you pulled the trigger, so the danger to the girl had passed and there was no danger to you. They'll say the amount of force you used was unreasonable, excessive under the circumstances. They'll talk to people at the sheriff's department and they'll find out about the accusation Holly made against Raleigh. Then they'll go back and talk to everybody you know and they'll find out you've been skipping school and basketball practice. They'll put it together, and when they do, they'll start screaming pre-meditation, especially since you were carrying the shotgun with you in a city park on a Monday morning. They'll say you were hunting Raleigh. They'll play up the pre-meditation to try to get a first-degree murder conviction. They probably won't ask for the death penalty, but you never know. If they convict you of first-degree murder, you won't be eligible for parole for fifty-one years. Did you see a weapon on Raleigh, by the way?"

"He had a knife."

"Did he make a move toward you? Were you afraid he was going to kill you?"

"I didn't know what he'd do. He was raping somebody. Was I just supposed to let him run away so he could rape somebody else?"

I shook my head. "I don't know what you should have done, but it doesn't matter now, does it? You did what you did. You shot him, you told them you shot him, and now you're going to have to deal with the consequences. Even if you're eventually found not guilty of murder, you're going to be in this place for months, maybe a year, probably in solitary confinement. You're also going to become the focus of a whole bunch of hatred, whether you deserve it or not. You think you killed a man, a rapist, but you also killed a symbol. Even if Raleigh was what you say he was, and believe me, we're going to have to find a way to prove it and find a way to get it admitted in court, you killed a representative of law and order, a *white* representative of law and order in a community that is dominated by whites. You've committed an act that flies in the face of their entire judicial system, and you're about to find out how brutal that system can be.

If everything is the way you say it is, and *if* we can get a fair trial in front of an impartial jury, then maybe you can walk away from this, but even if you do, I want you to know you're going to pay a steep price."

Tears welled in his eyes and they took on a luminescent glow.

"I don't know you, Mr. Dillard, but I want to ask you a question."

"Go ahead."

"Have you ever been in love?"

I thought about Caroline and the many years we'd been together, the trials and tribulations, the joy and the pain.

"Yes, Jordan, I've been in love for a long, long time."

"That's what he took from me, and no matter what the judicial system does to me, I don't think the price could be any steeper."

If you enjoyed the beginning of *Blood Money*, you can purchase here via Amazon:

<u>Blood Money</u>
Again, thank you for reading!

Scott

Made in the USA
Monee, IL
08 January 2024

20b0964c-c23a-4d2c-b197-f1a2683cf3ceR01